ANDREW G.
NELSON

AWAKENING

THE CRYSTAL COVEN SAGA

ANDREW G. NELSON

HUNTZMAN ENTERPRISES

AWAKENING: The Crystal Coven Saga

Copyright © 2020 by Andrew G. Nelson

Cover Design Copyright © 2020 by Huntzman Enterprises

Published by Huntzman Enterprises

First Edition: July 2020

ISBN-13: 978-0-9987562-9-5

Printed in the United States of America
1 3 5 7 9 10 8 6 4 2

<u>DEDICATION</u>

To my wife Nancy, without your love, support, and constant encouragement, this book would not have been possible.

Thank you for always believing in me.

And to God, through whom all things are possible.

In Loving Memory of Jax

(2011-2020)

Gone, but Never Forgotten.

.

Other Titles by Andrew G. Nelson

JAMES MAGUIRE SERIES

PERFECT PAWN

QUEEN'S GAMBIT

BISHOP'S GATE

KNIGHT FALL

GLASS CASTLE

ALEX TAYLOR SERIES

SMALL TOWN SECRETS

LITTLE BOY LOST

BROOKLYN BOUNCE

NYPD COLD CASE SERIES

THE KATHERINE WHITE MURDER

THE ROASRY BEAD MURDERS

THE CRYSTAL COVEN SAGA

AWAKENING

NON FICTION

UNCOMMON VALOR – Insignia of the NYPD ESU

UNCOMMON VALOR II – Challenge Coins of the NYPD ESU

WHERE WAS GOD? An NYPD first responder's search for answers following the terror attack of Sept 11th, 2001

PREFACE

For millennia, the young and old have been regaled with epic tales of mythical creatures and heroic champions.

For most it was merely entertainment; terrifying stories of dragons and bogeymen to be shared, with wild-eyed children, on a moonless night, around a roaring campfire. For others, it was to motivate or inspire them to greatness.

As we matured, we laid aside the old tales, relegating them to the deep recesses of our mind; nothing more than wistful fairy tales that harkened back to a much simpler time.

But what if we were wrong?

What if the stories were meant not to amuse us, but to warn us?

That these were cautionary tales, designed to counsel us to stay vigilant.

What if the man standing next to you at the grocery store, or the woman sitting at the desk behind you, were not what they appeared to be?

What if the smile they shared hid something darker, something much more sinister?

Be careful who you trust in the world, because even the devil was once an angel.

CHAPTER ONE

Serena de Mar sat on the parapet of the old Ford Bank Building, her legs dangling playfully over the side, and surveyed the garish street scene below her.

The buildings lining the block had been adorned with flickering light displays, typical for this time of the year, while strings of fake wreaths hung from the lampposts. Off in the distance the cheerful strains of *'Santa Claus is Coming to Town'* could be heard.

She didn't know why, but something about the holiday season disgusted her. Perhaps it was the fakeness, the whole *peace on Earth and goodwill to man* bullshit, which seemed to exist for only a few weeks before humanity went back to hating one another. Or maybe it was the commercialism; a way to rake in some extra bucks through some sense of faux charity. Whatever the case, it fueled her general contempt of the residents of the city and made her even less compassionate toward them.

"I'm bored," she announced, as a sudden gust of wind sent a flurry of snow swirling around her in the air.

"You're *always* bored," her sister, Gabrielle, groused, "which is usually what you proclaim just before you get *us* into trouble."

"I just don't understand the necessity to follow such archaic rules," Serena protested. "Let's be honest, this peace and harmony thing is designed strictly for *their* benefit, not ours. If the roles were reversed, I highly doubt they would be as benevolent to *us*."

"And yet here we are," Gabrielle replied as she sat down on the rooftop, her back resting against the parapet wall.

She knew exactly where this conversation was heading and she didn't like it.

Serena wasn't happy unless she was pushing the envelope; testing the boundaries of right and wrong, but what troubled Gabrielle most was that she often got away with it.

Serena had been blessed with a mix of beauty, brains, and a bohemian attitude, which seemed to charm even her most ardent critics.

Handwringing, scowls, and a dismissive, 'That's just Serena being Serena,' was the usual response to her latest flaunting of the rules. It amazed and often infuriated her as to just how much deference they gave to her dear, sweet sister.

"I want to remind you that there will come a time when you push things too far," Gabrielle warned, "and when that day comes I can't help but feel that you will not be happy with the consequences."

"See that's the problem with you, sis," Serena replied. "You worry more about the rules than the rewards. What is the purpose of all of this if we can't have a little fun from time to time?"

"You call this *fun*?"

"You say potato and I say *potahto*. Why the hell are you stressing over all of this anyway?"

"Because the games you play have real-world *consequences*," Gabrielle shot back. "In case you haven't noticed, the result of your *little fun* usually ends up disrupting many lives."

If Serena had noticed the anger in her sister's voice, she ignored it.

"Is your life disrupted, sis? Is mine?"

"Not yet, but if you keep this behavior up you might find that you've pushed the boundaries a little too far and then what? What happens when they decide to take action?"

"Then I will cross that particular bridge when I get to it. Besides, dangerous games like this make life more bearable."

"You have no fear of consequences, do you?" Gabrielle asked.

"No," Serena replied, "and why should I?"

"There will come a time when I can't protect you."

"I'm not asking you to protect me."

"That's because you know that you don't have to ask me; you already know that I will, but you're going to screw up one day and it will be out of my hands. After all, I am just one voice."

Serena closed her eyes and sighed loudly, as she leaned backward, balancing herself precariously on the ledge, and stretched her long, lithe body.

She knew Gabrielle was right, she always was, but that didn't mean she had to like it. She understood the reason for rules, especially the ones that directly affected them, but she questioned the necessity for some of the others. It felt like it was a one-sided construct which gave far too much consideration to *them*.

"I'm just asking you to stop for a moment and think about this," Gabrielle said, softening her tone a bit. "Remember, this isn't just about you, this affects me as well. If anyone finds out about your *proclivities*, they will want to know what I did to stop you and I won't have an answer. I will be just as guilty as you."

"I know, I know," Serena replied, a mix of annoyance and acceptance in her voice, as she sat back up. "I promise that I will *try* to be better."

It wasn't exactly what Gabrielle wanted to hear, but it was progress and she was willing to take it wherever it appeared.

"Thank you," Gabrielle said. "You know I am only telling you this because I love you."

Serena looked down at Gabrielle and smiled, "I love you to, sis."

"You and me against the world, isn't that right?" Gabrielle asked, as she reached out and took her sister's hand in hers.

"Just as it has been, so shall it always be," Serena replied.

Gabrielle was about to reply, when Serena's head snapped and she gazed intently into the distance; like a hawk who had detected the faintest movement of its prey.

"Hello there," Serena whispered with delight. "Sorry, love, but opportunity knocks."

And then she was gone.

Gabrielle closed her eyes in frustration and struck her head against the wall behind her, hard enough to knock some of the brittle coating from it.

"That girl will be the death of me yet."

CHAPTER TWO

A steady mix of *gurgling* and *hissing* noises emanated from the pressure relief valve on the large, antique cast-iron radiator, as Detective Karl Sigurdsson pecked away at the dilapidated typewriter on his desk.

The sound battled valiantly against the *ticking* of the 1980s era wall clock for the most monotonous sound in the Fifteenth Precinct's detective squad room.

Sigurdsson wasn't sure if the noises were by design, but he was convinced that if they piped the sound into the interrogation room he could elicit a confession, from even the most hardened criminal, within a half-hour. In fact, everything in the squad room, except for him, felt antiquated. From the battleship gray colored work desks, with their chipped Formica tops, to the decrepit filing cabinets that lined the far wall. Everything in the cavernous office space screamed *old*. Even the peeling, sea-foam green walls had seen their better days back in the 60s.

It often amazed Sigurdsson at just how little upkeep went into maintaining the precincts of the largest police department in the United States. Even when they built something new, it wasn't long till the roof leaked or the sewers backed up.

I bet they don't treat the fire department like this, he thought.

"You're up hot-shot," a gruff voice called out from across the room.

Sigurdsson glanced up from the report he was typing to see Sergeant Avery White standing in his office doorway.

Speaking of antiques.

White was one of those *old school* cops; the kind who had so much time on the job that when he put on his dress uniform, you thought he had a *railroad track* running up his left arm with all the hash marks sewn on his sleeve.

The other detectives joked that White had joined the department back when the precinct was brand new, but Sigurdsson also knew he wasn't a man to be trifled with either. Besides all his other medals, they had awarded him both the Police Combat Cross and the Medal of Valor. The man had been to hell and back, so there was little chance of getting over on him.

"Nope, that's where you're wrong, boss," Sigurdsson grinned as he swiveled around in his chair and pointed at the chalk board hanging on the far wall. "According to the assignment board, Janovic is up next."

"Maybe, but Janovic is driving the lieutenant tonight, smart-ass, so tag, *you're it.*"

The smile drained from his face as he slumped back in his chair.

"Come on, boss," he pleaded. "*Por favor, no mas.* I've caught the last eight cases and we're only mid-month. When do I catch a break?"

"Don't look at me, junior. I didn't tell you to shack up with the L.T.'s little sister."

"She was dancing at a club," Sigurdsson protested. "How the hell was I supposed to know who she was?"

"I guess the lieutenant figures that you're supposed to be a detective," White replied. "I mean did you even bother to ask her last name?"

"It didn't exactly come up in *conversation,*" Sigurdsson said sheepishly.

"Yeah, well your name obviously came up in *her* conversation, so now you know why he thinks you need to go out there and *detect.* You clearly need to hone your investigatory skills so you don't make any more stupid mistakes."

Sigurdsson let out a dejected sigh as he reluctantly came to terms with his fate.

"Look, Karl," White said, the tone of his voice changing into one that was *almost* compassionate. "I know you don't want to hear this, but I'm going to tell you anyway. Those pretty blue eyes and pearly white teeth might just make the girls go weak in the knees, but if you want to get your raggedy-ass out of the L.T.'s dog house, then you'd better start giving him something else to think about besides you and his kid sister getting jiggy with it; you know, like your stellar case clearance rate."

"I know," Sigurdsson pleaded, "but you have to believe me when I say that I didn't know who she was, sarge."

"It don't matter what *I* think, Karl. All that matters is that he doesn't care. So you have two choices, you can focus on your work, and become the all-star detective that he can't live without, or you can put in for a transfer back to patrol. I'm sure he would be more than happy to find you a nice A-house to keep you real busy."

"I did nine years in the Four-Four, boss," Sigurdsson replied. "I don't want to go *backward* in my career."

"Well, then I suggest you get out there and start earning that detective shield."

"Fine," Sigurdsson relented as he stood up and began putting on his jacket. "So where am I going to on this *lovely* evening?"

"Jennings Park," White replied. "Some dog walker thought she saw a homeless person sleeping on the bench and alerted a passing radio car. As it turns out, he was taking a *permanent* nap."

"He probably got drunk at the office Christmas party and froze to death."

"Then it should be an easy clearance for you, Karl."

"You want to back me up on this?" Sigurdsson asked as he made his way toward the door.

"Hell no, you're a big boy," White replied as he headed back into his office. "Besides, it's colder than a polar bear's balls out there."

"Thanks for nothing, sarge" Sigurdsson shot back as he walked out of the squad room; the door closing behind him just in time to cut-off White's smart-ass reply.

Jennings Park was only about a dozen blocks away from the precinct, but the holiday shopping rush made navigating the narrow city streets even more difficult than usual. Despite the red tear-drop light, oscillating frantically on the car's dashboard, it still took over twenty minutes for him to arrive at the crime scene.

As he pulled the unmarked Chevy Lumina onto the sidewalk, he could see that the entrance to the park was bathed in brilliant white light; courtesy of the telescoping light rack on one of the emergency vehicles. The familiar yellow crime scene tape cordoned off the surrounding sidewalks and entrance; holding back a group of curious onlookers, who stood on the other side hoping to catch a glimpse. Even the harsh winter chill wasn't enough to dampen the morbid curiosity of a city-dweller.

He lifted the tape and carefully slipped beneath it, before making his way over to where the uniformed cop, Officer Mike Sampson, stood guarding the perimeter.

"Hey, Mike," Sigurdsson said. "What have we got?"

"D.O.A., Karl," the cop replied. "Joe and I were headed in for meal when we got flagged down by a woman complaining of someone sleeping in the park."

"Do we have a name on the witness?"

"No," the man replied sheepishly. "She approached us and said she was walking her dog when she saw the man. Said she didn't want to get involved, just wanted him *gone*. We honestly thought it was another vagrant job. The locals have been bitching to the captain for months. We finally managed to chase them away from in front of the apartment buildings, but they just headed into the park. We rolled in to roust him, but he was unresponsive, so we called for EMS and they pronounced him at 2153 hours."

"Was there any ID on him?" Sigurdsson asked, as he opened his notebook and began taking notes.

"I did a cursory examination, but I didn't find anything," the cop replied. "I figured you guys would do a better search."

"Were there any obvious signs of trauma?"

"None that I could see," Sampson replied, "but he's bundled up pretty good."

Sigurdsson looked up from his notebook and frowned as he surveyed the area around the park.

The majority of the buildings in this area were commercial spaces on the street level, most of which were already closed, but apartments dotted the upper floors. He could make out the lights from a dozen plus residences and the thought of having to canvas each of them for potential witnesses made him cringe.

It wouldn't have been bad if he could just ask the simple question of, 'Did you see anything?' and get a yes or no response, but that only happened on television. In his world, there would be the crazy cat lady, the paranoid recluse, the angry octogenarian or any of several other sub-species of societal misfits who would look upon his visit as an opportunity to share with him every problem that had befallen the neighborhood for the last four decades. And the way his day was going so far, it would most likely be more tales rather than less.

Please, Lord, let him have died from natural causes, he thought.

He made his way into the park and located Sampson's partner, Joe Gentile, who was guarding the body of the deceased.

"Hey, Joe, what can you tell me about our vic?"

"Not much, Karl," the man replied. "Mike and I found him like this and called EMS. They rolled in, pronounced him, and then rolled right back out. They didn't disturb the body."

"Must be nice not having to hang around in the elements," Sigurdsson scoffed as he felt the wind kick up.

"I guess they have them running ragged," Gentile replied. "With this bitter weather, people are dropping like flies. All I'm hearing on the radio is aided cases and accidents."

"This weather continues like this and you can bet your ass the domestics will start piling up."

"Isn't that the truth," Gentile replied.

"Is the medical examiner on the way?"

"Yeah, we called them right after we notified you guys," the man replied.

"Well then, I guess it's time to get this party started," Sigurdsson said as he squatted down to examine the body.

The man was lying on one of the old wrought-iron and wood benches that dotted the interior of the park. His upper body was nearly horizontal while his legs were splayed out in front of him. It appeared as if he had sat down to take a rest and then fell over. His eyes were wide open, giving him a terrifying appearance, and his face had a grayish pallor. From what he could tell, the man appeared to be elderly, but it was obvious he wasn't your typical homeless person. For starters, he was too well dressed, wearing a three-quarter length, black cashmere jacket, with a knit cap and a thick wool scarf tied around his neck.

Sitting next to him on the bench were two giant shopping bags. Sigurdsson recognized the names on the bags as being from two high-end department stores in the area. He peered inside and saw several brightly wrapped packages.

Well, I guess that rules out a robbery, he thought. *Maybe it was natural causes.*

He stood up and took in the scene. It was in a desolate section of the park. They had erected several portable auxiliary lights to compensate for the broken bulbs in the street lamps that lined the walkway. Apparently, when people weren't dying there, the local kids used it as a hangout. If people couldn't see you, they were less likely to complain.

Sigurdsson looked back in the direction that he had come. The perimeter wall of the park was lined with two dozen or more London plane trees; their tall, thick branches obscuring any view from the neighboring buildings. He reasoned to himself that, judging from the remote location and lack of lighting, finding any witnesses was highly doubtful.

Just then, he heard the *crunching* sound of footsteps against the new fallen snow. He glanced over to see Doctor Andrea Reynolds, one of the city medical examiners, walking toward him.

"Hey, doc," he said, extending his hand to her.

"Good evening, Karl," she replied, shaking his hand. "What do we have?"

"First guess, I'm thinking he might have vapor-locked. It looks like he was out shopping and his heart probably gave out."

"Wouldn't surprise me," Reynolds replied as she kneeled down to take a closer look. "Frigid weather, exertion, and age don't mix well. Do we have an ID on him yet?"

"No, we didn't search the body yet. I wanted to wait for you."

"I'll check," she replied, slipping on a pair of blue nitrile examination gloves.

Sigurdsson retrieved an evidence bag from his coat pocket and held it open as Reynolds began her examination and started methodically removing several items from the deceased. First to be deposited in the evidence bag was the man's wedding ring and watch. Next she located a set of keys from the right front pant pocket and a wallet from the right rear pocket.

Sigurdsson examined the wallet, retrieving a driver's license from within. He examined the photo, matching it to the body in front of him, and then turned to Gentile.

"It looks like our victim's name is Benjamin Stein and he lives at 81-32 Pine Street. His date of birth is listed as October 13th, 1946."

"Got it," Gentile replied as he entered the information into his memo book.

"Nothing else," Reynolds said as she began unbuttoning the man's coat and removing the scarf. "Also not seeing any evidence of……. holy shit."

Sigurdsson pivoted sharply; first looking at Reynolds and then toward the man.

"What the heck is that?" he asked as his eyes locked on the long jagged wound across the left side of the man's neck.

"Well, I can tell you that it isn't a heart attack," she said as she stood up and removed the gloves. "I think I can go out on a limb and establish the cause of death."

"So much for natural causes," Sigurdsson grumbled.

"I'll be able to tell you more when I get him on the table, but I'm reasonably sure you will not be wrong with that guess."

"You know what I'm really interested in knowing?" he asked.

"What's that?"

"With a wound that bad, where the hell is all the blood?"

A quizzical look grew on Reynolds face as she examined the pristine area surrounding the body. "Well, if you ever find out who tied the scarf back around his neck, you might want to ask them that question."

CHAPTER THREE

Lieutenant Carlos Vega strolled into the squad room a little after 6:00 a.m., carrying a Styrofoam coffee cup in one hand and a brown paper bag, containing his breakfast, in the other, but abruptly stopped when he spotted Sigurdsson sitting at his desk.

"Damn, you're here early," Vega said sternly.

"That's because I never left, boss," Sigurdsson confessed.

"You better have a damn good reason, if you expect me to sign your overtime slip."

"Would the fact that I think we might have a vigilante killer on the loose be a good enough reason?" Sigurdsson asked.

Vega was about to jump ugly, but something in the man's voice made him realize it hadn't been a sarcastic reply.

"Oh, hell no," Vega replied, as he sat the items he'd been carrying on one of the vacant desks and pulled a chair over. "Please don't tell me this shit so early in the morning, Karl."

"Don't kill the messenger, L.T."

"Why do you think that?" Vega asked.

"I got back from the crime scene last night and I couldn't stop thinking of the apparent cause of death. I have a friend over in records and I asked her to do me a favor."

"You sure do have a lot of female *friends*, don't you, Karl?" Vega asked.

Sigurdsson turned around in his chair to face the man.

Vega wasn't much older than he was, probably in his mid-thirties, but he'd hit the promotional exams perfectly. In less than five years he'd gone from detective to sergeant and finally to lieutenant. Odds were strong that he would most likely be promoted in the first group of new captains as soon as they promulgated the test. So having him as an enemy, which was the spot he currently held in Vega's eyes, wasn't a good thing for his career. It was time to confront the 800lb gorilla in the room.

"Boss, I don't know what to say beyond I'm sorry," Sigurdsson said. "I swear on my mother that I did not know she was your sister."

"Her name is Gina," Vega snapped.

"I swear on my mother that I did not know *Gina* was your sister," he reiterated. "I was at the club with a bunch of guys I used to work with. She was with her friends, who apparently knew some of the cops I was with, and one thing led to another."

"You're not really helping your case here."

"Look, I get it, if the roles were reversed I would probably feel the same way, but you have to understand that the *last* thing I would ever want to do is piss you off."

"And yet here we are, Karl."

"Yes, you're right, here we are, but the problem is that I don't know how to make this *better*. The way I see it, there are three scenarios that are in-play; none of which are appealing. First is I hand in my shield and head back to some shit-hole precinct for the rest of my career, second I stay in your dog house until you get promoted, or third I screw up and you bust me back to a shit-hole precinct."

"She's my sister."

"And you have to believe me that if I had even the *slightest* inkling of who she was, I would have run out of that club and never looked back."

Vega's face contorted into a scowl and Sigurdsson could see the man's jaw clenching. For a moment he thought he had pushed Vega too far, but he knew he also couldn't work like this anymore.

As tough as it was for Vega to admit, Avery had been right when he'd counseled him that he had allowed his personal feelings to interfere with the professional and was punishing the kid more than he should have. Vega had always been an overprotective big-brother, but he reluctantly had to accept that his sister was an adult woman now. Besides, Gina had admitted that she'd never told Sigurdsson that her brother was his boss.

"What's done is done," Vega said stoically, but pointed his finger menacingly at Sigurdsson, "but let me make this perfectly clear, Karl. I swear to God, if I ever catch you with her again I'll chop it off myself and ship your eunuch ass back to patrol."

"Never going to happen, boss," Sigurdsson said, extending his hand.

Vega stared at him a moment longer before accepting his handshake, "So tell me again how you are going to ruin my day now."

"Well, like I said," Sigurdsson explained as he turned back toward the computer screen. "Something about our D.O.A. from last night wasn't sitting right with me. He wasn't a robbery victim, he still had all his personal belongings and packages he was carrying, but it was clear he'd been assaulted. What shocked me was that whoever did it went the extra mile to cover it up so neatly."

"Gang hit?" Vega asked. "Maybe an unknown group laid claim to the park as their territory?"

"Maybe," Sigurdsson replied, "but it feels wrong. At the very least, a street gang would have grabbed the packages. If it was professionals, they would have just put two to the chest or head and called it a day. This just didn't have that feel, so I had my friend run a search for any deaths that were *unusual*. Not surprisingly, it was a rather *long* list. You can't imagine how many unique ways people meet their demise in this city."

"Are you kidding me?" Vega asked wryly. "I once chased a robbery suspect through a church. The idiot thought he could escape by jumping through a window in the choir loft. Unfortunately for him it was at 3 a.m. and he never saw the wrought-iron fence until he landed on it, face first; the pike went in under the jaw and came out the top of his head."

"Ouch," Sigurdsson replied, with a pained expression. "I guess a Band-Aid was out of the question on that one."

"Indeed," Vega replied. "ESU had to cut the section of fence out and sent him to the morgue with it."

"I didn't come across anything quite that *unusual*, but I found a few that seem to show we might have a problem."

"Okay, well start with the details of last night's victim and give me your theory," Vega said.

"Last night was Benjamin Stein," Sigurdsson replied. "There was nothing remarkable except that he had a severe laceration to the neck which is the most likely cause of death, but right now I'm not sure how he fits the pattern."

"What about the others?"

"So far I have identified five potential homicides that concern me. The first occurred back in 2014. The cops in the One-Two-Three responded to a call for a burglary; homeowners said they heard someone at their backdoor trying to jimmy the lock. When the cops arrived there was signs of an attempted entry, so they canvassed the area and came up with the body of Nate Belkin, a twenty-eight-year-old, white male, in an alley about a block away. They labeled the cause of death as a homicide, because of a deep laceration to the neck. Belkin was from Newark and had a rap sheet a mile long with burglary arrests in both Jersey and New York."

"No real great loss to humanity," Vega replied.

"Agreed," Sigurdsson said as he continued. "The next case was in 2015. Jason Whittle, a forty-three-year-old, white male, had a long history of sex abuse and assault charges. He did a nine-year stint in Sing-Sing for rape and within a week of being paroled tried it again, when he attacked Mary Jane Burns in Prospect

Park. As luck would have it, Burns was a Krav Maga instructor. Whittle ended up on the ground and she ran for help. When the Seven-Eight showed up he was gone, or so they thought. Two days later a park worker found his body in a drainage ditch and his throat had been slashed."

"It's a long way from the One-Two-Three to the Seven-Eight, Karl," Vega said.

"I know, but there's more. Three months later Jermaine Butler, a twenty-one-year-old, black male, was found beaten to death just over the border in the Seven-Nine. Butler was a known pedophile. He'd been caught peeking into a six-year-old's bedroom and had some instant street justice delivered before he ran away. When the cops arrived, they canvassed the area and found his body two blocks away. Besides the severe contusions and broken bones, he also had a deep laceration to the right side of his neck. No one was collared, but word on the street was pretty emphatic, while he might have been handed a beating, the parties involved had not killed him."

"Let's be honest, who's going to admit to committing murder?" Vega asked derisively.

"Well, the detectives who investigated seemed pretty convinced that his death was done after the fact and their case is still open."

Sigurdsson looked at Vega and could see the scowl had returned to his face.

At least it's not directed at me this time, he thought, before continuing.

"The next one occurred in late 2016. Brittany Adams and her husband, Ryan, got into a verbal altercation in an upscale restaurant on the Upper East Side, and he ended up slapping her face. Ryan was a male white, fifty-six-years-old. The restaurant staff kicked him out and called the cops. The Two-Oh responded, but when they went out to interview him in the parking lot, they found him lying next to his car with his throat slashed. In that particular case his wallet was missing, so they just chalked it up to a robbery that went south."

"The next case I came up with is almost two years later," Sigurdsson continued. "Cops in the One-Oh-Two got a report of a homeless man, named Michael Paine, sleeping on a bench in Forest Park. Apparently this guy was a *frequent flyer* in the precinct. He had a rap sheet with about a dozen and a half collars for petty stuff; mostly dis-con and shoplifting arrests. Anyway, they locate him, but when they tried to roust him they realized he was D.O.A."

"Let me take a guess," Vega said, "he had his throat slashed?"

"Bingo," Sigurdsson replied.

"I'm not thrilled, but it still sounds kind of sketchy."

"Here's the weird thing, boss. All the autopsies were inconclusive for a weapon and each of the victims had what was deemed to be *significantly low* levels of blood."

"What do you mean by significant?"

"Looking over the reports, the blood loss was estimated to be between three and four liters of blood."

"Couldn't they have just bled out at the scene?" Vega asked.

"That was my initial guess, but none of the crime scene photos show any serious pooling of blood. Even a blind detective would notice that kind of mess."

"What did the autopsy reports say about it?"

"They had no answer."

"So what about our vic from last night?"

"Benjamin Stein? He's the anomaly," Sigurdsson said. "Unlike the others, he had no criminal history. He was a seventy-three-year-old, white male. I interviewed his wife, Lilian, last night. She told me he was a Vietnam vet who suffered from COPD. After he left the army, he got a job working as a banker. They moved to Florida when he retired, but they kept an apartment up here to spend holidays with the kids and grandchildren. He'd gone out shopping for some last minute gifts, even though she had asked him not to because of the bad weather. He most likely stopped to rest when he was attacked."

"And he had no criminal record?" Vega asked.

"None that I could find," Sigurdsson replied. "And just like the others, he'd had his throat slashed yet there was no discernable blood loss at the wound site. That's what ties them all together."

"You know, I liked it better when you were on my shit list, Karl."

"The problem is that these are just the ones I could identify. Who knows how many others we might ID, if we look harder, not to mention any potential bodies that haven't been found yet."

Vega let out a sigh and stood up. He retrieved his coffee and breakfast before heading toward his office.

"Where are you going, boss?" Sigurdsson asked quizzically.

"To call the chief of detectives and ruin her morning with your *delightful news*."

CHAPTER FOUR

"**I** hope you're happy," Gabrielle groused as Serena entered the kitchen.

"What's got your knickers in a knot?" Serena replied as she poured herself a cup of coffee.

"I don't know about you, but I'm not fond of being on page one," Gabrielle said as she laid the paper on the table and pushed it toward her sister.

Serena glanced down and looked at the headline. "It's a big, bad city. I still don't see what's bothering you."

"Call me crazy, but explain to me again how *publicity* is a good thing?"

Serena scanned the story as she stirred her coffee. "Are you named in this?"

"No," Gabi replied.

"Am I?"

"No," Gabrielle repeated tersely.

"Gabi, over a hundred people die in this city every single day. Some die of old age, some die because they got shot, some fall in front of a drain, and some fall down elevator shafts. It was a slow news day and this one made the morning papers. Nothing sells better than a little death with your Danish, but it will be forgotten long before the first dinner plate hits the table."

"It's not the death, but the fact that it was done out in the open."

Serena sat down at the table and sipped her coffee. "Is there anything in the article about the cause of death?"

"No, they said it was an active investigation. They wouldn't release any details pending notification to the next of kin and an autopsy."

"So they do an autopsy and what do you think they will find?"

"You know damn well what they will find," Gabi barked.

"Indeed I do," Serena replied. "Nothing."

"Nothing?" Gabi asked incredulously. "You can't be serious."

"I can and I am. Tell me, sis, what will they find?"

"I'm not interested in playing any of your mind games, Serena. You can mock me all you want, but you know what is at stake."

"All I am saying is that they have a mystery they can never solve, because it doesn't fit the mold."

"So that's your answer? Because you're *unique* they won't investigate it?"

"They'll investigate it; they just won't find any clues that their inherent biases will allow them to entertain."

"What if you're wrong? What if someone does entertain it?" Gabi asked.

"Do you know what happens to a pilot who claims they saw a UFO?" Serena asked. "Even if they don't lose their career, they are ostracized. Now imagine what would happen to a cop who claimed that some unidentified *monster* was terrorizing the city."

Gabrielle got up from the chair and stormed into the kitchen, tossing her coffee cup into the sink where it shattered. Before heading down the hallway, she turned and looked back at Serena. "Just for the record, I don't care what the police think about the monsters. I'm more concerned of what the monsters will think of us."

Serena watched as she marched down the hallway and slammed the bedroom door shut. She rolled her eyes and took a drink.

God, you can be so damn draining at times, she thought.

CHAPTER FIVE

Sigurdsson laid the crime scene photo, taken at the Stein homicide, onto the coffee table and rubbed his weary eyes.

He'd only gotten a few hours of sleep, since he had been assigned the case, and it was taking its toll on him.

Despite his gut feeling that these cases were all somehow related, the links were tenuous. The only commonality among them seemed to be the underlying criminal history of most of the victims, and the cause of death. But according to the chief, while there was no plausible medical explanation for the significant blood loss, there wasn't enough reason to warrant additional manpower. So, at least for the time being, it was his ball to run with.

A few years back he had gone to a training session during which he recalled the instructor discussing the differences between the organized and disorganized serial killer.

At first glance, there were many aspects to the crime scenes that matched the category of the *disorganized* killer, such as the victims apparently being chosen at random and no attempt made to hide the bodies, but, at the same time, there seemed to be a certain methodology to these killings which suggested that it might fit the category of the *organized* killer. Whoever it was had left no physical evidence or weapons behind and the murders were spread out over ethnically diverse neighborhoods. Whoever was doing this had no fear of moving around, which suggested a well thought out plan.

During the presentation, the instructor had pointed out that some killers returned to the crime scene for a variety of different reasons. Some wanted to re-live the moment, while others wanted to watch how law enforcement responded to their work. So he had tracked down video copies of the news coverage, from several of the murder scenes, and hoped that watching them might generate a clue.

Sigurdsson reached over to pick up the television remote and hit play. He muted the sound and watched, hoping his eyes would pick up something that seemed out of place, without the distraction of the audio commentary.

The first video was of the Nate Belkin murder. The camera panned from the reporter to the tarp draped body of Belkin. Then the video changed to show the crowd, gathered at the far end of the alley, as cops with flashlights examined the crime scene. Sigurdsson watched it till the end and then rewound it until it returned to the spectators and hit pause. He scanned the images of the crowd, looking for the one individual who seemed *out of place.*

It often amazed him at some of the theatrics that went on at these scenes. A person could be lying dead in the street, but put a camera on some people and they would perform like they were on stage at the circus. As he watched each video, the same type of coverage was duplicated at the other locations, but there didn't seem to be anything amiss, nor could he discern any *familiar* faces amongst the onlookers.

The last video was from the Stein murder, but as the camera panned away, Sigurdsson's attention was immediately drawn to the image of two women standing in front. The cameraman must have felt the same way, because he chose that exact moment to focus on them and pull the image in for a close-up shot.

Sigurdsson hit the pause button and studied the faces on the screen. Both women appeared to be in their late twenties or early thirties. One had long, black hair, which shimmered in the camera's light, and dark eyes that gazed at the scene in front of her. But it was the woman beside her that had caught his attention. She had long blonde hair, which cascaded over the shoulders of the black leather jacket she was wearing, and complemented her high cheekbones and bronze colored complexion. She had an exotic look to her, as if she had stepped off the cover of a magazine.

Well, it's not like there aren't a million models running around this city, he thought as he gazed at the woman.

After a few more moments, he hit the play button and continued to watch. Just as the camera pulled back she turned, looking right into the lens, and he saw her piercing blue eyes.

"Damn," he said out loud as the camera continued to pan down the line of gawkers. When it finally pulled back for a wide shot, the women were gone.

Sigurdsson let out a sigh as he turned the television off. He heard his stomach grumble loudly and realized that he hadn't eaten yet. He glanced at his watch and frowned; it was already half-past nine.

Fuck it, he thought as he got up from the couch, grabbed his jacket, and headed toward the door.

Once outside the apartment building he paused and looked up and down the street.

The problem with living in the city was that you almost had *too many* choices for food. There was Napoli Pizza on the corner and Wu Ming's Chinese takeout in the middle of the block. Good options on most days, but after slogging through endless crime scene photos and video, what he really craved was comfort food.

Out of nowhere he felt a sudden *rush* of wind pass by, strong enough to make him think someone had pushed him, and it startled him.

Great, now you're starting to imagine things, he thought, as he scanned the deserted street.

He adjusted the collar of his coat to fend off the frigid night air. Then he turned right and began making his way toward the bright neon sign that beckoned to him.

Nainsi MacNeighill's Pub was a staple of this Upper Eastside neighborhood. As he walked inside he was hit with the familiar odor of stale beer and cigarettes. Despite the ban on smoking, the regular patrons didn't seem inclined to cooperate. Rumor was that the head of the health department was friends with the owner and got tipped off to any inspections. Sigurdsson didn't care, as he appreciated the quaintness of the place.

The interior of the bar had changed little in over a century of operation. Along one wall was an old bar, whose wood had aged to a near black color over the decades, with about two dozen stools lined up in front of it. Behind the bar was a mirrored wall that had well over a hundred bottles of various liquors and spirits. Across from it were several booths that had been added when the pub expanded their food service.

Jimmy O'Toole stood behind the bar, washing a glass, and gave him a hearty wave as he walked in.

If there was ever a caricature of the quintessential bar keep, O'Toole would have been the living embodiment of it. He was a short, but powerfully built man, with a ruddy face, pot-belly, and white hair that framed his balding head in such a way that it gave him the appearance of a modern-day *Friar Tuck*. On the bar sat an ashtray playing host to one of the Pall Mall cigarettes that he habitually smoked.

Sigurdsson had never once seen the man cross, but tales among some of the regulars told about the *Mighty* O'Toole single-handily clearing the bar out of about a dozen hooligans. Word was that Jimmy had once worked as a ship builder in Belfast, Northern Ireland. During the period known as *the Troubles*, he and several hundred Catholic workers had lost their jobs. So Jimmy had packed up his bags, like so many of his ancestors before him, and headed off to chase the American dream.

"*How in the name of Jaysus are you, Karl?*" the man asked cheerfully, with his thick Irish accent.

"I'm doing well, Jimmy," he replied as he took his customary seat at the far end of the bar, "how about you?"

"I've got me health and I'm keeping the devil at bay," the man replied as he poured a pint of Guinness and handed it to Karl. "So it's a right grand day to be alive."

"Hear, hear," Sigurdsson replied as he raised the glass up in a toast.

"Hey, I got a joke for you," O'Toole said. "How do we know that *Jaysus* was Irish?"

"I don't know, Jimmy, how do we know that Jesus was Irish?"

"Because he was thirty-three, still lived at home, thought his mother was a virgin, and she thought he was the son of God."

The man burst out in laughter, which was so infectious that it made Sigurdsson laugh as well.

"You're going to hell, Jimmy."

"*Ai, boyo*, but hopefully not today," O'Toole replied. "What else can I get you?"

"Let me have the shepherd's pie."

"Coming right up," the man replied, before disappearing into the kitchen.

Sigurdsson took a sip of his beer and surveyed the bar. It was a quiet night and there were only a handful of regulars, who sat talking amongst themselves at the other end. Sigurdsson liked MacNeighill's because it was the kind of place where no one bothered you, even if they knew what you did for a living. There were no cop questions or complaints. When you were here, you were just another familiar face.

He raised his glass to take a sip when his attention was drawn to the ringing of the bell above the door. Sigurdsson's eyes went wide in shock as the tall, statuesque blonde walked in.

You've got to be kidding me, he thought as he recalled the woman he had seen minutes earlier on the video.

27

He watched as she removed her coat and took a seat at one of the booths.

"You're gawking, *boyo*," he heard Jimmy whisper.

"Do you know her?"

The man looked over, without trying to look too obvious, and then shook his head. "Nope, never seen her before, but she's a grand one, isn't she?"

"Yeah," Sigurdsson replied, "she sure is."

"Well go on, ya *eejit*, before she catches ya looking at her and calls the *guards*."

Sigurdsson took a sip of his beer for courage and got up. "Keep my dinner warm."

"*Ai*," O'Toole replied with a wink and a smile, "that I will."

Sigurdsson cautiously approached the table. The last thing he wanted to do was scare her off. "Excuse me, miss."

The woman glanced up from the menu she'd been reading and looked at him. "Yes?"

Sigurdsson felt his legs get a bit wobbly, as he stared into her eyes longer than he should have. The video didn't do justice to them. Her eyes sparkled, even in the poor lighting of the bar, like exquisitely cut aquamarine. It was all he could do to focus his attention away from them.

"Hi, I'm terribly sorry to bother you, but by any chance were you at Jennings Park the other night?"

The woman's indifference turned to one of caution. "I'm sorry, who are you?"

"Oh, pardon me, my name is Karl Sigurdsson, I'm a detective," he said, fishing his shield case out of his pocket and showing it to her. "I'm investigating the incident."

The woman examined the gold shield and identification card, before looking back at him.

"I'm so sorry," she said, the wary look turning warmer. "You just can't be too careful these days."

"No, I understand completely," he said.

"Please, have a seat," she said, motioning to the seat across from her.

"Thank you," Sigurdsson replied as he sat down, doing his best to avoid staring into her eyes.

"My name is Gabrielle and, to answer your question, yes, I was there. My sister and I were walking by when we saw all the activity and stopped to see what was going on."

"You didn't happen to notice anything *unusual* while you were there?" he asked. "Anyone that might have looked suspicious to you or perhaps seemed out of place?"

"No, not really," she replied. "Like I said, we were just out shopping and saw all the police cars. Curiosity got the better of us, so we stopped to see what was going on. One of the other people said that someone had died."

"Yeah, an older gentleman," he replied.

"Can you tell me what happened?"

"Right now we are still investigating, but it doesn't appear to have been natural."

"Oh, wow, that's terrible," she replied. "I guess no time is good to die, but it seems so much more tragic during this time of year."

"Do you mind if I ask you your last name?" Sigurdsson asked.

The woman smiled warmly and Sigurdsson felt his heart beating in his chest.

"No, not at all," she replied. "It's de Mar, Gabrielle de Mar, but my friends call me Gabi."

Sigurdsson pulled a pen and notebook out of his jacket pocket and began writing.

"I suppose you need my information for your report?"

"It would help," he replied.

She extended her hand and he gave her the notebook and pen; watching as she wrote down the address and phone number.

"What about your sister?"

"Serena? I'm sorry, but she left this morning to go out of town," Gabi replied. "She's visiting friends for the holidays and I don't expect her back till after the New Year. If you'd like, the next time I talk to her I can ask her if she remembers anything."

"That would be great," he replied. "Do you mind if I ask you a question?"

"Of course," she replied.

Something about the way she spoke was mesmerizing. Her voice had an almost melodic tone that had him listening intently to every word.

"You're not originally from around here, are you?"

Gabi chuckled. "No, I'm not. How could you tell?"

"You just don't strike me as the typical New Yorker."

"Is that good or bad?" she asked.

"Uhm,…. No, it's just…," he stammered, trying not to sound too much like an idiot and failing.

"It's okay, Karl," she replied. "Actually, I was born in Spain. My father was in the military, so we traveled a lot when I was younger."

"How did you end up in New York?"

"My sister and I came for a visit and we liked it so much we stayed."

"That must have been hard on your parents."

"They passed," she said softly.

"Oh, I'm sorry,… I didn't mean to…"

Gabi held up her hand. "Don't worry; it was a long time ago."

"So how do you like the city?" he asked, doing his best to change the subject as quickly as possible.

"It's nice, it has a good energy," she replied, "but it can also be a *lonely* place at times."

He perked up at that bit of information. "I have a hard time believing that you would ever be lonely."

"Is that your best pickup line?" she grinned.

Sigurdsson felt a burning sensation as his cheeks began to redden. For someone who had always been carefree and confident around women, he seemed to be bombing with her.

"I didn't mean to pry," he said nervously.

"No, you're not prying," Gabi said, trying to ease his obvious discomfort. "Believe it or not, I don't get out much. I'm not big into the club scene or whatever it is they are doing these days."

"So there's no….."

Gabi shook her head, "No, there isn't. When I was younger yes, but now I guess I'm more of a homebody."

"You're not exactly *old*," he replied.

"I guess I just wear it well," Gabi said with an impish smile.

"I guess you do," Sigurdsson replied.

"Now, do you mind if I ask you a question?"

"No, not at all," he replied.

"Is there a *Mrs. Detective*?"

"No, there isn't. Police work and relationships don't seem to mesh well. Most seem to like the attraction to the job, but very few like the job itself."

"Or, maybe you just haven't met the right woman yet."

"*Ah hem.*"

Sigurdsson and Gabrielle both looked up to see O'Toole standing next to the table.

"I don't mean to interrupt, but do either of you fancy a drink?"

"I'll have a glass of wine," Gabi replied.

"And what can I get for you, *sir*?" Jimmy asked with a wry smile.

"I'll have a Guinness," Sigurdsson said, giving the man a side-eyed *get the hell out of here* look.

After O'Toole had brought their drinks, they resumed their conversation. Three hours later they were still sitting there talking when, much to their dismay, O'Toole announced the last call.

"I can't believe how late it is," Sigurdsson said. "I didn't mean to keep you this long."

"No need to apologize," she replied. "In fact, I should be thanking you; I had an enjoyable evening with you."

"It was my pleasure, Gabi. I did as well."

The two of them stood up and he helped her with her coat.

"Thank you," she replied. "It's nice to see that chivalry still exists."

"My mother would never forgive me," he said, as he turned to look back toward the bar. "Hey, Jimmy, put this on my tab."

"Sure thing, *boyo*," the man called back with a wave.

"You didn't have to do that," she said as they walked outside.

"I'll bill the department," Sigurdsson laughed. "After all, I was interviewing a potential witness."

"I don't think you got enough information from me to warrant that kind of bill," she replied as she buttoned up her jacket.

"Well, maybe I should interview you again, in case you remember something else."

"Maybe you should," she replied.

"You think so?" Sigurdsson asked, shocked at her response.

"Yeah, I think so," Gabi said, giving him a wink. "Don't lose my number."

"No, I…. I won't," he stammered.

"Good. Then I will look forward to hearing from you," Gabi said as she leaned in close and gave him a quick kiss. "Goodnight, Karl."

Then she turned and walked away, disappearing around the corner.

"Goodnight, Gabi," he said, his voice almost a whisper in the cold December air as the heat from her lips lingered on his.

CHAPTER SIX

"**W**here the hell have you been?"

Her sister's pointed question caught Gabi off-guard as she set her shopping bags down and shut the apartment's door behind her.

"I went shopping," she answered as she made her way into the kitchen and poured herself a cup of coffee.

Gabi could see that Serena was annoyed. She was sitting at the table, smoking a cigarette. Her eyes were dark and she was clenching her jaw; causing the muscles in her cheeks to ripple.

"And where were you *last night*?" Serena asked.

"I went out," she said defensively.

"Where did you go?" Serena demanded.

"What is this, the *inquisition*?" Gabi snapped. "I told you, I went *out*. Why do you want to know?"

"Because it's completely out of character for you and I was *worried*," Serena replied, her tone mellowing slightly.

Gabi snickered, not entirely convinced of the second half of her sister's statement. "I needed some time out to think about things."

"You spent all those hours thinking *alone*?" Serena asked.

"I didn't say I was alone," she replied, sitting down at the table across from her sister.

A quizzical look came across Serena's face as she tried to make sense of what Gabi had just said to her. "You weren't *alone*? What the hell do you mean by that?"

"I met someone last night?"

"*Who*?" Serena asked, the question coming out as more of an immediate demand for an answer rather than a curious inquiry.

Gabi hesitated, considering how much she should share, but realized that there was no point in beating around the bush. Serena was like a dog with a bone; if she felt she was being lied to or misled, she would become tenacious and wouldn't stop until she got every last detail.

"Remember that cop from the park the other night?"

Gabi watched as her sister's eyes went wide in shock.

"No," Serena exclaimed, leaping out of her chair and began pacing around the kitchen. "Please tell me this is some kind of bad joke."

"No, why would I joke about that?" Gabi asked.

Serena paused in mid-stride and looked over at her sister; her expression was a mix of shock and incredulity.

"Are you out of your mind?" she asked. "We don't interact with *them*!"

"Well you've certainly *interacted* with one of them the other night," Gabi shot back angrily, "and what about the one last week? In fact, while we are taking this little *walk down memory lane*, how about the one last month? As I recall, you had a particularly *fun* time interacting with him, although I doubt the same could be said for *his* experience."

"That's different," Serena said sharply as she crushed her cigarette out in the ashtray. "They were just marks."

"Marks?" Gabi repeated, her eyebrows arching upward as she took a sip of coffee. "Oh, is that the colloquialism you're using to describe your victims now? *Bravo*! It makes it sound so much better."

"You know what I mean. They serve a purpose."

"Well, maybe I was looking for someone to *serve a purpose* as well."

"What do you think the council will say when they find out you're having a relationship with not only a human, but a *cop*?"

"I don't know, *sister*. Maybe you should explain how the council would ever *find out* about what I am doing in the first place?"

The accusation hung in the air between them, escalating the tension that already dominated the small room. After a few moments it was Serena who finally broke it.

"Look, Gabi, all I am saying is that this is risky."

"Life is risky, Serena. That doesn't mean we stay locked away behind the apartment door. If that's what this life is going to be, than I would rather die today."

"Don't say that," Serena replied, her voice tinged with a mix of anger and pain.

"Why not?"

"Because it's stupid," Serena said dismissively.

"It's not stupid," Gabi replied, her tone softening. "We act like we're not human, like we are something different—"

"We are," Serena shot back.

"Maybe we are, but that doesn't mean that we still don't have desires and needs."

Serena walked over to the large dining-room window and stared silently as she struggled with her own thoughts.

"If they find out……" she whispered.

"Who will tell them?" Gabi asked. "It's not like I'm the only one breaking the rules. I'm sure they wouldn't be thrilled with *any* of the antics going on."

Serena turned her head, looking back over her shoulder at Gabrielle. "Is that a threat?"

"Of course not," Gabi scoffed. "I'm just stating the obvious. You know I support you; all the time. I might not agree, but I would never turn my back on you. All I am asking is for you to support me."

"Fine," Serena said tersely. "But just remember that I warned you about the dangerous game you are playing."

"Aren't you also the one who said that 'dangerous games make this life more bearable'?"

Serena's eyes narrowed as she felt a rush of anger inside her. She hated the thought of her own words coming back to bite her in the ass, especially since it was true.

"Fine," she said.

"Don't be mad," Gabi pleaded. "In fact, I have a bit of an ulterior motive."

"Really?" Serena asked. "And what, pray tell, would that be?"

"I thought, being that you insist on playing your dangerous games, that it might be a smart move to monitor the local authorities."

Serena let out a laugh; the suddenness of which startled Gabi.

"Monitor? Is that what you're calling it now? You're *monitoring* him?"

"You know what I mean."

"Do whatever you have to do, Gabi," Serena said in annoyance as she spun around and headed toward the front door.

"Where are you going?"

"Out," she replied, as she put on her coat. "I need some fresh air."

"Want me to come with you?" Gabi asked.

"No, maybe I will meet someone I can *monitor*, like you have."

"Don't—" Gabi cried out, but the slamming of the door cutoff the rest of her sentence. "*Damnit*, Serena!"

CHAPTER SEVEN

Gabrielle poured herself a glass of wine and walked over to the window where her sister had stood a few moments earlier.

The city skyline twinkled with bright lights, keeping the darkness at bay, but it did nothing for her mood.

"What a whiny little bitch," she muttered as she sipped her drink.

Serena had always been impulsive. She was never one to give a second thought to any decision she made, but what infuriated Gabrielle was the obvious double standard for her.

Even though they were the same age, Serena always seemed to treat her like the *younger* sibling; something that annoyed her to no end. Now that she had done something for herself, it was like she had broken some cardinal rule. Yes, on one hand Serena was right, the council was against any personal interaction with humans, but who gave them the right to decide what relationships were acceptable? She knew for a fact that several of them were fond of *blurring the lines*. And who was Serena to judge what she did? She always acted as though she was *above* the law.

It was frustrating and infuriating.

The chirping of her cellphone interrupted her thoughts. Few people had her number, but when she looked at the screen, she didn't recognize the caller.

"Hello?" she asked cautiously.

"Hi, Gabi, it's Karl," the voice on the other end said.

"Karl, hey, how are you?" she asked, feeling a mix of relief and excitement.

"I'm doing well," he replied. "Look, I hope I'm not being pushy, but you gave me your number and I was wondering if you were free tonight?

"No, you're not being pushy, and yes, as luck would have it I am."

"Would you like to go to dinner with me or maybe catch a movie?"

"I'd love to."

"Which one?" he asked.

"Either, both," she replied, feeling a bit brazen. "Your call, just tell me what time to be ready by."

"Well, I get off work at five," he replied. "I can swing by and pick you up around five thirty; if that's all right with you?"

"Do you know where I live?"

"Uhm, yeah, you gave me the address for my report, remember?"

"Oh, right," Gabi said, feeling a wave of embarrassment wash over her. "I guess I had a blonde moment."

"We all have them," he replied. "So does five thirty work for you?"

"Yes, I'll be waiting."

"Great, I'll see you then."

"Bye," Gabi said, before ending the call.

She did a little pirouette in the living room, feeling a girlish-giddiness coursing through her body.

How long has it been? she wondered, before pushing the thought away.

Times had changed and people had changed. This was the present and she knew that she had to live in the moment; for as ever long as that moment lasted.

CHAPTER EIGHT

Serena made her way across the city as effortlessly as a sleek jungle cat sliding through the forest.

There was anger raging inside of her, something that felt almost primordial, and she struggled to maintain control, even as it threatened to spill over.

She paused for a moment, hunkering down on the transept of St. Patrick's Cathedral, and glared down at the pedestrians who were making their way along Fifth Avenue. Something about their naïve ignorance of the deadly threat, which stalked them from two hundred feet above, made her smile.

Normally this would be the *fun* part of the game for her, picking out her latest victim, but tonight was different. Tonight wasn't about enjoyment, it was about exacting revenge.

The irony that she was hunting from atop the largest cathedral in North America was not lost on her.

It's all Your fault, she thought as she gazed up into the blackness of the night sky with condemnation. *You allowed me to become this… this thing.*

She leaned back, slipping into the shadows, as she sat against one of the spires.

Any other time she would have selected her prey and followed them, waiting for just the right moment to swoop down and satisfy her needs, but tonight her emotions were hindering her ability to stay focused.

It wasn't like her and Gabi hadn't had their disagreements in the past, but this felt different; Gabi was different. Ever since she'd gotten her stupid little *promotion,* things had changed between them.

Did she really change or did you?

Serena's eyes went wide in panic and she jerked her head, scanning the rooftop for the source of the disembodied voice that she had heard in her head.

"Yes," she retorted as she stared down the deserted roofline. "Yes, she has changed,"

But even as the words came out, she knew they were a lie.

As equal as they were, she had always embraced her role as the older sister in their relationship. She had enjoyed being a mentor and had envisioned a time when the two of them could do great things together, but she realized now that it would never happen. Despite what she'd always wished for, they would never be alike. She was bold, and willing to take risks, but Gabi was more unassuming, compliant, and willing to support the status quo.

Serena missed the old Gabi; when she was young and filled with the same passion fervor, but she grudgingly accepted that person was gone now. Gabi had embraced the rules, and that was something Serena could not do.

That's not true, she thought. *Even before all the rules were put in place, Gabi never enjoyed the hunt; not the way I do.*

Now that Gabi had moved up the ladder, the fissure in their relationship had only grown wider. Serena was happy for her, but she couldn't quite stave off the pangs of jealousy she felt over Gabi's achievement. Not that she felt Gabi was better than she was; it was just that it should have been her and it was a feeling shared by others. On top of that, she now had to contend with this new *relationship* that had appeared out of the blue.

Well, it wasn't entirely out of the blue, she thought.

Serena had seen that *look* in her eyes when Gabi had first caught sight of the detective. At first she had mistaken it for the same look she had when she had found a new victim, but she soon realized just how wrong she was.

She was shocked when she realized that Gabi was smitten by the tall, blonde-haired detective. To be fair, the man was handsome, but he was still a human. What concerned her most was that she had never known Gabi to be enamored by one of *them*, let alone pursue it as she apparently had. And she certainly didn't buy her story that she was looking for *information*.

Gabi always seemed to be in control; almost to the point of being calculating. Rarely had she ever seen her give in to anything that would even be remotely considered impulsive.

"Stupid people sometimes do stupid things," she said flatly.

And that really was the problem.

She wasn't a leader, not like she was. It had always been her who'd paved the way for them. Sure she cared about her, in the same way anyone would care about someone less fortunate. Gabi didn't have the same world view as she did. She seemed to be more inclined to heed the *live and let live* orthodoxy that was being pushed these days, but Serena couldn't understand why.

Why do I have to suffer because of their inferiority? Why do any of us have to take a back seat to them?

Serena knew that she wasn't the only one who felt this way, but, unlike the others, she seemed to be the only one willing to push the boundaries; to take the chances necessary to bring about change. That was because she was a real leader, and it was that lack of deserved recognition that angered her most.

She loved Gabi, but that didn't mean she had to love the things her sister did. If she wanted to embrace Janus' philosophy of peace and love, she could, but that didn't give them a right to force it upon her and the rest of them.

There came a point in every life where you had to choose what side you stood with. Gabi had chosen her side and now she would have to choose hers.

History had proven that life *never* favored the submissive. Weak people elevated other weak people, who in-turn promoted ineffectual ideas that never lasted. Eventually, all those who laid down their arms, and embraced the mantra of *peace at all costs,* perished because they lacked the conviction and ability to defend themselves when it mattered most.

She would not be counted among those who went quietly into the night.

A successful rebellion needed a champion; somebody willing to take the reins and make the difficult choices. She was that somebody. She'd been through the fire, faced all the obstacles, and emerged victorious. She knew that there were others, waiting for the right opportunity, and once she proved that Janus and his ilk didn't have the temerity to lead, it wouldn't be long before they would follow the path she had carved out. Then life could decide who the rightful victors and losers would be.

Still, she knew that this wasn't a choice to be taken lightly.

As amicable as Janus and the others appeared to be, she also knew *what* they were. Even the most easy-going among them could be pushed into action from a direct assault. No, if she would enjoy any measure of success she would have to be smart.

What was the saying? 'How can anyone enter a strong man's house and steal his possessions, unless he first ties up the strong man? Then he can plunder his house.'

She would first have to tie them up and what better way to do that than with their own rules. Perhaps when Gabi saw first-hand how her beloved rules could be manipulated against her, she would have her own change of heart.

Serena smiled as the seed of discontent took shape in her mind.

The anger that had previously gripped her took flight, carried aloft by the wind and out of her mind. In its wake something else took hold; a hunger that yearned to be quenched.

She stood up and stretched as a smile grew on her face. She felt a sense of freedom that came from being unencumbered by the petty rules and politics of the coven.

No longer burdened by the need to *hide* her unseemly behavior, she set out to satisfy her needs and to strike the first *spark* of her rebellion.

CHAPTER NINE

Sigurdsson walked up the old wrought-iron staircase, which led up to the squad room, with a newfound spring in his step and a smile on his face; all while his mind played out the events of the previous night.

A part of him wanted to play it off as being normal, that this was something he was accustomed to, but Gabi was unlike anyone he'd ever known before. Not only was she extremely attractive, but she was equally intelligent and funny.

He'd picked her up, intending to take her out to dinner and a movie, but they ended up spending the night at a local coffee bar engrossed in conversation. They had found a booth near the back, away from the hustle and bustle of the counter, and got lost in each other's stories.

The more she shared about herself, the more he wanted to know. A part of him was envious, as she shared all the places that she and her sister had visited, but she was much more tightlipped with information about her parents or any other family members. He got the impression that there was some drama there, which she wasn't quite ready to share yet, and he made a point to not press the issue. It wasn't hard, because he was more interested in her than anything else. Sigurdsson couldn't help but get the feeling that she was an *old soul* trapped in a young woman's body.

She seemed equally interested in learning more about him; wanting to know what it was like to be a *big city* detective.

"Well, I can tell you that it is nothing like what they show you on television," he said with a laugh. "It's three times the work, a quarter of the help, and it takes more than an hour or two to solve things."

"You're crushing my fantasies," she said as she took a sip of her drink.

"You?" he asked lightheartedly. "Imagine how I felt when I realized all the shows I grew up on were a lie. They never show you the mountain of paperwork that is generated by even the simplest call."

"That had to be utterly devastating," Gabi laughed. "So what made you want to become a cop?"

"I guess deep down inside there was always a part of me that wanted to help people," he confessed. "My mom, Helga, used to say it was the warrior spirit that ran in our blood."

"She sounds like an amazing person," Gabi said. "I'd love to meet her someday."

"I wish you could, but she passed away."

Gabi cringed inwardly and wished she could take the words back. "Oh, Karl, I am sorry, I didn't mean—"

"No, don't be sorry," he interrupted. "You didn't know and I truly wish you could have met her. She was an amazing woman and I think she would have liked you."

"That's sweet of you to say, especially after I stuck my foot in my mouth."

"Mom had an adventurous spirit. She was not happy unless she was outdoors being one with nature."

"That must have been a wonderful experience for you growing up," Gabi replied.

"It was, but it could also be tough," he said thoughtfully. "Mom was not one of those touchy-feely, helicopter parents; in fact, she was the antithesis of that. Growing up in the Sigurdsson household was about hard work and respect. I remember one time we were eating dinner and my brother, Arne, told a story about a kid who was being bullied at school. According to Arne, some kids at another table were picking on this kid because he was poor.

Without even looking up from her plate, mom asked, 'So what did you do?' I remember Arne looking over at me with a confused look on his face. Mom repeated the question again and he said, 'Nothing, it wasn't my table, I wasn't involved.' Mom folded her napkin and set it on the table and asked him what he would have done if it had been Gunnar, our younger brother. Arne says that he would have taught them a lesson. Mom looked at him and said, 'In this life you have two choices: do what you know is right or sit back and let evil win. Today, by choosing to do nothing, you sided with evil.'"

"Wow," Gabi said. "That's pretty powerful."

"The next day mom got a call from the school that Arne had gotten in a fight and was being suspended. She asked them what happened and they told her he had intervened on behalf of the kid who had been bullied. Mom asked them if they had monitors in the lunchroom and they told her they did. Then she asked them what the monitors had been doing to stop the bullying from happening in the first place. Apparently they didn't have a good answer, so she informed them that if they suspended Arne, for doing what the monitors were being paid to prevent, then they needed to send that to her in writing and to get ready for a lawsuit. Needless to say, Arne didn't get suspended and the bullying stopped."

"She doesn't sound like the average mom," Gabi said.

"She wasn't," Sigurdsson replied. "In fact, none of my family was what you would call average. My aunts and uncles were a fun loving bunch, but there was also an unmistakable hardness to them. Most of my family are first or second generation Danes who came over to America for a better life. I can remember growing up and listening to them talk around the table. They would drink and tell stories about their homeland and the more they drank the wilder the stories grew. If you listened long enough, you would undoubtedly hear one of them proclaim that we were descendants of Vikings."

A faint smile appeared on his face as he relived the memory.

"You're very lucky to have those memories."

"I miss those days," he said wistfully. "Things seemed so much simpler back then. It's hard to grow up, to give up on all the things you once believed."

"It sounds like you had a great life," Gabi said.

"I did," he replied as he took a drink and reminisced, "but as much as I enjoyed the family tales, it was the times spent with my mom, sitting out by the fire, when she told me stories from Norse mythology that have always stayed with me. While other kids grew up playing *Cowboys and Indians*, I would imagine myself fighting alongside the likes of *Balder, Vale, Heimdall,* and *Thor*. It was fun to imagine myself being transported to faraway lands, where I could battle epic foes. I grew up wanting to be that hero, which is why I joined the department."

Out of habit, and in memory of his mother, he touched his chest, pressing the pendent he wore against his heart.

It was his most treasured possession; a hand-carved bronze pendant depicting *Mjöllnir*, Thor's hammer, which she had given to him when he graduated from the police academy.

"Any weapon, even the great ones, is only as effective as the person who wields them, Karl," she told him, as she placed it around his neck, "but remember, with great strength also comes great responsibility; when you have to, always use it wisely and justly."

Sigurdsson could feel tears begin to well up in his eyes and he swallowed hard, as he recalled her untimely death just a few months after his graduation.

Gabi recognized that he was having a personal moment and held her silence.

"The hardest thing for a cop is that you learn early on that most people don't want help," he continued, pushing the memories away. "At least not until it is too late, and even then you get blamed for their misfortune. You're either too oppressive or you're never around."

"That must be frustrating," she replied.

"It can be, if you take it to heart, but you come to realize that you do a thankless job and the measure of your success doesn't come from outside, but from within. Besides, sometimes, if you're lucky, you have a chance to meet someone who makes it all seem worthwhile."

A smile grew on her face, and her eyes twinkled at his compliment. "You're very sweet, Karl. I'm sure your mother is very pleased by the man you've become."

"Thank you," Sigurdsson replied.

It was a quarter after eleven, and the shop was getting ready to close, when they realized how long they'd been talking. With reluctance, Sigurdsson drove her back to the apartment and walked her to the front door.

"I had a wonderful time, Gabi," he said, not wanting the night to end.

"I did as well, Karl," she replied. "You're a truly special person."

"*Special*, huh," he said jokingly. "Special, as in I should clear my social calendar or I should get some professional help?"

Without saying a word, Gabi leaned in and kissed him.

It was a long, lingering kiss; the kind that seemed electric and had the ability to stop time. For a moment it was only them in the world and he wrapped his arms around her.

When their kiss finally came to an end, she took a step back and looked at him with smoldering eyes, "Does that answer your question, Karl?"

"My calendar is all yours," he whispered.

"Smart man," she smiled, before heading back into the apartment building.

His reverie of the past night's activities lasted just long enough until he saw the dour looking face of Sergeant White peeking out from his office.

"You've got another body," the man said gruffly.

"Oh, for the love of God," Sigurdsson replied, setting the container of coffee he was carrying on the nearest desk. "What am I, the *homicide whisperer* now?"

"Call it the fruits of your labor, Karl," White replied, as he walked into the squad room. "The L.T. had a chat with the Chief of D's, who found your theory amusing, but apparently worthy of further consideration. She was quick to point out that bad guys died all the time, and the department didn't view them as being committed by one person, but she agreed to have you follow-up with any unusual homicides that come in to see if there is any correlation. This one is about as *unusual* as they come."

"So I'm getting this dumped on me?"

"The Chief is concerned that there is the *potential*, however slight, that you might be right and that we may have a serial killer running loose. Those things tend to generate a lot of unwelcome news for the department."

"Do I get help at least?"

"No, after all it is just a weak-ass *theory*. If you can come up with some conclusive evidence linking them I'm sure they'll consider putting a task force together, but until that time comes, you're *the* man."

"That's awesome."

"Well, maybe next time you'll want to consider keeping those hunches to yourself until you have solid evidence to back them up," White replied. "But there is a bright side to all of this."

"Really? I can't wait to hear about it."

"I guess you're talk with the L.T. did the trick. You're out of his shit house. So, for the time being, he's pulling you off of the case assignment loop; at least for the moment, but the clock is ticking. I don't think Janovic is too happy about the extra workload, but it's about time his useless ass did some real police work."

"That's fine, but my cases will start getting backed up."

"Go through them and give me anything that is time sensitive," White said. "I'll pass them out to the others."

"Thanks, boss," Sigurdsson replied. "So what's the story with this one?"

"From what Operations told me it sounds like our stiff tried to hop the fence over at the zoo and become the next *Daniel*, but I guess the lions didn't get the memo from on high."

"That's great," Sigurdsson said sarcastically, envisioning the carnage that would most likely limit his breakfast options.

"Looks like you're the L.T.'s new favorite detective," White laughed, "so get out there and start detecting, son."

CHAPTER TEN

The service road, leading into the zoo, was blocked off by a marked patrol car.

Sigurdsson pulled his unmarked squad to a stop, as the uniformed officer exited his vehicle and approached him. Sigurdsson lowered the window and held his shield out in his left hand.

"Fifteenth Squad," he said to the cop. "They told me you have a D.O.A. here?"

"Yeah, over in the lion's pen," the cop confirmed. "Just head through the gate and take the left access road, you can't miss it. Everyone, and their pet dog, is already there."

"Thanks," Sigurdsson replied, as he contemplated how messy the scene would be.

In the past he'd heard horror stories from the old timers about how crime scenes would be rendered useless by the flood of cops traipsing through; especially on *photo worthy* homicides. Every profession had some folks who enjoyed the *macabre*. Over the years, techniques had improved considerably, but a scene like this would be messy enough without having to waste time eliminating the tracks of the responding police, EMS, and zoo personnel.

A few moments later he arrived at the *Serengeti Safari* exhibit; a large, two-story building, that was located in the center of the sprawling park.

He pulled in behind a morgue wagon and stepped out into the frigid morning air.

"Doesn't feel much like Africa to me," he muttered as he made his way toward the front door. Once inside, he felt a thermal blast hit him in the face, shocking his senses.

Well, that's more like it, he thought as he walked over toward a group of people gathered by a display window.

A man in a suit noticed him approaching and waived him over.

"Are you the detective they were sending over?" he asked.

"Yeah, I'm Detective Sigurdsson, Fifteenth Squad."

"I'm Sergeant O'Donohue," the man replied. "The Chief said she was sending someone over to look at what we had. Other than having crime scene photos taken, I told my guys to stand down until you got here."

"Thanks."

"Do you have any idea why this one is so special?" O'Donohue asked.

"It's probably not," Sigurdsson replied, not wanting to give away too many details. "It's just that I had a homicide the other day and the Chief wanted me to take a look to make sure they weren't connected."

"Well, to be honest with you, this one is kind of weird."

"Why do you say that?"

"They found the night-shift security officer dead in the lion enclosure. The lions were in there, but we don't think they attacked him."

"How does that happen?"

"Beats the hell out of me, but I'll let them explain the details," O'Donohue replied as he motioned for one of the zoo employees to join them.

"Ashley, this is Detective Sigurdsson, can you tell him how you found the deceased?"

"Hi, I'm Ashley Cannon," she replied, shaking Sigurdsson's hand. "I'm the director of the Serengeti Safari exhibit."

"Sorry to meet you under the circumstances," he said. "Do we know how this happened?"

"Normally, Mel, our night security guard, is waiting for us in the morning to open the front gate, but when we arrived, it was still closed and he was nowhere in sight. We tried to call him on the radio, but there was no reply."

"Is that unusual?"

"For him, yes," she replied. "If it had been anyone else, I would have thought they had just fallen asleep, but Mel was always Johnny-on-the-spot. So it worried me that something had happened to him. I had one of my guys climb the fence and he opened the gate from the main control room. I immediately ordered a search of the grounds, while I continued to try to raise him on the radio."

"Where did you find him?"

"Inside the exhibit," she replied. "I can show you."

The three of them walked out of the main room and down a long service tunnel. She paused at a large steel door and lifted the portable radio from her belt.

"This is Ashley, I'm entering the enclosure," she said.

"Copy, enclosure is clear," a man's voice replied.

"Protocol," she explained to Sigurdsson. "Even when we know the animals aren't outside, no one enters without confirmation that they are secure."

She turned back toward the door, removing the safety latch that held a thick steel sliding bolt in place, and opened it.

They felt a blast of frigid air rush by them.

"Excuse my ignorance, but why were the lions out in this environment overnight?"

"They weren't," she replied, leading them down a rocky path to where the body of Melvin Brooks lay. "Or at least they shouldn't have been. I checked the records and they haven't been outside since before Thanksgiving."

Sigurdsson glanced around, taking notes on the exhibit. It was a wide open area that stretched for as far as he could see. There was a viewing area, where visitors could look into the exhibit, but beyond that there was a fence that he guessed to be nearly twenty feet high. At the top of the fence were poles that had large, inverted u-shaped anti-climbing rods, facing both inward and outward; making it doubtful that the security guard would have been able to scale the fence.

"How big is the exhibit, Ashley?" he asked.

"Just about three acres," she replied.

"And the same fence configuration runs the whole length?"

"Yes, it starts from the visitor center on one side," she replied, pointing up toward the building, "then runs the entire length of the enclosure and returns to the center on the other side."

Sigurdsson kneeled down next to the body and began taking notes. He hadn't known what to expect when he arrived, but as he examined the man, he was certain that this wasn't it. The body of the deceased seemed normal, with no visible injuries, except that his eyes were open and glazed over.

Realizing that you're about to have an unexpected meeting with your maker will do that, he thought.

He was an older man, probably in his late 60s or early 70s, and was still attired in his security uniform. He was wearing a thick parka and the fur-lined hood was pulled up securely over his head. Sigurdsson noticed that he was still wearing his watch. He examined the face, noting the cracked glass which had stopped the hands at the 10:18 mark. As he examined it closer, he recognized the small silver shield in the center with the letters PBA on it.

Sigurdsson glanced up at O'Donohue, "Was he a cop?"

O'Donohue shrugged his shoulders and looked over at Canon.

"I think he was at one time," she replied, "but I believe he was retired. He's been working here for almost fifteen years now."

Sigurdsson began a search of the body, finding a .38 Cal revolver in an ankle holster and a small leather wallet containing a silver police officer's shield.

"*Jesus H. Christ*," O'Donohue said somberly as Sigurdsson handed him the man's gun and shield. "I've got to notify Operations."

He watched as the sergeant walked back up the path, then turned to look at Canon.

"Why would he come in here, Ashley?"

"That's the part I don't get," she replied. "He shouldn't have. Mel knew the rules better than anyone. Even if there was a disturbance in here, the protocol is that no one goes inside alone and without first notifying control."

"Even if the park is closed?" Sigurdsson asked.

"Especially if the park is closed," she replied. "There is a list of emergency numbers in the security office that he would have known to contact."

"So take me through this from the beginning, Ashley. I want all the details from the time the body was first discovered."

"Well, like I said, I started the search and it was about fifteen minutes before I got the call on the radio. One of my techs, Javier Rodriguez, said that he'd found Mel's body. I rushed over to the exhibit and we could see him lying there. We immediately went into the stalls and realized that several of the lions were missing."

"Missing?" Sigurdsson asked.

"Yes, the cage doors had all been opened. So we began to do a visual check and found them huddling near the service door that we just came through."

"*Huddling*?"

"Yeah, they were gathered in a group in the corner; it was like they were afraid to move."

"I've watched my fair of nature shows and I've never seen a lion afraid of anything."

"Neither had I," she replied. "At least not until this morning,"

"Then what happened?"

"Well, we put in a call to 911 and then took steps to get the lions back in their cages. Not that it was hard, because the minute we opened the door they rushed back in. After that we waited until you guys arrived."

"Any idea on how he got in there?" Sigurdsson asked.

"No, the door to the enclosure was unlocked when we arrived, but there is no way that he would have been able to release them."

"Why is that?"

"Because the cage doors work off a two-man system," she replied. "The control room has to release the electronic safeguard of the lock, but someone has to be here physically, in order to disengage the door lock. You can't have one without the other. The system was specifically designed to prevent something like this from happening. So even if the electronic safeguard was tripped, it automatically resets in 15 seconds."

"And you're positive that there was no one else here last night?"

"No, he was the only one here," she replied. "I want to help, but we just don't understand how Mel, or the lions, got inside."

Sigurdsson looked around the enclosure and noticed a small, fisheye lens camera in the overhang's corner.

"Do those security cameras work?"

"Yes, they do," she replied, "but they're not the greatest quality. They allow us to monitor the goings on in and around the park."

"Do they record?"

"I believe they do, at least for several days, and then they record over them."

"Well if he was on the overnight shift, then there should still be time," Sigurdsson replied. "Can you show them to me?"

"Sure, come with me."

Five minutes later, Canon pulled her golf cart up to the administration building, where the security office was located, and led Sigurdsson inside.

An older, gray haired man sat behind a desk monitoring a bank of grainy, black and white security monitors.

Sigurdsson tried to contain his dismay when he realized that the video set-up appeared to be, at best, late twentieth century tech.

"Tony, this is Detective Sigurdsson," she said by way of introduction. "Can you pull up the Serengeti feed for last night?"

"Sure thing, Ash," the man replied, before tapping several keys on the board in front of him.

Sigurdsson watched as the live feed on several of the monitors went dark and were replaced a moment later with taped footage. The man fast forwarded the video until they saw the lights of a golf cart appear in the distance and then pulled up outside the exhibit.

"Okay, can we see this in regular speed?" Sigurdsson asked.

The man slowed the speed to normal and they watched as Melvin Brooks got out of the cart. The man pulled the hood of his parka up, before removing an old *Maglite* flashlight from his pocket and turned it on.

"Something seems to have gotten his attention," Sigurdsson said.

"There's no entry in the security logs," Tony said matter-of-factly. "I checked this morning when I came in."

"Maybe a routine check then?"

"It's December, it was cold as a witch's tit last night," Tony said, before realizing who was in the room. "Pardon my French, ma'am."

"Don't worry, Tony, my dad also speaks fluent *French*."

"Anyway," the security man continued. "Short of the park being on fire, I can't imagine Melvin leaving this office."

"Well it appears that he was checking something out," Sigurdsson replied.

As they watched the man walk around the exterior fence, the screen rippled slightly, as if a sudden gust of wind had passed by it, and then Melvin disappeared from the screen.

"What the fuck?" Tony said, with a mix of confusion and anger in his voice.

He tapped several keys, rewinding the video, and watched as the same scene repeated itself. Then he slowed it down further, watching the time stamp on the bottom.

"Glitch?" Sigurdsson asked.

"I got nothing," Tony said as he slumped back in his chair, raising his hands in a display of exasperation, "According to the time stamp there's no missing footage."

"People don't just disappear, Tony," Ashley said.

The security man swiveled around in his chair to look at her, "I know that, you know that, but apparently the video system disagrees with us."

"What's the time that he disappears from the screen?" Sigurdsson asked.

"10:17:15," Tony replied.

"What about the interior?" Sigurdsson asked. "I saw a camera that leads into the enclosure."

"Yeah, but it's a limited field of view," he said, returning to the keyboard. "I've been complaining to the administration about this system for years, but they keep telling me, 'If it isn't broke, we're not gonna fix it.'"

"I'm pretty sure they might change their minds now," Ashley replied.

"Good luck with that," he said as he brought the new video feed on-line.

Sigurdsson realized what he meant by a limited view. Rather than have a full shot of the door and hallway, the camera was perched above it, offering only an angled image. They could see just the upper part of the door and a short stretch of the hallway, but only in one direction.

"Can we go back to about a half an hour before Melvin arrived?" Sigurdsson asked.

The man entered some information and hit play. The three of them watched intently, and then the screen *rippled* again. For several moments the enclosure door was wide open and then, in an instant, it was closed again.

"*Sonofabitch*," Tony said.

"That's an understatement," Sigurdsson replied, before turning to look at Ashley. "So how does a door open and close on their own?"

"They don't," she replied. "It's impossible, unless the park has suddenly become haunted."

Sigurdsson stared at her for a moment as the thought of a murderous ghost played out in his head.

"Can you pull up the feeds and see where Melvin was before this happened?" Sigurdsson asked.

"Sure," Tony replied.

A moment later Sigurdsson watched as an external shot of the administration building appeared on one screen and an interior view of the lobby on another. He could see a golf cart with security markings parked outside the front door. As they watched, the same rippling appeared on the screens and the front door swung open violently.

"Could the wind have done that?" Sigurdsson asked.

"No," Ashley replied without taking her eyes off the video monitors. "Those doors lock tight. Maybe, if the door was already ajar and a gust of wind caught, but not from a locked position."

It clearly caught the attention of Melvin, because he exited the office a few seconds later. He scanned the interior of the lobby first, then grabbed his coat and headed outside. The three of them watched as the man walked around and then his head snapped around, looking at something off screen. A moment later he jumped into the golf cart and headed off in the direction of the lion exhibit.

"Well he saw *something*," Sigurdsson said.

"Tony, can you bring up the remote cameras by the ornithology building?" Ashley asked.

The image changed again and they watched as the screen once again rippled, before the golf cart passed by.

"What the hell is that?" Ashley asked.

"Do you think the video has been manipulated?" Sigurdsson asked. "Or maybe there was some form of electronic interference?"

"If you asked me this yesterday, I would have said no," the man replied. "Today, I can't come up with any other plausible explanation."

"Okay, I need you to save these videos; all of them and for as far back as you have. I will have our technical unit look them over to see if they have been altered or if they can find any other *unusual* activity."

"I'll swap out the hard drives and save them," Tony said.

The crackle of the portable radio interrupted the conversation.

"Ashley, is Detective Sigurdsson with you?" a man's voice asked.

"Yes he is," she replied into the radio.

"The medical examiner's office is asking if they can take Mel's body."

Canon looked over at Sigurdsson, who nodded yes.

"Yeah, they can remove the body," she said into the radio.

"Thanks, over," the man replied.

"So what do you think happened to Mel?" she asked.

"I don't know," Sigurdsson replied. "It clearly wasn't a robbery, but something got Melvin's attention and led him to the exhibit. How exactly he got into the cage with the lions, I don't have a clue, but I need to figure out how and why."

CHAPTER ELEVEN

Jack Smith sat at the head of the conference table, in his Park Avenue office, going over a merger proposal.

As president & chief executive officer of Smith-Cabott Pharmaceuticals, he had the final say on all new acquisitions. Normally he was inclined to pass off the grunt work to one of the firm's executive vice-presidents, but this deal was special for him.

Smith-Cabott was poised to take over Leaf Spring, the world's largest on-line ancestral history company. It might seem odd for a pharmaceutical company to want to acquire a firm devoted to family-tree history, unless you considered that they had also pioneered the use of DNA research. Gaining Leaf Spring would allow Smith-Cabott to tap into an area of science never before imagined.

This had been a long-term project for Smith and he knew of the implications. Five years prior he had directed the creation of an off-the-books project known as *My Tree*. It mimicked Leaf Spring's ancestral platform, *sans* the DNA network. The company was moderately successful, but he knew that Leaf Spring had already cornered the DNA market and it would have been foolish to try to re-invent the wheel. He allowed enough time to pass until My Tree was seen as a successful, second-tier company offering *free* family-tree hosting with an industry recognized user-friendly interface. Then he arranged for a substantial endowment, from a dying philanthropist, to make its way into the company's coffers. All that was left was to dangle the bait in front of Leaf Spring's ownership.

Knowing that they now faced a formidable opponent, with a solid web platform and a large bank account, they did the smart thing and agreed to a buy-out. At face value it was a win-win. Leaf Spring walked away with billions in profit and the company was merged without any employee layoffs, including their senior management. Of course, there would be proper oversight conducted by Smith's hand-picked executive staff, who would covertly funnel the DNA information directly to Smith-Cabott's R&D team.

"This looks good, ladies and gentlemen," he said, closing the cover on the leather-bound portfolio. "When can we expect the ink to be dry?"

"Leaf Spring has a ten-day window to approve, but that's just a formality," said Brian Lee, vice-president of mergers & acquisitions, whom Smith had tasked with overseeing the project. "We've been in direct talks and their board is eager to close the deal."

"When can we expect access to their database?" Smith asked.

"Realistically, we're looking at mid-January," Lee replied.

"That will work. Do we have the programming in place to begin research?" Smith asked, directing the question to Arianna Laurent, his vice-president of information technology.

"Yes," Laurent replied. "About a year and a half ago I brought over a senior programmer who previously worked for the *Combined DNA Index System*. Since Leaf Spring is a provider to CODIS, he was already familiar with their uploading system."

CODIS was the database created and maintained by the Federal Bureau of Investigation, and it comprised three different levels of information. One was called the *Local DNA Index Systems* (LDIS), which was where the DNA profiles originated. The second was the *State DNA Index Systems* (SDIS), which allowed state based laboratories to share information, and the final one was the *National DNA Index System* (NDIS), which was an interface that allowed states to compare information with one another.

Because of privacy issues, the database did not contain any personal identifying information, such as the name associated with the DNA profile. Hits were sent back to the individual labs who would then contact the appropriate authorities. The bulk of identifications relied on what they called STRs, or *short tandem repeats*, which were scattered throughout the human genome, and on statistics that were used to calculate the rarity of that specific profile in the population. They considered it a *benign* system, used primarily to catch criminals and find missing persons, but in the age of ballooning technology it was only a matter of time before the software was manipulated.

What was more alarming to Smith, and something that the customers of Leaf Spring didn't know, was that the company had quietly created a health and wellness division. The helpful sounding moniker masked a more intrusive program that was using DNA information to create a massive medical database that was directly linked to user names. The last thing Smith wanted was an information index which might identify a marker that could expose *them*.

"Is he one of us?" Smith asked with a measure of concern.

"No, sir, but it's not a problem," she assured him. "His programming work is compartmentalized, but we have a Trojan horse in place that allows direct mirroring of the data. In addition, any uploads to CODIS will be filtered to remove any of those we have positively identified. The more we can remove from our system, the less likely it is that they will find a questionable pattern to pursue."

"What about our ability to access data directly in CODIS?" Smith asked.

"We won't be able to gauge that until we have access to the system," she replied, "but, at least theoretically, our people should be able manipulate data if needed."

"Fair enough," Smith said, before turning his head toward the closed conference door, beyond which a loud, muffled conversation was taking place.

"Brian, see what is going on," he fumed.

"Yes, sir," the man replied, but just as he got up to investigate the door flung open wide and Serena de Mar strode in, followed by Janus' harried-looking secretary.

"Sir, I told her you were busy," the woman said, her voice cracking with panic.

"It's okay, Brielle," Smith said as he watched Serena stroll over to an empty seat at the far end of the table and sit down. "I think now would be a good time for us to take a break."

The assembled executives quickly gathered their belongings and took their leave. Each of them was familiar with Serena and none of them wanted to be a witness to what was about to transpire.

"What in the hell do you think you are doing, Serena?" Smith snarled, after the last person had left the room and closed the door behind them.

"We have a problem," she replied, her voice flat and even.

"There is *always* a problem, somewhere," he replied, his voice betraying the exasperation he felt. "That doesn't mean you can come bursting through my door—"

"It's Gabrielle," she said, cutting him off.

"Gabrielle?" he asked, his voice reflecting genuine concern. "What's wrong?"

Serena did her best to suppress the wave of contempt she felt for him at the moment.

"I think your *precious little princess* has embraced her darker side."

"What do you mean?"

"I believe she is engaging in unsanctioned killings."

If the statement had caught him by surprise, he didn't show it. His face remained calm and neutral.

"That's a serious accusation," he replied. "I hope that you have more evidence than just your beliefs."

"Don't you have *one* damn television in this entire building?" she asked accusatorily.

"I don't have the *luxury* for television, Serena," he said with annoyance. "So please spare me the melodramatics and just tell me why you believe that your sister is breaking our laws."

Serena softened her demeanor. There was no point in provoking him further; especially since she didn't exactly occupy a spot on his *good* list. In fact, she was convinced that he barely tolerated her because of his affinity for Gabrielle. So this accusation was bound to have struck a nerve.

"I didn't at first, but lately her mood has changed. She seems capricious, almost angry, at times. I just chalked it up to her being cranky over her latest project. You know how impossible those artsy-types can be, but then she began to disappear for hours on end and whenever she came back, she would get defensive when I asked where she had been."

"That's hardly evidence of a crime," he pushed back.

"True, but the other morning I was reading the paper and there had been a murder reported close to our place. It piqued my curiosity, so I started doing a little digging and realized that there had been several others which all occurred around the times of her disappearances."

"That's still nothing more than speculation," he replied, but she could tell she had set the gears where in motion.

"Still, if it turns out to be *more* than just speculation, she will have potentially compromised all of us," Serena insisted. "If word gets out, it could endanger the community we have built and it could endanger you."

"Me?"

"Once rumors spread that you can't control your people, than who knows what could happen," Serena pointed out. "As much as I am loath to say it, laws only work if there is respect for them or, at the very least, a fear of punishment."

Smith stood up and made his way over to the panoramic window that overlooked the city and stared outside. It was one of the trappings of his position, but this position was only his public persona and the private one was a much more complicated one.

While the person of Jack Smith was a recent creation, his true identity, Janus Graf Schmidt von Bad Tölz, had been around for substantially longer. There were times he wished he could go back to when his word was the only one that mattered. Not that he found the responsibilities of leadership displeasing, quite the contrary. Unlike many of his noble peers, who preferred to bask in the opulence of their positions, he believed that a ruler led from the front. He'd taken men into battle countless times, sometimes to their death, but more often to their victory. In a way, he relished the simplicity of war; you gave an order and it was followed. It was the life he had always known.

But the times had changed and, much to his chagrin, *they* had changed as well. He would have much preferred the *one man, one voice* approach to problem solving, but now everything was dealt with by committee. The very thought sent a wave of revulsion through him. While many deferred to his experience, he understood that he only presided over a *thin* majority. He couldn't help but admit that some of the dissenting voices were already nipping at his coattails. Something like what Serena was alleging could easily tilt the tenuous balance of power he currently enjoyed. Despite his affinity for Gabrielle, he needed to protect his position; not for his own sake, but for the sake of them all.

When he turned back to look at her, Serena could tell that he had taken the hook. Now all she needed to do was set it.

"I'll take your suspicions under advisement, but I don't believe there is enough evidence at this point to move forward with a formal accusation."

"What do you want me to do?" Serena asked, tossing the ball back into his court.

"Monitor your sister," he replied, "but I caution you to exercise the utmost discretion, Serena."

"Of course, Janus," she said. "You know me."

"Indeed I do, Serena," he sneered, "which is why I am *telling* you to be cautious. These are merely suspicions and I will not have this community torn into opposing camps without just cause."

"I will be the embodiment of discretion, I promise. After all, Gabrielle is my sister and I love her, which is why I came to you with my concerns in the first place. But, if my suspicions are warranted, we both know that finding evidence won't be hard. Once the blood lust takes hold, the body count will begin to rise rapidly."

"Then I pray that you are wrong," he replied.

"Don't be silly, Janus. You know that no one listens to *our* prayers."

CHAPTER TWELVE

Sigurdsson stepped out the door of the 15th Precinct and zipped up his jacket. He was just about to walk down the staircase when he spotted Gabrielle standing by the car holding up two coffee containers.

"Gabi, what are you doing here?" he asked with concern as he walked over to her. "Are you okay?"

"Yes,..... No," she smiled weakly, handing him one of the coffee containers.

"What's wrong?"

"No, it's nothing, I'm just being silly. I shouldn't have come here unannounced. I don't even know if I'm messing up any plans you might have had."

"It's fine," he reassured her as he opened the car door and let her get in. "I'd cancel any plans I had to be with you, but let's get you out of the cold."

"You're so sweet, Karl," Gabi smiled, as he held the car door open for her.

A moment later he got in and started the engine, turning up the heat. "So tell me what's bothering you."

"It's Serena," she replied.

"Your sister? I thought she was away?"

"She is, but we talk a lot, or at least we did. Lately she seems distant and I guess being stuck in the apartment alone has gotten to me."

"Was it anything specific?" he asked as he peeled the lid back on the coffee container and took a sip.

"I love my sister, but she can be very narcissistic. I always chalked it up to the fact that she was a model and they are used to the attention, but lately it seems that it has become a bit too personal."

"What do you mean?"

"Let's just say I recently had a certain level of professional success—"

"And she got jealous?"

"Exactly," Gabi agreed. "I guess I just got my feelings hurt"

"That's completely understandable," Sigurdsson replied. "Sometimes it's the ones closest to us that hurt us the most."

"Yes, but now it's like she is throwing it back in my face and making me feel as if I don't deserve it."

"Some people take a bit more time than others to warm up to someone else's success and sometimes they never do. Trust me, I know firsthand about envy."

"Sounds like there's a story there," Gabi replied.

"It was a few years ago," he explained. "I was a cop in a precinct anti-crime unit. The guy I was working with was one of those 'look at me' folks. He'd stop a guy for jay-waking and he'd write it up like he was the last man standing at the Alamo. Anyway, we stopped this guy for a broken taillight and when we ran the name he was wanted on a warrant. Instead of sticking around to help with the arrest, he told the sergeant he needed to leave early so he could pack for vacation. The boss cut him loose and left me with the paperwork. The perp is acting real hinky and I'm getting a weird vibe. So when I go to inventory his car, I go over it with a fine-toothed comb. I find a box of credit cards and some electronic device in a secret compartment in the center console. When I bring it in, this guy offers me twenty-five grand cash to forget about it. Says he has it at home, all I have to do is swing by on the way to booking and he'll give it to me. I tell him sure and then tell the sergeant. Next thing I know everyone is there, IAB, FBI, hell even the Federal Trade Commission showed up. It turns out this guy was a runner for a phony credit card ring. He sang like a bird and gave up all the main players in a multi-million dollar operation. Next thing I know I'm getting called down to the police commissioner's office and he promotes me to detective."

"Wow, that's amazing, Karl."

"Yeah, except the guy I was working with proceeds to trash me as soon as he gets back from vacation. Apparently he was getting texts while on vacation and lost his shit."

"I guess there are people like that in every walk of life," she replied as she sipped her coffee.

"You know what you need?" he asked.

"What?" she smiled.

"A glass of wine and a home cooked meal."

"You cook?" she asked.

"I haven't poisoned anyone recently, but I don't think my culinary skills are ready to be showcased on the Food Network anytime soon."

"I'm willing to take the chance," she smiled.

A half hour later he opened the door to the apartment and motioned her inside.

"Wow, you have a beautiful place, Karl," she said as she stepped into the apartment.

Sigurdsson helped her take off her jacket and hung it on the coat rack before leading her into the Livingroom.

"What an amazing view," she said as she walked out toward the patio overlooking the park.

"My brother, Arne, is an executive for the company that owns the building. I could have never afforded it on a cop's salary, but he got me an amazing deal."

"You have a wonderful brother."

"Please don't let him hear you say that," Sigurdsson laughed as he handed Gabrielle a glass of wine. "He's insufferable as it is."

"I doubt that," she scoffed.

"Enjoy the view. How do you like your steak?"

"Rare."

"Coming right up."

Sigurdsson returned to the kitchen to prepare dinner.

"How are things going at work?" she asked, taking a seat at the island.

"Eh, they're working me like a dog," he replied as he seasoned the steaks and set them onto the cast-iron skillet.

"The murder in the park? How is that going?"

"I kind of hit a brick wall with that one," he replied as the steaks sizzled in the pan.

"I take it that isn't good?" she asked.

"No, but nothing about this case is good. Usually you have certain facts that you can follow, but from everything I have uncovered this man shouldn't be dead, but he is."

"That has to be terribly frustrating."

"That it is and, to make matters worse, I had another one dropped into my lap."

"Anything you want to talk about?" she asked, taking a sip of her wine.

"We might want to skip the details on that until after dinner," he laughed as he flipped the steaks. "The one thing you learn is that crime never takes a break, even when the weather is crap."

"I guess you never have to worry about job security."

"This is very true," he replied.

After they finished eating, they retreated to the living room couch in front of the gas fireplace.

"So how long have you and Serena been having problems?" he asked.

"Oh, you know how it goes. Things are never easy with sisters and I'm probably reading too much into all of this. I think I just sat in the apartment alone too long and my mind started to mess with me."

"Well, you're always welcome here," he said.

Gabi looked over at him and smiled as she took a sip of her wine. "Oh really? That sounds like a pretty serious invitation."

Sigurdsson raised his hand and gently brushed a stray strand of blonde hair from her face. "I really like you, Gabi."

She set her glass of wine on the coffee table and shifted in her seat so she could face him. "Well, I really like you to, Karl. I just need to be honest with you."

"Uh oh," he said, recoiling a bit. "You're not sending me to the *friend zone* this quick, are you?"

Gabi slapped his leg playfully. "No silly, I didn't mean it like that. It's just that I'm a bit rusty when it comes to relationships. I don't want to move to fast and screw this up."

"You could never screw it up," he argued.

"Let's just say that I'm a bit *complicated*."

"Wow, that's a word I have *never* heard used to describe a woman."

Gabi socked him in the shoulder, just hard enough to illicit a genuine 'Ow!' from Sigurdsson.

"Oh, suck it up cupcake," she teased.

"Damn, you hit hard for a girl," he replied as he rubbed his shoulder.

"I told you, my father was in the military," Gabi said as she leaned over, moving his hand out of the way, and playfully kissed his shoulder. "Weakness was not allowed in the de Mar household."

"What was he, Spanish Special Forces?"

"No, just a stern, but very protective and loving father," she replied.

"At least I don't have to worry about you being able to protect yourself."

"I'm also very competitive," she snickered. "So don't expect me to play easy."

"Perish the thought," he said as he felt her body nestle against his and her head rested on his shoulder.

"I just want to take things slow," she whispered.

"I've got all the time in the world for you," he said as he wrapped his arm around her shoulder and gently kissed her head.

Gabi closed her eyes and did her best to ignore the lie.

CHAPTER THIRTEEN

Dr. Andrea Reynolds heard the knock on her office door and glanced up from her computer screen.

"Come in," she said.

The door opened and Karl Sigurdsson stepped into the small office.

"Hey Doc, I hope I'm not bothering you," he said.

"Not at all, what's up?"

"I was in the area and wanted to ask if you'd had a chance to examine the victim from the zoo?"

A frown grew on Reynolds' face as she removed her glass and set them down on the desk. "I have, and I think we have a problem, Karl."

"It's never good news when a doctor says you have a problem."

"No, it's not," she said, getting up from her chair, "but I think it will be easier for me to show you. Come with me."

Reynolds led him out of the office and down a long hallway.

The morgue had been built back in the late 1950s and the walls were lined with white ceramic tile, which amplified the sound of their footsteps as they made their way toward the autopsy room. It always had a thick scent of industrial cleaner; like antiseptic mixed with Pine-Sol, but as they drew closer to the room, the air was filled with an almost sickeningly sweet pungent odor.

"Got a ripe one?" he asked.

"Yeah, deceased from up in the Two-Eight," Reynolds replied as she paused outside the door and slipped on a disposable exam gown. "Family hadn't heard from him in three weeks. The heat in the apartment wasn't kind to him, but neither were the cats."

"That's why I don't have pets," Sigurdsson said.

"You want a mask?" she asked.

"Nah, I'm good," he replied.

No cop wanted it to appear that they were a wimp, especially when it came to the macabre, so they generally masked their disgust with a false bravado. Besides, the mask would only slightly damper the smell and he would still carry the odor on his clothes for the rest of the day.

"Suit yourself," Reynolds said as she opened the door and led him into the cavernous autopsy room.

A dozen steel beds, most of which were empty, were spaced out evenly throughout the room and she motioned him toward the farthest one on the left.

As he followed her, he glanced back to the opposite end where the active autopsy was being conducted.

"Ouch," he muttered, as he glimpsed a bloated, discolored body.

What a way to go.

He turned his head away and spied the naked body of Melvin Brooks lying on the last table. Even in death there was no dignity.

"So what do we have?" he asked.

"Well, I can tell you that the lions didn't kill him, that's for sure."

"Yeah, otherwise he'd be a helluva lot worse off than him," Sigurdsson said, hooking his thumb back toward the other end of the room. "So if *Mufasa* and *Sarabi* didn't kill him, how did he die?"

"He had what can only be described as a cardiac event," Reynolds replied.

"A heart attack?" Sigurdsson asked, trying not to sound too optimistic that Melvin's demise appeared to be from natural causes.

"No, that's not what I said," Reynolds replied. "Best I can tell is that Mr. Brooks' heart stopped beating because it ran out of blood."

"You're shitting me?"

"I wish I was, Karl, but I don't have an answer for this."

"We have a time of death?" Sigurdsson asked.

"Between nine and eleven last night," she replied. "But I didn't ask you to come down here for the basics; I actually want to show you something."

"What?"

"Well, when we got him on the table, I found something strange."

"Let me guess; he had a neck laceration?" Sigurdsson asked.

"No, but you're close," she replied. "Take a look at this."

Reynolds motioned him over to the top of the table and tilted Brooks' head to the side.

"What the fuck are those?" Sigurdsson asked in disbelief as he stared down at two small puncture wounds on the man's neck.

"Holes," she answered matter-of-factly. "And before you ask, no I don't know why they are there."

"How much blood loss?" he asked.

Reynolds picked up the clipboard from the table; not that she couldn't recall the number off the top of her head, but because she needed a physical reminder that she wasn't crazy. "Four and a half liters."

"You're telling me that this man lost nearly all of his blood without a trace?"

"Like I said, I don't have an answer for this. All I know is that he is dead and his blood is missing. Aside from the difference in wounds, the cause of death is the same for Brooks and Stein."

"You think those holes were used to drain his blood?"

"I can't rule it out," she replied, "but this whole thing has me perplexed."

"Why?" Sigurdsson asked.

"Draining blood isn't all that hard," she said. "We do it here daily, but there is a process to it. I've also seen folks who have bled out after being shot in their femoral artery. But I'm at a loss to explain how this was done, out in the open, with no visible sign of blood loss at either scene."

Sigurdsson jaw clenched, as he stared at Reynolds, and he felt the hairs on the back of his neck bristle. He reached into his pocket and removed the piece of paper containing a list of the previous victims he had compiled.

"They're not the only ones, doc," he said, handing her the paper.

Reynolds glanced down at the names on the list and then looked back at him with a quizzical look. "What does this mean?"

"Take a walk with me, Doc. We need to have a chat about something."

CHAPTER FOURTEEN

Gabi tapped methodically at the keys on her laptop computer, which was perched precariously in her lap, as she lay on the couch, her feet propped up on one of the armrests.

"I'm going out," Serena said as she made her way through the living room.

"This late?" Gabi asked suspiciously.

"Easy, sis," she replied. "Don't get your knickers in a knot; it's not what *you* think."

"And what do *I* think, Serena?"

"That I'm going for some *takeout*, but I'm not."

"So where are you going?" Gabi asked.

"I got a call regarding a potential modeling job that's coming up in January," Serena explained. "Monique is heading out of town for Christmas, so I agreed to meet up with her before she leaves to discuss the details."

"Do you want me to tag along?"

"No, you're writing. Besides, you know how much Monique likes to talk. It will probably end up being a long night with her drunk-crying about which guy left her this month."

"Are you sure? I don't mind."

"Positive," Serena replied as she slipped on her leather jacket. "Besides, aren't you the one who is always telling me how important it is to write when your *imaginary* friends are talking to you? Look at it as a chance to have some quality alone time with them."

"One day I am going to make you a character in a book and torture you slowly," Gabi laughed.

"Is there any *other* way to torture someone?" Serena asked mischievously. "You just relax and spend some time with the voices in your head."

"Have it your way," Gabi said, shrugging her shoulders as she turned her attention back to the laptop.

A moment later she heard the apartment door open and then close.

She stared down at the screen for a minute before picking it up the setting it down on the coffee table. Then she got up and went to the kitchen to get a glass of wine.

As much as she wanted to write, her heart wasn't into it. She'd already re-written the current chapter twice and she just wasn't feeling it.

You'd better start feeling it soon, she thought as she took a sip.

The bitchy phone calls from her literary agent were already beginning to come in as the deadline for the submission of her latest manuscript approached; something which she always dreaded. It was hard enough to write without all the added pressure and the fact that she had other things on her mind lately wasn't helping matters.

Gabrielle walked over to the window and stared out. She knew that the responsible thing to do would be to go back to writing, but at the moment being responsible was the last thing on her mind. Her mind was occupied with thoughts of him and the night they had shared.

For the moment, it was enough to feel his arms around her and his gentle kisses, but she wanted more. It wasn't fair to be given this and not be able to have it all.

Technically, you weren't given this, she scolded herself. *You pursued it. You knew the dangers and you ignored them.*

She gazed out into the night sky, looking for an answer to her problem. Across the street, in one of the other apartment buildings, she could make out a brightly lit Christmas tree and two people cuddled together on the couch. It always amazed her how people who lived in high-rise apartments never considered closing their blinds, as if their perch above the city somehow made them immune from voyeurs.

Or maybe they just like the idea of being watched, she thought.

Something about watching them made her feel melancholy, as if their happiness was just highlighting what she didn't have. She chased the thought from her head, as she turned and made her way back over to the couch and sat down. She placed the wine glass on the table, while her eyes darted back and forth between the laptop and her cellphone. She knew what she should do, but instead picked up her cellphone and stared at the blank screen.

This is nuts, she chided herself. *You're an adult woman. It's the twenty-first century for crying out loud.*

She steeled her nerves and selected a number from her contact list. It rang several times before she heard the call connect.

"Sigurdsson," the familiar voice said gruffly.

"Hey there, I hope I didn't catch you at a bad time," she replied.

"Gabi, hi, how are you," he said, his voice softening measurably. "No, it's not a bad time at all. I was just sitting here going through some reports."

"I'm sorry," she said. "I didn't mean to bother you; I just wanted to see how you were doing."

"I'm good," Sigurdsson replied. "It has just been a busy day. I've done so much reading that my eyes are starting to go blurry."

"Nothing good, I assume."

"Oh, you know, just man's inhumanity to man," he said dismissively. "A cop's world is like a Shakespearean play, filled with moments of tragedy and comedy, often at the same time."

"I've wondered why cops do what they do," she said.

"So have I," he laughed. "So how has your day been?"

"Honestly? I should be working, but I can't seem to concentrate on anything."

"I know the feeling."

"I know I should do something productive, but I just can't seem to focus on it."

"Boy, can I relate. I've been having that feeling a *lot* lately. Well, at least for the last week."

Gabi smiled. "Well, if I may be so bold, what are your plans for this evening? Are you free?"

"I can be," he replied. "In fact, I could use a break from all this paperwork and clear my mind a bit."

"Well, maybe we can commiserate about our mutual *problem*."

"That sounds like a great idea. Technically my shift ended about an hour ago, so how about I grab my coat and pick you up?"

"That works for me," she replied.

"Are you hungry?" Sigurdsson asked. "I could take you out to dinner; what do you like?"

"Anything would be fine."

"Well, then go and get ready," he said. "I'll pick you up in about a half an hour."

"I can't wait," she replied. "See you soon, Karl."

Gabi ended the call and laid the phone on the table.

She could feel a flutter inside her, as if a million butterflies had suddenly taken flight.

She lifted the wine glass to her lips and took one last drink, finishing it, before going to get dressed.

CHAPTER FIFTEEN

Serena's hands were clasped together, the tips of her index fingers pressed firmly against her lips, as she stared at the sidewalk below. Inside her mind, dark thoughts wrestled with her emotions as she cast out the last remnants of doubt.

She loved Gabi, but tough times required one to make tough choices.

But you don't really love her, do you?

This time she didn't search for the disembodied voice, she just gritted her teeth and remained focused.

A part of her wanted to protest, to argue that she did in fact love Gabrielle, but she knew that it was a lie.

Not that she *hated* her, but, if she was being completely honest, she had to admit that her affection toward Gabi had always been tied to ulterior motives.

Their relationship had always been complex, like yin and yang. They were the epitome of duality; summer and winter, light and dark, order and chaos. Where Serena had thoroughly embraced who she was, Gabi always seemed to be at odds with herself.

Of course, there were times when she had enjoyed Gabi's benevolence and her standing within the community, but the time had come to upset the status quo. Serena didn't want forgiveness from the council, she wanted to topple it; to tear it to the ground and build a better one.

Now that the dynamic of their relationship had changed, there didn't seem to be anything left to hold it together and she had to resolve herself to make the tough decisions. The time for action was upon her. She needed to act decisively and with extreme prejudice.

This time there could be no mistakes; no second guessing. If there was any hesitation, any last momentary spark of affinity, than her plan would fail and it would be her that would face the wrath of the council.

She had already won the victory in her mind; all she had to do now was to wage it with ruthless efficiency. She would miss her sister, but she wouldn't miss who she had become. Besides, she argued, there would always be new ones; those who needed a mentor and who better to serve in that capacity than the one who made the rules.

Her contemplation was cut short as she watched the dark colored vehicle pull up to the curb and the cop got out.

"I guess your imaginary friends weren't talkative tonight," she said sarcastically as ¡she watched Gabi come out of the apartment building and walk straight into his arms.

Something about watching them kiss sent a wave of anger and revulsion coursing through her. Not that she didn't have desires, she did, but there was no point in pursuing it the way they did.

It annoyed her that Gabi could even entertain the notion of having a relationship with someone so inferior; someone who couldn't even protect themselves, let alone anyone else.

At its heart, humanity was weak and if there was one thing she detested, above everything else, it was a weakness.

It was so unbecoming.

Even animals had more dignity. They fought till they could no longer fight and they either emerged victorious or they died.

She recalled the countless times she had listened to their sniveling whimpers and pleas for mercy; even when they knew what was about to happen. There blubbering didn't make her feel pity on them, it made her feel contempt.

"You'll learn soon enough, sister," she sneered as she watched them get in the car and pull away.

Even without the benefit of heavy traffic, Serena followed them with ease; leaping from rooftop to rooftop, like a panther bounding through the air.

Serena had no fear of being seen by anyone; she knew that she moved to fast for the human eye to capture. If anyone had caught a *glimpse*, it would appear to be nothing more than a fleeting shadow; a wayward glint of light that was easily dismissed as the mind playing tricks.

Several minutes later she found herself perched atop a building; watching as the car pulled into a dimly lit alley in the city's restaurant district.

"Oh, you are making this far too easy," she said malevolently as she watched the couple exit the vehicle and head inside.

CHAPTER SIXTEEN

"**S**o where are you taking me?" Gabi asked as her fingers toyed playfully with the police radio mic's coil.

"I know this little hole-in-the-wall, family owned Italian restaurant that has decent food," Sigurdsson said.

A few minutes later he pulled up in front of *La Bella Vita* restaurant.

"This is your idea of a *hole-in-the-wall*?" Gabi asked incredulously. "I'm not sure if you know this, but they have a waiting list three months out just to get reservations."

"Details," he said, waving his hand dismissively.

"Well, you're nuts if you think you will find a parking spot anywhere near here tonight," Gabi said.

"Don't you worry," Sigurdsson replied. "I still have a few tricks up my sleeve."

"Oh, really?" she asked curiously. "Can you make cars disappear, Karl?"

"No, but I have something even better," he replied as he removed a laminated placard from the visor. "I have an official free parking pass."

"Who knew there were so many *perks* to dating a cop?" Gabi laughed.

Sigurdsson smiled as he pulled the car around the corner and slipped into the alley behind the restaurant.

He didn't want to admit it, but hearing her say they were *dating* made him feel like a kid again.

Don't flatter yourself, he thought. *You never got the hot chick when you were in school.*

He parked the car across from the restaurant's back door and hopped out, hurrying around the car to open the door for her.

"*Merci beaucoup*," she said, the words rolling off her tongue as if she were fluent in French.

"My pleasure, *mademoiselle*," he replied, taking her by the hand and leading her toward the door.

"I don't think I have ever entered a restaurant through the backdoor."

"It's okay," he replied as he opened the door for her. "I know the owner."

Sigurdsson led her through a long hallway filled with the raucous sounds typical in a busy kitchen. About halfway down he paused outside the doorway to a small office and peered inside, spotting a large man seated behind a desk.

The man's appearance seemed almost comically. He had a bald head and his skin was as dark as coal, while his enormous, muscular body seemed as if it had been *stuffed* behind the tiny wooden desk. If that wasn't strange enough, the man's hands, which appeared to be the size of frying pans, struggled to navigate the diminutive buttons on the computer keyboard.

"You gonna do any damn work today or just sit on your ass?" Karl said loudly as he rapped his knuckles on the door frame.

The man looked up angrily, but his demeanor changed instantly when he saw who was standing there.

"My brother," he exclaimed as he stood up and moved toward Sigurdsson, taking him in his arms and lifting him up off the ground in a bear hug.

"You're killing me, Monte," Karl gasped as he felt his chest compress.

"Suck it up, buttercup," the man replied, dropping him to his feet.

Karl swallowed hard before turning toward Gabi.

"Gabi, this big dummy is my old partner, Lamont Jefferson," he exclaimed. "He was a shitty cop, but he's an amazing chef."

"It's a pleasure to meet you, Ms. Gabi," Lamont said, extending his hand out to hers. "And I was great at both until the job paired me up with Karl."

Gabi smiled. "It's a pleasure to make your acquaintance as well, Mr. Jefferson."

"Please, call me Monte. It's nice to see Karl with someone who has charm and class. Hopefully it rubs off on him."

"Ignore him, Gabi," Karl said. "He's just angry because I'm his mama's favorite and they stopped making cars big enough to haul his grumpy ass around in."

"If you want to know the truth, you just come look me up, Gabi," Lamont replied. "I got *stories*."

"I will remember that," Gabi giggled.

"That's enough," Karl blurted out. "You got a table available in this dive or are we going to have to eat in my car?"

"I got a table for *her*," Lamont said. "So you better hope she still wants *your* company."

"You know I love you, man," Karl said with a wink.

"Uh huh," the man replied, before turning toward Gabrielle. "Please allow me to take you to your seat, ma'am."

Lamont held out his arm, which Gabi accepted, and he led her out into the packed restaurant.

He led them over to a section of the restaurant where there were several empty tables that were kept in reserve, much to the chagrin of the people who'd waited in line. *La Bella Vita* was already a 2-star Michelin restaurant and Jefferson was hell bent and determined to snatch up that last star. The last thing he wanted was to have an influential food critic or celebrity have to wait to be seated, but Sigurdsson was family and they always came first.

"Ms. Gabi, you're welcome here anytime," Lamont said, after he'd helped Gabi into her seat, "with or *without* him. You just ask for me."

"Thank you," she replied. "That's very kind of you."

Lamont turned to face Sigurdsson, "You need me to help you with your chair too?"

"Nah, I'm good," Karl replied. "Thank you again, Monte."

"Anytime, brother," the man said affectionately. "You be careful out there and let's get together soon."

"Will do."

"You two have a great evening," Lamont said, and then took his leave from the couple.

"He's quite the character," Gabi whispered.

"You don't know the half of it," Sigurdsson replied. "He saved my life."

"Are you serious?"

"Like a heart attack," Sigurdsson replied. "I was a wet-behind-the-ears rookie with about six months in the street. One night we were working a midnight shift during a hurricane. It was around two a.m. when we got a call for a burglary at a beer distributor. It was one of those old places that had an alarm system that was state-of-the-art in 1969. We were always getting chronic calls for the location, especially when it was windy. The old glass panes would rattle around and set off the window sensors. Despite all the warnings we issued, the owner never bothered to fix it."

"Typical," Gabi said.

"So this one night we get a call and we are already strapped thin because of the weather. Most of the shift was out handling motor vehicle accidents and fallen trees. Monte and I take the job and head over, thinking this is just another bullshit alarm call. When we get there, we start walking around, because we need to cover our asses, and we find the back door ajar. So we put over the air that we have an open door and head inside. It's a cavernous storage area, with a maze of beer cases stacked eight feet high. Did I mention it was dark as hell?"

"Not exactly."

"Well it was," Sigurdsson replied. "We couldn't find a light switch, so we had to rely on the moonlight that was coming through the old windows that were about fifteen feet above us and it created these eerie shadows. I was scared shitless, but I wasn't about to show it and certainly not in front of Monte. We're walking down these make-shift corridors, dimly scanning the rows with what passed for light from our beat-up department flashlights, but there's nothing amiss. I'm starting to think one of the knuckle-head employees left the back door open, but then I hear a noise about thirty feet in front of me. At this point my adrenaline is pumping and my common sense goes right out the window. I run forward, thinking I'm going to catch this perp and be the cop of the month. Only problem was that he wasn't thirty feet ahead of me, he was about twenty-five and I shot right past him. Guy pops out of the shadows and levels a gun at my back."

"Holy shit," Gabi exclaimed.

"Yeah, and if I had realized he was back there, I probably would have shit. All I hear is this ungodly roar and I turn back just in time to see Monte lift the guy clear off the ground and slam him to the floor with a sickening thud. I mean, it was like some old school pro-wrestling shit. I just stood there frozen."

"Dear Lord, that had to be terrifying."

"It was, but it also taught me an incredible lesson."

"Well I'm glad it turned out all right," Gabi said as she reached across the table and took his hand. "And let it be a reminder not to do anything stupid in the future."

Sigurdsson smiled as he squeezed her hand. "I promise."

"So whatever happened to him?" she asked.

"Monte broke his back. He ended up spending eight weeks in the correction's hospital ward over in Brooklyn. He was a career criminal who'd been out on parole at the time for a string of burglaries, so he ended up getting remanded back to state and got himself shanked in a mess hall fight; he bled out before they could restore order."

"What a way to go."

Sigurdsson shrugged his shoulders. "One could say that justice was ultimately served. Had he gotten out he would have done it again and maybe his next victim wouldn't have been so lucky."

"I guess that is true," she said. "I live in my own little world, so I often forget how violent the rest of it can be."

"Stay there, you'll be much happier. I wish I could unplug myself from the case I'm working on and find a cozier world to get lost in."

Just then a waiter appeared with a bottle of wine, *courtesy of the owner*, pouring each of them a glass and then took their order.

After the man had departed, Sigurdsson picked up his glass and raised it in a toast. "Here's to a beautiful evening with an even more beautiful lady."

"Aw, thank you, Karl," she said, gently tapping the rim of her glass against his. "You're so sweet."

"You make it very easy, Gabi."

"So is it bad?" she asked. "The case you're working on?"

"I don't know if I would call it bad, but it is *confusing*," he replied.

"How so?"

"Well, without getting too into the gory details, the deaths don't seem possible."

"Like they shouldn't be dead?" she asked.

"No, I know what killed them, I just can't figure out exactly how it was accomplished."

"Okay, now you've piqued my curiosity. You've got to tell me what's so strange about these cases?"

Sigurdsson pondered her request as he scanned the room to ensure no one was listening and then leaned in closer.

"It's the way the bodies were found," he said in a hushed tone. "They were missing a lot of blood."

"Missing blood?" she replied, acting surprised. "You mean like someone took it?"

"It might sound strange," he said, nodding his head, "but people do weird shit. There was a case back in the 70s that involved a guy who would abduct women so he could sexually assault them. While he held them captive, he used needles and tubing to drain their blood, almost to the point of death, so he could drink it. The tabloids labeled him the *vampire rapist* for obvious reasons."

"Oh my God," she replied as the waiter brought out their appetizers and set them on the table. "That sounds like a Patterson novel."

"Yeah, it's just too bad I'm not getting paid his salary to solve it."

"Is that what you think is going on here?" she asked. "That someone is draining their blood?"

"No," he replied. "Maybe,... I don't know. This one really has me confused. Under the circumstances, it doesn't seem plausible, but the bodies tell a different story. The biggest hurdle I am dealing with is that these deaths happened in the open and within a fairly short amount of time. That's the part that has me scratching my head. There's no way that it could have happened, but it did."

"Well, we do live in the age of *big-brother*," she said. "Any chance you can find video?"

"I have video," Sigurdsson replied, "at least on the latest death."

Gabi took a sip of her drink, trying hard not to appear overly curious. She knew where this investigation was heading and the thought that a video existed concerned her beyond words; especially since she had a good idea of who the prime suspect was.

"You do?" Gabi finally asked.

"Yeah, but it's not helping."

"I don't understand; why wouldn't it help you identify who is behind this?"

"I think the video might have been tampered with," he explained.

"What makes you think that?"

"Because there seems to be some form of electronic interference going on," he replied. "I've watched the tape and every time something happens the screen gets distorted. It's strange, it's like one second my victim is standing there and the next he disappeared."

"Maybe you're dealing with *alien abductions*," she joked.

"At this point I am willing to think anything is plausible."

"Well, just for the record, I have every confidence in your investigative skills, Karl."

"Thanks, I just wish my boss shared your enthusiasm for my skills."

"Well he doesn't know you the way I know you," she said, a mischievous smile on her face.

"And I would be happy to keep it that way."

"Don't worry," she replied. "I promise I won't kiss and tell."

CHAPTER SEVENTEEN

"Excuse me, sir."

Janus looked up from the report he was reading to see Roderick Luther, his assistant, standing in the doorway to the study.

"Yes, Roderick, what is it?"

"I'm sorry to bother you, sir, but you have a visitor," the man said. "It's Serena."

"Oh, dear Lord," Janus fumed, dropping the papers into his lap.

"I don't hold myself in such an exalted position," Serena said cheerfully as she brushed past Luther and strode into the room, "but I like your enthusiasm."

"Why are you here?" Janus asked in annoyance at the intrusion into his inner sanctum.

"I happened to be in the neighborhood and just wanted to deliver a personal reminder that the body count is growing," Serena replied as she sat down on the couch across from him.

"I am sure you will find this amusing, but there are some of us who have actually chosen to be productive members of society. So if there is something you wish to say, please do so and let me get back to my work."

"Janus, you're the *Doyen* of this coven," Serena replied accusatorily. "Are you telling me that you are not aware of what is going on in the world around you?"

"Yes I am the Doyen," he roared, slamming the dossier he'd been holding onto the coffee table. "And you'd be best to remember that. There is more going on in this world than your fashion shoots and vacations. So please pardon me if I don't have the luxury of *your* free time."

"*Fine*," she said irritably, "but you told me to monitor Gabrielle and I'm just here to give you an update."

"Well then I suggest you do so."

Serena reached into her jacket pocket and removed a copy of a newspaper cover, which she proceeded to lay on top of the table.

Janus glanced down and read the headline: *Death in the Lion's Den*. The picture under the caption showed a grainy photograph of the body of Melvin Brooks.

"This is why you're here; because an elderly security guard died?"

"After our prior discussion I would think you would be more *concerned*."

"Evidence, Serena," he said. "I told you that you needed evidence if your accusations were to be taken seriously."

"You also told me to monitor Gabrielle, *discretely*, and that is what I am doing. Short of catching her in the act, I can only provide you with the information I get, but there is more."

"More what?" he asked, "more innuendo, supposition, and rumor? Please humor me."

"She's dating one of *them*," Serena replied in disgust. "On top of that, he's a cop."

"What did you just say?" Janus asked, a look of shock on his face.

"You heard me," she replied. "She's dating a cop."

"This had better not be some kind of game," he said. "How do you know?"

"She told me," Serena said. "As I explained to you she has been acting strange lately, so I confronted her about what was going on; under the guise of sisterly concern. She was evasive at first, but eventually she confessed that she was having a relationship with him."

A tense silence gripped the room as Janus stared at Serena, who held his steely gaze impassively. She knew he was ruminating on what he was being told and she wasn't about to give him any help.

There was no hard and fast rule against interacting with humans, but it was frowned upon when it went beyond the professional. Some covens, like the West Coast ones, were more lax, but Janus had recognized the danger posed by such *social* interaction and he'd strongly discouraged it. Humans, by their very nature, tended to be curious and jealous. Eventually they began to see the signs that something wasn't *right* and they began to ask unnecessary questions. It was bad enough when those questions came from an ordinary human, let alone a government official. If Serena's accusations were correct, and Gabrielle was engaged in a personal relationship with a law enforcement officer, then it could jeopardize all of them.

"What was her reasoning," he asked thoughtfully.

"She claims that she wanted insight into the killings," Serena replied. "Although, it does make you wonder why she would need that, if she wasn't involved in anything?"

Janus reached over and picked up the newspaper clipping, scanning the article about the security officer's mysterious death. Something wasn't sitting right with him. If Gabrielle was aware of some mysterious killings, why hadn't she come to him with her concerns?

"What was she doing Tuesday night?"

"Beats the hell out of me," Serena said dismissively. "I had to run over and review some photo shoot proofs. When I left the apartment she was there, but she was gone when I returned about an hour later. All I know is that she went *out* and didn't come back until almost midnight."

"Where is she now?" Janus asked.

"I assume at the apartment writing," Serena replied. "She has a deadline approaching and was working on her latest manuscript when I left, why?"

Janus picked up his cellphone and placed a call. His jaw clenched tightly as he listened to it ring several times before going to voicemail.

"No answer," he said as he ended the call.

"That's not like her," Serena replied. "She always has her phone nearby and I can't imagine her not taking a call from *you*."

The *evidence*, if that was what you could call it, was circumstantial at best, but it was still disturbing. Gabrielle was highly respected among the members of the Crystal Coven and if the allegations turned out to be true, then it would send shock waves through their community. There were always murmurs from dissenting members, who felt the rules of the coven were tougher than they needed to be, and some might feel emboldened to embrace more liberal reforms; especially when it came to hunting.

"I want you to go home and let me know if she is there," he replied. "Perhaps she is too engrossed in her writing to answer her phone."

"And if she isn't?"

"You've done enough already," he said. "I think this matter needs a fresh set of eyes."

"As you wish," Serena said, while quelling the urge to celebrate. "Does this mean you're going to convene a tribunal?"

"No, it's too soon for that, but I will have the matter looked into. The accusation you raise is serious, but the actual evidence is lacking. I won't empanel a tribunal without additional proof of wrongdoing."

"Oh, I don't foresee that being much of a problem," Serena said as she stood up and began walking toward the door. "We both know that if Gabi has gotten the urge to hunt, she won't be able to control it."

"Goodnight, Serena," Janus replied.

The dismissive tone of his voice made it clear that their conversation was over, but she couldn't help herself from getting one last final jab.

"Goodnight, *sir*," Serena said with a cheerful smile.

Janus glared at her as she walked out of the room and then looked down at the newspaper lying on the table.

Just the idea that he might have *lost* Gabrielle was almost debilitating. She was one of the most trusted and beloved members of the coven, not to mention his own affection for her, which is what made his next choice so difficult.

He picked up his cellphone and selected a number from the contacts list. A moment later he heard the voice of his *Regent*, Emilio Rossi, come on the line.

"Good evening, sir," the man said.

"We have a potential problem, Emilio."

"And what might that be?"

"I've received an allegation that Gabrielle de Mar may be involved in unsanctioned killings."

Janus spent the next several minutes sharing the information Serena had given him.

"Pardon my disbelief, sir," Rossi said, "but that doesn't sound like Gabrielle."

"I agree," Janus replied, "and that is precisely why I want you to look into this matter, Emilio. I can't allow my affinity for her to cloud my judgment. If the accusations are baseless, then the truth will come out, but if there *is* merit to them—"

"I understand, sir," Rossi replied. "Do you want me to notify Michael about your concerns?"

Janus closed his eyes and took a deep breath. It was a question that had already crossed his mind and one that he was struggling with.

Michael Orlov was the coven's *head sentry*. It was his job to maintain order and security. Typically, this was a case that would normally be referred to him for investigation, but Janus had his concerns. Orlov was effective in his role as head sentry, but he also had a reputation of being heavy-handed at times and Janus was hesitant to involve him in such a *delicate* matter. He didn't need a case of *punishment in search of a crime*.

"No, not right now," he replied. "I don't want to put the cart before the proverbial horse. This could simply be a case of misunderstanding on the part of Serena. After all, she isn't the textbook example of propriety herself. I'd rather have you look into the matter and see if there is any merit to the accusations."

"Certainly," Rossi replied.

"Do you still have your connection at the police department?" Janus asked.

"Yes."

"I want you to make some discrete inquires and see if you can find out what is going on with the investigations. Let me know whether there is anything *unusual* about these deaths that would be cause for concern."

"I'll let you know what I find out."

"Thank you, Emilio," Janus said. "Goodnight."

"Goodnight, sir."

Janus ended the call and stared at the blank screen.

A part of him wanted to find Gabrielle and just flat out ask her if there was any truth to what Serena was accusing her of, but he knew he couldn't. Despite their closeness, he couldn't allow it to interfere with his responsibility as the head of the coven. Like a father facing the dilemma of a wayward daughter, he had to think about the ramifications to the entire family; not that it made his choice any easier.

Setting this investigation into motion was the hardest thing he had done in a long time; perhaps the hardest of his tenure. It was times like this that made him long for the old days, but he knew that you couldn't live in the past. There was too much at stake now to risk it over the reckless acts of any member, including her.

"Roderick!" he exclaimed as he rose from his chair.

A moment later the man appeared in the doorway. "Yes, sir?"

"Get the car. I need to go for a ride."

CHAPTER EIGHTEEN

"This may sound sophomoric, but I don't want tonight to end," Gabi said as she finished the last of her wine.

"Well, who said it has to end?" Karl asked with a wink.

"Oh, am I starting to see the *bad boy* side of you?"

"Is that a good or a bad thing?" he asked.

"I'll let you know," she replied, a coy smile growing on her face.

"This is going to sound impossibly immature, but can we take a picture?"

Gabi giggled. "What like a *selfie*?"

"Well, yeah, I guess…. Because saying it that way doesn't sound *immature*."

"I think it's adorable," she replied. "Come over here."

Sigurdsson got up and moved his chair next to Gabi. He took out his cellphone, as she leaned in closer, and put his arm around his shoulder.

"Smile," he said, holding up the phone and snapped a picture.

A second later he felt her lips on his ear, kissing him playfully.

"*Everyone* has a bad side, Karl," she whispered.

"I thought you wanted to take things slow?"

"Slow has different *levels*," she said, biting her lip.

Sigurdsson swallowed hard. "Then what are we still doing here?"

"I was just thinking that myself," Gabi purred.

"I think it's time we leave and go somewhere quieter."

They quickly gathered up their belongings and headed back in the direction they had first come; the tension between them growing more palpable with every step they took.

"Leaving so soon?" Monte's loud voice bellowed from the office.

"Hey, yeah, sorry, uhm,...." Sigurdsson stammered as they stood in the doorway. "Work called.... I gotta run."

The man stared at them in silence for a moment, his eyes reading the *harried* look that was evident on both their faces. He may have left the police department, but his ability to *read* people remained.

"Uh huh," he said with a knowing smile. "Well you too just get to work then."

"Thanks, brother, talk soon."

"Oh, we will definitely talk soon," Sigurdsson heard Monte call out as they continued down the hallway.

By the time they hit the backdoor they were almost at a full run. As soon as the door swung open, they felt a rush of cold air hit them in the face. Sigurdsson took her by the hand and pulled her close, their lips pressing hard against one another's in a passion fueled kiss. He wrapped his arms around her tightly, feeling her body press against his.

"We have to go —" he muttered.

"Uh huh," she replied, before resuming their kiss.

Sigurdsson pushed her back against the wall as the sexual tension reached a fevered pitch.

"Oh, how cute," a voice called out, snapping them from their embrace.

Sigurdsson pivoted and he recognized that things had taken a serious turn for the worse.

There were three of them in the alley.

The two men closest to them stood on the other side of the restaurant's doorway, partly obscured by the shadows, while the third man, the one who'd spoken, was across from them leaning against the unmarked car.

"C'mon guys, the shows over," Sigurdsson said authoritatively as his mind raced to evaluate the potential threat facing them.

"That's funny, it looks to me like it was just getting started," the man replied as he stood up and began walking toward them.

Sigurdsson surmised that they were all about the same age, somewhere in their late twenties or early thirties, and they all had a distinct disheveled look to them. They weren't the normal homeless types, who called the city's back alleys *home*, but the hardened, down-on-their-luck kind that looked to make a quick buck wherever they could.

"I don't care what you and your girlfriend do, but this is our alley you're parked in, fella," the man continued, "and I don't recall you paying the parking fee."

Sigurdsson felt Gabi grip his hand firmly and, out of the corner of his eye, he caught motion of the other two men drifting toward them.

"Let's not be stupid here," Sigurdsson warned as he turned his back toward the alley's entrance and began to ease Gabi behind him, toward safety. "You're smart enough to know what kind of car that is. Why don't you take your act to another alley?"

"You hear that, Johnny Lee," one of the men in front of him said, with a maniacal laugh. "He called you stupid."

"Well, I guess he's going to owe us *interest* with that parking fee," the man said angrily.

Even in the noisy urban environment, Sigurdsson could still make out the telltale *ping* of the spring-assisted knife opening, followed a second later by another.

It was a worst-case scenario for Sigurdsson.

He knew he couldn't get to the .9mm on his hip in time, not with the jacket he was wearing, before they could close the gap. On top of that, he had to contend with his adversaries advancing toward him from two different directions. Every strategic response that crossed his mind ended up with him being cut or worse; so he did the only thing he could do and spun around, pushing Gabi out of harm's way.

"Run!" he yelled, before turning back to face his attackers head-on; putting himself between them and her.

Years of training kicked in and his left hand shot forward, in a blocking maneuver, as he took a step back, blading his body, to minimize the target he presented to his attackers. At the same time, his right hand fumbled with his coat as he attempted to retrieve his gun.

The man called Johnny Lee was almost upon him. Even in the dimly lit alley he could see that the man was no match for him physically, but they had positioned themselves in such a way that no matter which direction he turned, he risked exposing himself to a knife. He needed to be lucky three times, but they only needed to be once.

The barrel of the pistol had just cleared the holster when a sudden rush of air buffeted his body, as if he had been standing too close to a subway station platform when a train passed through. He watched in shock as some unseen force propelled Johnny Lee's body backward until it slammed against the wall, on the opposite side of the alley, with a nauseating thud. The body hung in the air for a split second before it crumpled to the ground.

Sigurdsson blinked and when his eyes opened, he saw that Gabi was now standing in front of him. Her back was toward him and she was squaring off against the other two men.

Before he could say a word, one of the men let out an angry roar and rushed toward her, his knife wildly slashing in her direction.

Gabi held her ground as her hand thrust forward, grabbing the man by his forearm and squeezed. He held onto the knife for a second longer until his fingers gave up their grip on the deadly weapon. A moment later, the alley was filled with the sound of agonized screaming, as the bones in in the man's arm were crushed. As Sigurdsson stood, immobilized by shock, she pulled the man toward her and then flung him backward; sending his body crashing headfirst into a large, industrial-sized garbage dumpster twenty feet away.

The speed and violence of Gabrielle's attack hadn't just caught Sigurdsson by surprise, but the remaining attacker as well, who was now backing away from her. For a moment, an eerie silence gripped the alley, but it ended just as abruptly.

The man had had only gotten a few feet before he backed into the brick wall and had nowhere else to go. It was at that moment that the man opened his knife with a flick of his wrist, but before Sigurdsson could aim down the sights of the pistol, and order the man to *freeze*, Gabrielle pounced.

She closed the distance, faster than his brain could process, and grabbed the man by the throat. Sigurdsson watched in stunned horror as she lifted the man into the air and pinned him against the brick wall; his feet dangling three feet off the ground.

"No, please, don't kill me," he choked, his voice cracking with pain and fear. "She made us do it."

"Who made you?" Gabrielle snarled, in a voice so dark and menacing it sounded demonic.

"Her," he whimpered, "the woman with the black hair."

"Gabi, stop, let him go!" Sigurdsson yelled.

Her head snapped around and she glared at Sigurdsson, who had his gun leveled in her direction.

The woman in the restaurant was gone now, replaced by something he couldn't begin to comprehend. The sparkling blue eyes, that had previously left him speechless, were replaced by two obsidian orbs that sent a chill coursing through his body.

With her attention diverted, the man seized the opportunity to strike; raising the knife he'd been holding and sliced at her arm.

It was the last poor decision he would ever make.

A blind rage came over her; as she felt the blade cut through her jacket and tear at her skin. She drove her face into the man's neck and her teeth ripped into his flesh.

The man's body flailed about, his arms and legs shaking violently, as a loud gurgling sound ushered in his demise.

"Gabi, let him go!" Sigurdsson ordered.

She released the man's body and let it drop to the pavement. Then she turned slowly to look at Sigurdsson and the last thing he saw, before she disappeared, was the bright red blood that stained her *fangs*.

And then an eerie silence gripped the alleyway, leaving him standing alone as his eyes darted from body to body, unable to process the carnage he had just witnessed.

"What... the... fuck...?" he whispered in disbelief.

CHAPTER NINETEEN

"Jesus H. Christ," Vega said as he slid beneath the crime scene tape and walked into the alley, which was lit up with a mix of portable spotlights and the emergency lights of several patrol cars. Three yellow tarps covered the bodies as crime scene techs processed the area.

He spotted Sigurdsson leaning against the wall, standing next to a man who bore a striking resemblance to a mountain.

"What the hell happened here, Karl?" Vega asked as he approached the two men.

"It beats the hell out of me, boss. I stopped by to have dinner and when I came out I stumbled into this shit show."

"Who are you?" Vega asked the man.

"This is Lamont Jefferson," Sigurdsson replied. "He's my old partner. He retired from the job and owns this restaurant. Monte, this is my boss, Lt. Vega."

"Did you see anything, Mr. Jefferson?" Vega asked.

"No, sir," the man replied. "I'd just said goodbye to Karl, when he came running back inside and told me to call 911."

"What did you see when you walked out, Karl?" Vega asked.

"Three bodies," Sigurdsson replied. "One on the opposite side of the alley and two were lying by the back door. My first thought was that it might be gang related, but after I did a quick assessment, it became obvious that something else went down."

"And you heard nothing?"

Both men shook their heads.

"Were you here alone?" Vega asked.

"No," Sigurdsson said. "I met a friend for dinner."

"Where are they?" Vega asked. "Did they witness this?"

"No, we said our goodbyes inside the restaurant and she left through the front door. I couldn't find an empty spot when I first arrived, so that was why I was parked in the alley."

"Another female friend, huh?"

Sigurdsson remained silent.

"And nothing else was going on when you first got here?" Vega asked.

"No, when I arrived the alley was empty."

"Hey, pardon me, but I'm going to head back inside if you don't need me anymore," Lamont said. "I do have a restaurant to run."

"No, you're good, Monte, thanks for keeping me company."

"Anytime, brother," he replied.

"Thanks," Sigurdsson replied.

"Call me," the man whispered, as he gave Karl a hug, and then slipped back inside the restaurant.

"Christ, this is a damn massacre," Vega said as he scanned the crime scene, catching sight of the media that had assembled at the opposite end of the alley. "Those vultures will have a field day. Nothing sells better than death."

"That isn't the worst of our problems, boss," Sigurdsson replied. "You really need to look at these bodies."

He led the lieutenant over to the nearest body and kneeled down, pulling back the covering.

"You've got to be kidding me," Vega exclaimed as he stared down at the grotesque wound on the man's neck.

"This wasn't death; this was a goddamn horror movie."

"What about the other ones?" Vega asked.

"They're busted up, but not like this guy," Sigurdsson replied as they walked over to the body lying next to the garbage dumpster, "but you need to see this."

He kneeled down and removed the tarp covering the victim.

"Holy shit," Vega exclaimed as he stared at the man's deformed skull. "What the hell did that?"

"Well, take a look at this," Sigurdsson said, pointing toward the steel bin. "I'm not positive, but I'm willing to take a bet and say that was the cause of death."

Vega's eyes darted back and forth between the victim and the garbage container; as his brain tried to calculate how much force it would take to dent the steel panel.

"What about him?" Vega asked, pointing toward the body across the alley.

"Looks normal, aside from some obvious head trauma, but the point of impact appears to be about a dozen or so feet up the wall," Sigurdsson replied as he stood back up. "Crime scene took hair and blood samples, so we will see if we get a match."

"Did they find any weapons?"

"Several spring-assisted knives, but nothing that would have done this kind of damage. The blades were all open, so it seems to show that they knew something was going down."

"Do we have any names?" Vega asked.

"One, so far," Sigurdsson replied. "The guy across the alley is named John Lee Dupree according to the driver's license in his wallet. I ran his name. It turns out that he's a small-time thief with about a dozen arrests. He did six years in *Sing-Sing* for burglary and aggravated assault."

"Maybe this was a type of retribution?" Vega asked.

"At this point any theory is plausible," Sigurdsson replied, "but I don't know how to explain these deaths."

Vega scanned the alleyway, examining the doors and windows which overlooked the scene.

"Any chance of video?" he asked.

"I walked the alley, but I didn't see any sign of cameras. It looks like everything here is commercial businesses and they were already closed for the evening."

"How the hell am I going to spin this?" Vega asked.

"I don't know, boss, but for once I'm glad I'm the detective and you're the lieutenant."

Vega looked over at Sigurdsson with a scowl on his face. "Karl, I'm starting to think, that with you in my squad, I'm going to be a lieutenant for life."

CHAPTER TWENTY

Andrea Reynolds examined the findings of the latest autopsy she had performed; as if it was going to somehow *miraculously* change.

It didn't.

She removed her glasses, setting them down onto the desktop, and rubbed her weary eyes.

A career in the medical field, including four years spent working trauma cases in an E.R., told her that everything she was reading was a lie, but the bodies told a different story.

This doesn't happen, she thought as she looked past her desk at the body of John Lee Dupree lying on the table nearest to her.

She stared at it for several minutes, as if searching to find a clue she had missed which would shed light on the mystery in front of her.

The bodies that had been brought in over the weekend were an enigma. So much so that she had gotten into her car and visited the crime scene; certain that the details they had given her were wrong. Unfortunately, that trip left her with even more questions than she already had.

As horrific as the injuries were they could all be *explained*, but there was no explanation as to how they could have occurred under the circumstances they did; unless you first suspended the laws of physics.

"Hey, doc," a voice called out, jarring her from her thoughts.

Reynolds looked up to see Sigurdsson and Vega walking across the autopsy room toward her.

"Good afternoon, gentlemen," she replied.

"What can you tell us about our victims from Friday night," Sigurdsson asked.

"A lot," she replied, "but I am not sure how much of it will make sense."

"What do you mean?" Vega asked.

"I mean I can't match the injuries to the circumstances under which they were supposedly received, Carlos. None of this makes sense."

"Not to be rude, but I don't need *another* mystery to solve, Andrea," Vega replied. "Can you explain what you're talking about?"

"How about I just show you?" she asked as she stood up and led them over to the body furthest away from her desk.

Reynolds stopped at the table and removed the sheet, revealing the body of a young man in his twenties. Sigurdsson recognized him as the man who'd been sent flying into the dumpster.

"John Doe #1," Reynolds said. "His cause of death was traumatic brain injury. This guy was the easiest one and I say easy, because his head struck the dumpster with such force that his skull erupted into his brain."

"So he fell and struck his head or someone pushed him?" Vega asked.

"Nice try, but no to both those theories," she replied with a tinge of sarcasm. "His injuries were consistent with a fall from a ten story building."

"But there are no buildings that tall at the location," Sigurdsson interjected.

"No, there aren't," Reynolds replied. "He also had acute trauma to the chest. His sternum was shattered, his ribs were broken; hell, it looked like someone drove a pile driver into him. Which I guess would explain why his head hit the dumpster so hard."

"Could he have been hit by a car?" Vega asked.

"Damage was too localized for that," Reynolds replied, pointing to the man's chest. "Whatever hit him was a blunt instrument. Picture a fist traveling at the speed of a train. It's the only answer I have for why he could have dented the steel wall of that garbage bin."

Sigurdsson's face remained impassive as the image replayed in his mind.

Vega's brow furrowed and a scowl grew on his face, "What you're describing is physically impossible."

"Welcome to my world," Reynolds replied.

"What about him?" Sigurdsson asked, pointing to the adjoining table.

"*Johnnie-bag-o-bones*?" Reynolds asked irreverently as she moved to the other table. "Oh, he's one for the medical journals. Out of the two hundred and six bones in the human body, he managed to fracture or break one hundred and thirty-seven, including a majority of the ones that made up his axial skeleton."

"How the hell does that happen?" Vega asked.

"It doesn't," Reynolds replied. "This guy had worse luck than Evel Knievel jumping the fountains at Caesars. Which is kind of ironic because the blood and hair fibers from the wall show the impact height was about the same as the fountains. The only consolation was that, unlike Knievel, he didn't know it, because he was dead before he hit the ground."

"I hope you have *some* better news in all of this," Vega said.

"Well, John Doe #2 isn't *as* bad," she said cheerfully.

Sigurdsson steeled himself as they moved over to the last table. This was the one that bothered him the most, because he was the one that…

He chased the gruesome image from his mind.

"Cause of death was a gross laceration of the neck, resulting in irreparable damage to the carotid artery," Reynolds said, pulling back the sheet to reveal the man.

Sigurdsson swallowed hard as he stared down at the jagged, gaping wound on the left side of the man's neck.

"Judging from the wound I would say death occurred almost instantly."

"What would cause that kind of wound?" Vega asked.

"I don't know, Carlos," she replied. "The flippant answer would be a lion, bear, or a wolf, but the bite radius doesn't support that conclusion, although it looks to be consistent with a bite."

"Human?" he asked.

Reynolds shrugged her shoulders. "I wish I could give you an answer, but the wounds aren't consistent with a human bite. All I can tell you is that, unless someone's exotic pet got loose, and decided on takeout, some *thing* tore his neck open."

Vega let out an exasperated sigh.

"Oh, wait, there's one more thing," she said. "His arm."

Reynold pulled the sheet away to expose the man's right arm. There was a massive discolored bruise that encircled almost the entirety of his left forearm and the skin within the bruised area appeared collapsed in relation to the rest of his arm.

"What the hell is that?" Vega asked.

"The remnants of what were his ulna and radius bones. About a three inch section was completely pulverized; not fractured, not broken, *crushed*."

Vega stared down at the arm, and then back up at her, a baffled look on his face.

"To put it succinctly, your killer is someone who possesses the appetite of a ravenous bear, the brute strength of a blue whale, and the crushing force of a T-Rex," she explained. "I wish you good luck in your pursuit."

"Thanks for nothing, Andrea," Vega grumbled.

"Trust me when I say that this is as frustrating for me as it is for you, Carlos. I just don't have any explanation for what happened; at least none that make any sense medically."

"I'm sorry for snapping. I'm just trying to figure out how the hell I'm going to explain this to the chief."

"I wish I could give you a better answer," she replied.

"If you do come up with anything else, please call me."

"I will," Reynolds said.

"Thanks, Doc," Sigurdsson said as he and Vega turned and walked out of the autopsy room. Once outside, Sigurdsson paused for a moment.

"Hey, boss, I have to hit the head."

"Go ahead, I'll meet you out in the car," Vega replied as he continued down the hallway. "I've got some calls to make."

Once he was out of eyesight, Sigurdsson turned and headed back into the autopsy room.

"Doc, I wanted to see if you had a chance to look over those other cases."

"I did," she replied. "Prior to last night's event, I would have said that those bodies had to have been dumped. There was no explanation for that kind of massive blood loss, without any signs at the crime scene, but now,…"

Reynolds paused for a moment as she contemplated the things she knew, "Look, I just don't have any answers, Karl. This defies everything I know. This isn't a homicide, it's in a category all its own."

"I was afraid you were going to say that," Sigurdsson replied.

"It might have sounded sarcastic, when I said, 'good luck in your pursuit,' but I meant it. Whoever, or whatever, did this isn't something I would want to trifle with."

Sigurdsson nodded his head before turning and heading back out the door.

"Happy hunting," she said as the door closed behind him.

CHAPTER TWENTY-ONE

Janus and Emilio sat in the study, with the latter discussing what he had learned.

"After we spoke, I contacted my friend at the police department. He said there had been some *unusual* deaths reported recently; ones that have the investigators perplexed."

"How many?" Janus inquired with a concerned look.

"Two recently," Emilio replied. "Although there is some speculation that several others might be connected."

"Do they have any suspects?"

"No, not at this time," Emilio said. "The impression I got was that they are quite unsettled by all of it and don't appear to have a cohesive strategy for investigating it."

"How long has this been going on?"

"It's hard to say, sir. This could be a new phenomenon or it could have been happening for years."

"How is it that we are only learning about this *now*?" Janus snapped as he reached over and poured himself another cognac. "I mean what is the purpose of having liaisons and sentries if we are in the dark?"

"I understand your frustration, sir, but the system has never been foolproof."

The statement made Janus frown; because he knew it was true.

Emilio had been his friend for a long time and was his most trusted confident. He relied heavily on him for the most sensitive issues and he had always been diligent, but he could not deny that his world walked a fine line with that of humanity. There was only so much that could be done, only so many questions that could be asked, before suspicions began to take hold and it was generally best to avoid those scenarios, even when it meant you didn't have all the answers you would like. Humanity didn't believe in *them* and it was an illusion they needed to protect at all costs.

"Could there be a nomad running around?" Janus asked.

"That is one possibility."

Nomads had always been a problem for their kind. They were not part of any coven and therefore were not obliged to follow any of their rules; especially as it pertained to killing humans. In most cases, those who were traveling through an area, or taking up a *temporary* residence, would show their respect by checking in with the local coven. It gave the coven an opportunity to see who was operating in their area, and, more importantly, it gave the sentries a face to watch out for. But there was a small percentage that chose to operate entirely in the shadows, and they didn't concern themselves with the law of the land.

When a coven was put in danger by the actions of a nomad, then it became the duty of the sentries to address the problem. They operated as the enforcement arm for the doyen and Janus' head sentry, Michael Orlov, was particularly effective at maintaining control. It was the primary reason they had not had any problems; until now.

"Whether it is a nomad or someone else," Emilio continued, "then we will need to get Orlov involved. If someone is hunting in our area, we need to put a stop to it before they attract any more unwelcomed attention.

"Agreed," Janus reluctantly replied, "but I would prefer that involvement to wait until we know definitively that these deaths aren't a *man-made* phenomenon."

"Do we have the luxury for that?" Emilio asked.

"Perhaps not," Janus said somberly, "but I would prefer not to preside over a witch-hunt."

Emilio lifted his glass and took a drink as he reflected on the issue at hand. Beyond his friendship with Janus, he deeply respected the man for his integrity and intellect. More than anyone else, he was responsible for elevating the Crystal Coven to its position of preeminence; much to the chagrin of some of the more senior doyens.

The difference between Janus and the others was that he was not enamored by his own success. He never set out to do something with the thought of how it would elevate his own status, but how it would enhance the coven. Nevertheless, even if he wasn't interested in his own prosperity, that didn't mean others weren't and that enmity put a target on his friends back.

"Janus, you know I deeply respect our friendship," Emilio said, "but, as your regent, I feel that I must also provide you with my best possible counsel. It is with that position in mind that I must warn you to proceed carefully. You are loved by most, feared by some, and envied by many. It is those latter two groups that you must remain always mindful of. Nothing would bring them greater happiness than to see you fall; especially if that failure was rooted in your *compassion*. A leader must always remember the adage, '*It is the greatest good to the greatest number of people which is the measure of right and wrong.*'"

"So you're telling me that I should sacrifice Gabrielle just because it will make me look better to those who dislike me?" Janus asked, doing his best to hide his irritation. "That's not a leader, Emilio, that's a tyrant."

"I'm saying that you need to temper any decision you make to deny them material for their cause."

"That's like telling a firefighter he has to put out the flames, but he can't use water," Janus said.

"No, that only means he has to find an *alternative* method to succeed," Emilio replied.

Janus was about to reply, when their conversation was interrupted by a knock at the door.

"Come in," Janus called out.

The door opened and he saw Luther step inside. "Sorry to disturb you, sir, but Serena is here and she said it was important."

Janus gritted his teeth as his annoyance grew. The appearance of Serena so late in the evening could only be considered a harbinger of further bad news.

"Let her in," he said, doing his best to conceal his displeasure.

A moment later, Serena marched into the room; a scowl on her face making it apparent she was in a foul mood.

"Well I hope you're happy now, Janus," she said sharply. "You demanded proof and now you have it."

She slammed a copy of the evening newspaper on the coffee table. The sensational headline read: *Terror Strikes the City*.

"Where did you get this?" Janus asked, his anger quickly changing to concern as he picked up the paper.

"It just came out," she replied, "and by tomorrow morning the city will be in a state of panic."

Janus turned the page and began reading, *'According to sources within the Medical Examiner's Office, one victim had his throat ripped open, while two others sustained traumatic internal injuries to their bodies that resembled victims of a plane crash. One unnamed employee, speaking on a condition of anonymity, said, "It was as if every bone in his body was broken." A statement from the Chief Medical Examiner, Dr. Andrea Reynolds, stated that her office was investigating the suspicious deaths of three men that had been ruled a homicide, but that no official cause of death had been determined at this time.'*

"This will be more than panic," Janus said furiously, handing the paper to Emilio.

"I warned you last night that your little pet had gone rogue," Serena chimed in, her voice filled with contempt, "but *no*, you didn't want to hear it. While I was here trying to convince you to take action, she was out *dining* on the locals."

The strain of his prior conversation with Emilio, coupled with Serena's insolence, was more than Janus could stand and he lashed out.

"Enough!" he roared as he leaped from the couch and came face-to-face with her, baring his fangs. "Remember your place, Serena, before I have to *remind* you of it."

The words pulsed through the air between them like a shock wave, and she swallowed hard as she quickly took a step backward and bowed her head meekly.

"Please forgive me, I didn't mean to," she apologized, her voice quivering. "I'm... sorry."

Serena realized that in her zeal she had made a gross miscalculation and pushed her luck. Janus was a man who prided himself on always being in control, but that control had its limitations. The idea of a physical confrontation with Janus would have been suicidal.

"Stop this," Emilio said softly, "*both* of you. This bickering between us will not resolve this problem."

The standoff continued for several long seconds before Janus finally nodded his head.

"Where is Gabrielle now?" he asked as he regained control over his emotions.

"I don't know," Serena said, her voice taking on a more modest tone. "After I left here last night, I went home and waited, but she never returned and she's not answering my calls."

"If what Serena has said is true, and it appears that it might be, our coven is in danger," Emilio said. "We cannot hesitate to take action."

"What do you recommend we do?" Janus asked.

"We have to notify the council, *tonight*."

Janus walked over to his desk and sat down, his body collapsing into the leather chair.

For the first time, in his reign as doyen, he felt an incredible weight on his shoulders. He had never been opposed to taking action, but the circumstances that he now faced were beyond anything he had ever expected to face. He knew Emilio had been right, that he'd been slow to act because of who it was, but now he was forced to come to terms with the fact that who he knew might no longer exist.

"Call the council, Emilio," he said wearily. "Tell them I am calling an emergency meeting."

"When?" the man asked.

"Tonight," Janus replied. "You're right; this matter cannot wait any longer. I don't want there to be any rumors circulating that I made any attempt to keep the council in the dark."

"And what about Orlov?" the man asked.

"That is a decision I will leave up to the council."

"Yes, sir," Emilio replied.

"And when you're done, I want you to reach back to your contact and get as much information as you can. If the council is to reach a decision, I want them to be armed with as much information as possible."

"What do you want me to do?" Serena asked.

"Testify against your sister," Janus said sternly.

CHAPTER TWENTY-TWO

Janus caught his reflection in the rain-stippled window of his study and for the first time he suddenly felt *old*.

He'd been gazing out the window, watching as a steady procession of vehicles arrived at the mansion and pulled into the parking area adjacent to the council hall. For the first time, he felt the full weight of being the doyen resting heavily on his shoulders.

How long has it been? he wondered.

The Crystal Coven had been formed in 1643, by Pier Gerritse, who had presided over it for nearly 300 years. In the waning days of World War I, Gerritse had been elected to the Grand Council and passed the torched to Janus.

The war had created unique opportunities for their kind and certain risks. A proposal was put forth, and a decision was made, by all the major covens, that a permanent council would be created to oversee the needs of their *community*. Its membership was made up of selected members of both the old and new worlds.

Unlike the League of Nations, or its modern-day counterpart the United Nations, the Grand Council took its role seriously. If the council was forced to intervene in the affairs of a coven, its ruling was absolute and the outcome was rarely welcomed.

The *iron fist* approach, while universally unpopular, proved to be ruthlessly effective at maintaining order. No coven wanted the threat of the Grand Council meddling in their affairs, so they went to great lengths to handle their issues judiciously and efficiently; sometimes too *efficiently*.

Right or wrong, sacrifices were made, figuratively and literally, to settle disputes and ensure to keep any problems off the Council's radar.

In all his years as doyen, Janus had never had any apprehension about calling a meeting to order; until today.

"Excuse me, sir."

Janus turned to see his assistant standing in the doorway.

"All of them, Roderick?" he inquired.

"No, sir," the man replied, "but there are enough for a quorum."

Janus nodded his head. "Then I guess it is time."

He made his way to the council chambers via an underground tunnel. Even with Roderick accompanying him, he felt alone.

Everyone wants to be a leader, he thought, as his footfalls echoed off the stone walls, *but few actually know how to lead*.

A few moments later he emerged inside a small anteroom. Almost immediately open entering the room he could *sense* the muffled conversations taking place in the adjacent hall. Confusion seemed to be the primary focus, although others were furious at being summoned without explanation.

Would you be any different if the roles were reversed? he wondered.

"Shall I notify them, sir?"

"Yes, please," Janus said as he buttoned his jacket and steeled himself for what would come next.

Roderick opened the door and stepped inside the chamber. "Please rise."

The act was strictly one of etiquette, since each member of the council was considered an equal, but it served as a measure of respect for the titular head of the coven; since he potentially held the deciding vote on all matters.

"Please be seated, my friends," Janus said as he strode over to his seat, taking a silent head count of those assembled.

The full council of the Crystal Coven consisted of thirteen members who were elected to their positions by a majority vote among the community. But tonight there were only seven members seated at the large, horseshoe shaped oak table. It met the threshold to hold a quorum, but just barely. What troubled him more than the number of those in attendance was who they were.

Several of those gathered tonight held positions that often seemed contrary to that of the council at large. In the event of a four-three split, Janus recognized that his vote might cause a tie and that could not be an option. The matter before them was serious enough that it called for extraordinary measures.

"Thank you for your attendance this evening on such brief notice," he began as he assumed his place at the middle of the table. "But I can assure you that when you hear the matter we must discuss, you will understand the gravity of this situation."

Quizzically looks were passed back and forth among the assemblage as Janus continued.

"Before I begin, I want to address a matter that has rarely been instituted. While the number of council members in attendance this evening has fulfilled the requirements for a lawful meeting under our governing laws, I am moved to ask that we invoke article eighteen."

Murmurs filled the chamber as the members shared their shock and dismay with one another.

Under the laws of the coven, article eighteen gave the doyen the authority to seat an unelected member on the council *temporarily*. Normally this was done when a council member was incapacitated or was away for an extended period of time. The move was highly controversial, because of the fear that the temporary seating could be enacted to pass a particular agenda, and none of those gathered could recall it being implemented during modern times.

Janus sensed the hesitation and sought to mitigate it.

"I know that this request is unusual, and while I also have the authority to implement it on my discretion, I wish that this matter be resolved with the full consensus of the council. I ask that you respect the gravity of this situation and grant this request."

Jeremiah Blackstone was the first to stand up and address the gathering.

"I must strenuously object to this," Blackstone said. "We are the duly elected representatives of the coven and I believe that it is reckless to empanel someone who has not been selected through the ballot process."

"I understand your concerns, Jeremiah, and I take them to heart," Janus replied, "but as I said, I believe this matter is serious enough that it requires additional measures."

"And you may be right," Blackstone conceded, "but that does not mean that the council should act blindly. Perhaps if you shared the exigent circumstances, which you believe necessitate this radical action, we would agree."

"You have my word that this matter will be fully addressed in this meeting, but I do not want it to be the foundation for your decision. It is my strongly held belief that an impartial vote to move on this motion, absent any bias from the matter at hand, is in the best interests of the council and the coven."

Murmurs again filled the room.

Abigail Kensington rose from her chair to speak, "With all due respect, Janus, you are asking us to have blind faith that this matter is egregious enough to invoke a rule that is generally loathed by the majority of the council."

"Yes, I am, Abigail," Janus replied, "and I will note that I consider myself to be a part of that consensus. That being said, the authority to invoke article eighteen is solely invested in me, although, while I am inclined to invoke it at this juncture, I would prefer that the council stand with me."

Kensington sat back down, holding Janus' gaze, as she contemplated what he was asking.

She was considered one of the hardliners and she had clashed with Janus numerous times in the past. Kensington came from an aristocratic English background and it often showed. While she had been duly elected to the council, it had come at a time when many of the members had held similar positions and beliefs. As times had changed, she often found herself at odds with the slim majority and she seemed to take great pleasure when her vote upset the prevailing mood.

"For the record, I am in vehement opposition to any rules that provide additional authority to the doyen, above and beyond their permanent status as a council member," she said. "However, as often as I find myself in disagreement with you on the issues, I know you to be a man of honor, Janus, and I respect that. I will agree to your proposal with the stipulation that you give me your word that this matter is of such exigent circumstances that it requires an equal response and that this incident will not be used as a precedent for any similar action in the future."

"You have my word," Janus replied.

"Then I move to grant exception and call for a vote to affirm the temporary placement of an *ad hoc* council member."

"Will all those in favor of this motion, please raise your hand," Janus said.

He watched as each member gave thoughtful consideration to the measure and then voted their conscious. They passed the vote by a measure of five to two.

"Mr. Luther, would you please ask Mr. Rossi to come before the council?"

"Yes, sir," Roderick replied.

A few moments later the two men emerged from the waiting room and Emilio stood at the podium directly across from Janus.

"Mr. Rossi, you have been asked to appear before the council this evening to serve as a non-permanent council member; as outlined under article eighteen. You will be empowered with all the authority and standing of an elected representative, but your participation in this meeting is limited in its scope to the discussion at hand. Upon conclusion of this matter, your role will be completed and you will be relieved of your position. Do you understand and agree to these conditions?"

"I do," Emilio said.

"Then please take your seat," Janus said, pointing to the vacant chair next to him.

"Now that we have dispensed with the formalities," Kensington said, after Rossi had taken his seat, "would you be so kind as to explain the reason we are all here this evening?"

"I was recently approached by someone who shared with me her suspicions that a member of this coven has been engaging in unsanctioned murders," Janus explained.

Stunned silence filled the room.

"At first the allegation seemed baseless to me," Janus continued, "and I considered it nothing more than a misunderstanding, but now, in light of recent events that have occurred, I find myself concerned that there may be some merit to the accusations. I've called you here today so that you can hear these charges for yourself and make a decision as to the appropriate cause of action."

"And who has brought these claims to your attention?" Nicolaus Mavros asked.

"Someone close to the accused, Nico," Janus replied.

"It is customary for one accused of such a heinous crime to be heard," Kensington interjected. "Are they being afforded that opportunity?"

"At the present time, the whereabouts of the accused are unknown," Janus replied, "which is the reason for my dilemma.

Without the ability to hear directly from the accused, I believe that it is in the best interests of the coven that the council be allowed to hear the charges and decide on the proper cause of action."

"And is the accuser prepared to testify tonight?" Mavros asked.

"She is," Janus replied. "Mr. Luther, would you please present the witness to the council?"

Roderick opened the door to the chamber and motioned for Serena to come forward.

The appearance of Serena stepping up to the podium caused a buzz in the room among the council members; many of whom did not particularly like the woman.

"Ms. de Mar, would you please inform this council of the accusations you have made?" Janus asked.

Serena steeled herself, gripping the edges of the podium, and addressed the council. "It is my belief that my sister, Gabrielle de Mar, has broken our laws and has been killing innocent people."

The room erupted in raucous protests from several members.

Janus raised his hands to quell the objections.

"Enough," he exclaimed. "We are here to perform our duty and that requires us to put aside our personal feelings. There will be time for each of you to question the witness before making your decision, but I implore you to give this matter the serious attention it deserves."

A hush fell over the room, as each of the members focused their scrutiny back on Serena.

"Ms. de Mar, please explain to this council your basis for bringing this accusation."

Serena spent the next half-hour testifying to her *suspicions* and answering pointed questions from several of the council members. At times, the cross examination became heated, as several members brought up her past behavior and lack of candor.

"Did you *personally* witness any of these events?" Winston McFarlane asked.

"No," Serena replied. "I did not."

"You come before us today with the most serious allegations one can make, yet you have nothing substantive to back them up?"

"Gabrielle might be my sister, but it is not my job to keep track of her every waking moment," she said brusquely. "Her erratic behavior concerns me and I brought the matter to you. I am not the law, you are."

"Yes, we are," the man replied. "And I seem to recall you standing there as a defendant on several occasions."

"I am merely providing you with what I know," Serena declared. "Do with it as you please."

By the time she was dismissed, Janus concluded that they were no better off than where they had started.

"I am sorry, Janus," Kensington said, after Serena had left the room, "but considering the witnesses' questionable character, I am not convinced of Gabrielle's involvement."

"I share your sentiment, Abigail, which is why I wanted the council to make any decision. While I initially questioned the veracity of the original charges, I thought they were serious enough to warrant further investigation. On my orders, I had Mr. Rossi conduct some discreet inquires and I must say that I am troubled by his findings."

"What did you ascertain, Emilio?" Blackstone asked.

"According to my sources, the police department has been actively investigating a string of rather suspicious murders," Rossi explained. "Over the last few years they had several homicide investigations where the cause of death was listed as unknown.

Most of the victims had a criminal history, so there was not a lot of additional effort that went into solving them and most went *cold*. However, there have been several unexplained deaths lately that have put these cases back on the front burner and it appears one of their detectives has drawn a correlation. According to my source, the common factor in the overwhelming majority of these cases was a lack of blood in the victim's bodies."

Knowing looks were shared between the council members.

"The most recent attack involved three men outside a restaurant," Rossi continued. "The traumatic injuries they sustained leave little doubt as to whom, or rather *what*, the perpetrator is."

"And yet, this is all still supposition," Mavros added. "Just because a death occurs in a manner that is *familiar* to us, does not mean we know the identity of the perpetrator. I can point the finger at anyone in this room, each of whom has the capacity to inflict the same type of injuries, but it is still only an unsubstantiated accusation."

"I agree with you, Nico," Janus replied. "Even if I accept Serena's word, that Gabrielle was unaccounted for during the time of the murders, that still does not make her guilty. But, we are also left in a position where her sudden disappearance presents a problem we must address."

"Considering all this, what do you suggest we do?" Pavel Reznik asked.

"My opinion is that we must set aside our personal feelings for Gabrielle and do whatever it takes to either prove or disprove the charges against her. I believe that requires bringing her in for questioning. Uncertainty will only create division within the coven and lead to unrest."

"I ask the council to think long and hard about this," Nico interjected. "Consider for a moment how it would feel if you were brought before the council to prove you had done nothing wrong."

"I cannot disagree with you, Nico," Janus replied, "I have my doubts, but my fear is that if we are not proactive in this matter, then we will have wasted precious time. Having Gabrielle testify will allow us to address the matter directly and, if she is not guilty of the charges, then we can focus our attention on identifying the real culprit."

"For the record, I am going to voice my objection," Kensington said. "I might take issue with *them*, but I believe their principal of *innocent until proven guilty* has merit. What is being alleged is the most serious charge that can be brought upon one of us and we on this council know the penalty which is at stake, but, that being said, I agree that this matter needs to be examined further and we cannot adequately do that without Gabrielle's participation."

"I think it is only proper that we put a motion before the council for a vote," Janus said. "All those in favor of bringing Gabrielle de Mar before this council, to face the accusations against her, say 'aye.'"

Janus watched as Abigail, Pavel, and Emilio raised their hands, and were joined a moment later by Sophie Janssen.

"All those against bringing Gabrielle de Mar before this council, to face the accusations against her, say 'nay.'"

He watched again as Jeremiah, Nico, Winston, and Logan Tremblay raised their hands.

If he had hoped to avoid casting the deciding vote, he had failed. Now the eight members of the split council looked to him to decide.

Everyone wants to be a leader, but few actually know how to lead.

"Mr. Luther, as doyen of this coven, I am directing you to notify the head sentry to locate Gabrielle de Mar and immediately bring her in for questioning before this council."

"On your orders, it shall be done."

CHAPTER TWENTY-THREE

The *Order of the Sentry* had existed for over two hundred years.

It had been first established at the dawn of the 19th century, when mass immigration to the United States had forced the covens to take a more proactive role in maintaining control of the burgeoning population.

Dramatic increases in new arrivals, from disparate nations, had led to growing tensions, as each nationality fought to establish dominance in neighborhoods. Often these territorially disputes among humans would turn violent, effectively ringing the *dinner bell* for nearby vampires.

While they were obviously different than humans, vampires seemed to keep some remnant of national pride. As a result, they would delight in attacking those of other countries, especially if they were from a nation they had once been at war with and in the 19th century that included just about every country on the planet.

The coven soon realized that this reckless behavior threatened to expose them, so they codified a basic set of governing rules and laws.

In the beginning, the laws were simple:

1. *Do not kill another vampire.*
2. *Do not divulge the existence of vampires.*
3. *Do not put another vampire at risk.*
4. *Bear all responsibility for humans you have turned.*
5. *Bear all responsibility for humans taken into servitude.*
6. *Disagreements, which cannot be resolved, will be brought to the council.*
7. *The council has the final say on all matters.*

Then they established The Order of the Sentry as an enforcement arm to implement the rules.

The sentries were seen as a way to quash problems before they began. The first order of the Crystal Coven was established with the appointment of the twelve strongest vampires, with one of them being named the head sentry, and it was housed in a medieval stone structure in a remote section of the doyen's sprawling thirty acre compound.

The number was symbolic, as it was one less than the council and therefore subservient in nature. Each member of the sentry was required to swear an oath of fealty to the doyen, as the legal head of the council, and to enforce any lawful edict that the council issued. Violating one's oath was punishable by death.

In the beginning, the sentries were ruthless in their application of justice; because they had to be. Immigrant vampires were used to the free-reign they had enjoyed in Europe and were loath to *bend the knee* to the rules of their new homeland. Initially, the aim was to bring the offender before the council for trial and punishment, but violent resistance often ended in the swift administration of *street justice*.

Over time, the vampire population was brought into reluctant compliance, primarily through fear of the sentry.

As time passed, and the transitory nature of immigrants began to slow, the coven realized that excess killings would draw unwarranted attention on them. By the early part of the 20th century, advancements in medicine had led to the creation of the first blood bank and they seized on the opportunity. Now that they had a voluntary source of blood, they revised their laws to enact a *no-kill* policy within a specified geographical area.

Those living within the Crystal Coven's territory could use the donated blood available to them, source it from blood slaves, or choose to hunt only animals. The majority grudgingly complied with the law, and those who did not, chose to relocate *voluntarily* after being paid a visit from the sentry.

It did not completely eradicate the killing of humans, but it curbed it to an acceptable level. When it came to the killing of criminals, the council tended to turn a blind eye toward such matters.

The overall effectiveness of the sentries was so successful that they almost policed their way into obsolescence. While they continued in their role, they were now more like warriors without a conflict. Rather than sit around and wait for a problem to arise, they took on additional duties; such as providing security for the doyen and the council when it was in session. But the warrior mentality remained restless within them, and they champed at the bit as they waited for the next *assignment*.

Tonight they sat in their chamber, eagerly awaiting word of what tonight's emergency session was about, and speculated if they would be called upon for a new mission. They got their answer when the door to the head sentry's office opened and their leader entered the room.

At 6'8" tall, and tipping the scale at just over three hundred pounds, Michael Orlov would be physically intimidating to any human being, but when coupled with his superhuman strength and propensity toward violence, he was terrifying to nearly every other vampire as well. His jet black hair was slicked back, matching the all-black suit and shirt he wore. A long, jagged fencing scar ran from the center of his forehead, across his right eye, and ended at the jaw bone, just in front of his ear; an eternal reminder, skillfully delivered by the epee of an upper-classman at the *Universität Wien,* of his last lapse in judgment.

A quiet hush gripped the room as Orlov walked in, accompanied by his twin English Mastiff's, Castor and Pollux, each of which weighed almost as much as he did. The fact that the dogs had been his faithful companions for the last century left little doubt of their own immortality.

He strode over to head of the large oak conference table and sat down; the dogs flanking either side of his chair.

139

"We have a *delicate* problem that needs to be handled expeditiously," he said, "and it will require a measured response."

The assembled group exchanged curious looks with one another.

"For this assignment, I am selecting the following," he continued. "Antonis, Marcus, Zander, and Fiona; the rest of you are excused."

The remaining seven stood up and exited the room. If they had any objection to not being selected, it remained unspoken. As much as they had a reputation for being heavy-handed, in the application of *justice*, there was none who exemplified that characteristic more than the man at the head of the table.

In Orlov's sentry, orders were issued and they weren't up for debate.

While each of them was loyal to their mission, he was not naïve to the fact that they all had connections, especially when it came to certain members of the council. The four that remained were Orlov's inner circle; those whom he chose for the most *critical* missions. They were loyal to him alone and there would be no leaks, irrespective of the orders they were given.

Once the others had left the room, closing the door behind them, Orlov continued.

"The council has directed that we locate Gabrielle de Mar immediately and bring her before the council to face trial for the alleged crime of unsanctioned murder."

"That's a very serious charge," Fiona O'Dell replied. "Who's the accuser?"

O'Dell was the lone female member of the sentry. What she may have lacked in strength she made up for in cunning and sheer will.

"Who it is doesn't matter," Orlov replied, "but I can tell you that it is someone who is familiar enough that the information is deemed reliable."

"How long has this been going on" Marcus Dräger asked.

"It's believed to have been occurring discretely for at least several years," Orlov replied, "but it appears that the killings have begun to escalate in recent months."

The four sentries exchanged perplexed glances with one another.

It was possible, but highly unusual, for a killing spree to go unnoticed by the council or the sentry; unless someone was covering for the accused. If that were the case, then it made perfect sense that this matter would have to be investigated covertly.

"If the accusation is reliable," Zander Yatsko said, "then we must also consider the fact that the accused will not want to be taken into custody."

Orlov nodded his head.

"Under the circumstances, and considering her position on the council, I would have to agree," Orlov replied. "The truth is that this community does not need this type of drama, nor do *we*. We are all well aware of the tensions that exist, to this day, over some of the rules that the council has enacted. The trial of a council member, accused of such a heinous crime, will only serve to further polarize the situation and it presents an *imminent* threat to the fragile order that we maintain."

"So, we should assume that she will never see the inside of the council chamber?" Antonis Karas asked, but it was less a question and more of a statement.

"Someone who is consumed by blood lust can, and should, be considered dangerous," Orlov replied. "The last event involved the deaths of three humans. Under the circumstances, I wouldn't expect her to come quietly, so I would caution each of you to not take *any* chances. Is that understood?"

Each of the four nodded, and in doing so sealed the fate that awaited Gabrielle.

"Good," Orlov said. "Here is a summary of the last known kill and the location. She has apparently gone into hiding, so you will need to act quickly. Her abilities will make this track very difficult."

Each of them knew the hurdles they would face in their pursuit. Normally, they would be able to shake the tree, so to speak, reaching out to snitches, and those with a *past,* who would eagerly provide information if it meant keeping the sentries off their backs and out of their business. But doing this in the *dark* would require much more work. The only saving grace was that, when the moment came, there would only be one version of how the events unfolded; the one they chose to share with the council.

"If there are no other questions," Orlov said, "then you have your orders. Act swiftly."

"Yes, sir," four voices rang out in unison as they stood up and left the room.

Orlov waited several minutes, before removing the cellphone from his pocket and placed a call.

It rang three times before he heard the familiar voice on the other end.

"It's done," he said.

"Good," Serena replied. "I trust there won't be any problems."

"My people know their job," Orlov said brusquely.

"My dear Michael, this is not a *job*, this is a matter of life and death, namely ours," Serena scolded. "As good as you claim your sentries to be, I hope you're willing to place your life into their hands."

"Don't worry," the man replied. "They understand that this matter needs to be dealt with quickly and efficiently."

"I hope you're right, for both our sakes. Let me know as soon as it is finished."

"I will," he replied, just as the call disconnected.

Orlov put the phone back in his pocket and sat there; feeling the rage welling up inside him.

Serena was one of those galvanizing people; the ones you either loved, hated, or just barely tolerated, but she was also incredibly smart, cunning, and a master manipulator. To be on her bad side was foolish, but being her ally came with its own perils. He would need to stay on this investigation, and make sure the problem went away, before he ended up in her crosshairs.

"Let's go hunting," he said as he rose from the chair and headed toward the door; Castor and Pollux following closely at his side.

CHAPTER TWENTY-FOUR

Fear gripped Gabi as she dashed through the woods.

Peering over her shoulder, she would catch glimpses of light in the distance, watching as it bounced back and forth against the trees. Coming here to feed had been a horrible lapse in judgment and it appeared that she would pay dearly for it.

She paused for a moment, taking refuge behind a large oak tree, as she watched the lights flickering in the distance. The evening air was filled with a cacophony of noises. The sound of boots crunching loudly against the new-fallen snow mixed with the frantic barking of dogs. At any other time she could have easily avoided her mortal pursuers, but her escape tonight was made difficult because they were not the only ones looking for her.

How did they find me so quick? she wondered.

She knew the sentries were close by, she could sense them, so she played a calculated game. By keeping her human stalkers close, she could keep the sentries at bay, but she couldn't continue this game forever. Eventually the humans would tire or call off the pursuit, and then the others would descend. She needed to keep those on the ground in the chase long enough for her to formulate a plan of escape.

Gabi had done her best to flee, putting as much distance as she could between her and the crime scene, but it obviously hadn't been far or fast enough. She'd already been in a weakened state, having not eaten for several weeks, and knew that she needed to feed, if she had any hope of surviving the coming fight.

Her head snapped to the left as she detected movement and watched as a deer galloped across an open field.

She knew that the sentries were trying to funnel her into an area where she could be contained. Once they were sure there wouldn't be any outside human interference, they would descend upon her. That the council had mobilized them so fast didn't bode well for her. There were only two possible outcomes, which meant only a fifty/fifty chance she would be taken alive.

Gabi sprinted forward, in the direction of the flashlights, getting to within a hundred yards before turning right. Then she veered off toward the nearest mountain. Doing so put the humans between herself and the closest sentry, which meant the funnel would collapse and perhaps buy her enough time to formulate a plan.

Her escape was aided by the heavy cloud cover that dampened the moonlight. Near the base of the mountain she encountered a stream which gently sloped into a valley. She dashed ahead, finding a small, abandoned mill at the base. Gabi slipped inside and sat down on the floor, beneath one of the dilapidated building's broken windows, as she listened to the barking grow fainter. She glanced out through the remnant of a grime covered windowpane but didn't see any lights coming in her direction. For the moment they seem to have gotten slowed down in the hilly terrain.

Gabi knew she had bought herself extra minutes, but it wouldn't be long before they followed her track into the valley. She hoped that the water would slow them down a bit more, to give her time to think. The sentries were still around, but their signatures had grown weaker. This allowed her to take a rest and contemplate everything that had caused her to end up here.

The three men in the alley were common street thugs and she had a hard time believing that they would take orders from a woman unless they were deathly afraid. There was only one woman Gabi knew that could illicit that level of fear.

"*She made us do it…..The woman with the black hair.*" The words had sent a chill coursing through her.

As much as she didn't want to face it, everything pointed toward the fact that Serena had engineered the attack.

But why would she do it? Why would she want to hurt me?

The idea that Serena had betrayed her, after all they had been through together, was emotionally crushing. Despite her habit of skirting, if not out-right breaking, the rules; Gabi would never have imagined that she would turn on her.

You need to stay focused, she scolded herself. *You can work on that problem after you deal with the bigger one, which is getting out of this current situation.*

Gabi pulled out her cellphone and stared blankly at the screen.

She needed to reach out to him, to explain what had happened, but she was paralyzed with fear. It felt like she had been given a second chance at love, but at the very moment she had allowed herself to open up to him, to take a chance at some semblance of a relationship, it had been ripped away like some cruel joke.

How had everything so right, gone horribly wrong so fast? she wondered.

She selected his number from the contacts and was about to call him when the door to the small building flung open.

"Police, don't move," a disembodied voice commanded.

A bright light filled the room and she turned her head to avoid the beam of intense light. She couldn't see the gun, but knew there had to be one pointed in her direction.

No, no, no...... not like this.

"Stand up, slowly, and turn around," the cop commanded.

Gabi did as she was ordered, her mind racing. She didn't want to hurt him, that wasn't who she was, so she needed to find a way out this situation.

She forced herself to concentrate, allowing herself to take in everything.

The forest outside was still and she could no longer hear the dog's barking. She sensed only his presence. She could get to him, but if he got off a lucky shot, it would alert the others. Whatever she did, she needed to be perfect.

"Put your hands on top of your head," the man ordered, "and interlock your fingers."

Gabi raised her hands in compliance.

He must have gotten separated from the others, she thought.

She heard his cautious footfalls on the creaking floorboards as he approached.

Gabi swallowed hard as she felt him step behind her.

If they take you into custody, it's all over.

There was no way the sentries would allow her to be arrested; the risk was just too great.

It wasn't that her kind couldn't survive in jail; it was just that no one else would. Before long, especially in her weakened state, she would have to choose between escape and feeding. Even solitary confinement would not be enough to contain her when the need to survive took hold.

Oh, God, I don't want to do this.

The die was cast when she felt the man firmly grab one of her hands and started to twist it behind her back.

Gabi pivoted hard, pulling the man off balance and thrust her free hand into his chest. The man's body sailed backward, until it struck the opposite wall with a nauseating thud, and he let out a blood-curdling scream.

She picked up the discarded flashlight and shined it in his direction.

Gabi gaped in disbelief, her eyes wide in horror, as she stared at the body of Sigurdsson impaled on the far wall.

"Karl," she screamed as she rushed toward him.

A large, broken section of cross-beam extended from his chest by several inches.

"Oh my God,… I'm…. I'm so sorry, I didn't know it was you," she said, her voice cracking, as she tried to assess his injuries.

He was alive, but just barely.

Sigurdsson's eyes opened, but his unsteady gaze told her that he was losing his fight.

"Karl……"

He shook his head weakly as he stared at her. "It's okay."

"No, it's not okay," she replied frantically. "I've got to get you out of here."

She could sense them closing in now; drawn to the sound of his scream. They would seize this opportunity, while the humans were still far enough away, and try to grab her, but it was not her safety that she was concerned with at the moment.

"I won't let you die," she said

Sigurdsson raised his hand up, touching his finger to her lips. "No, it's better this way."

"No, it's not," she said desperately. "I can't lose you; I won't lose you."

"You… You don't understand,… Gabi…" Sigurdsson said, struggling to get the words out. "You already have."

"No,… No I haven't," she replied, a pained expression on her face. "I can stop this."

"And what?" he asked. "Turn me into a monster… like you? I'd rather die."

The cutting accusation caught her off-guard and she took a step backward.

"But I thought—"

"Thought what?" he asked. "That... That I cared for you?"

Sigurdsson coughed violently and frothy pink blood began to run down from his lips.

"How.... How could I ever care... for someone who isn't... Who isn't even human?"

Gabi stumbled backward, her mind reeling at his cruel rebuke.

"I'm sorry, Karl... I... I never... I never meant to hurt you," she stammered. "What can I do?"

Suddenly the room erupted with the sound of loud crashing noises as several dark forms assaulted the building. Two came in through the windows, while another through a jagged hole in the roof and a fourth through the door.

Gabi tried to fight them off, but in her debilitated state it was a futile attempt. Two of them grabbed her by her arms, holding her in place, while another stood behind her, their arm wrapped around her neck.

"Well now, isn't this cozy?" Michael Orlov said as he came into view.

"It's not what you think," she protested, struggling to free her arms from the sentries flanking her.

"Oh really?" he asked, grabbing her face roughly. "Then what is it, Gabrielle? Are you cleaning up your mess? Getting rid of witnesses?"

"No," she protested. "It's nothing like that. You know me, Michael. I would never do this."

Orlov looked at her with disdain and then glanced over his shoulder at Sigurdsson. "He might disagree with you."

149

"Ask him," Gabi demanded. "He'll tell you I'm innocent. This was an accident."

Orlov shrugged his shoulders and walked over to Sigurdsson.

"Are you still alive, human?"

Sigurdsson weakly nodded his ashen face.

"Well, I'm sorry to inform you, but you won't be for much longer," Orlov replied. "So I must ask, is she as innocent as she claims?"

"No," Sigurdsson replied. "She killed them… I watched her do it."

Orlov turned around to face Gabi and the others, a feigned look of shock on his face. "Well, that sounds like a death bed confession to me."

"Karl, tell them the truth," Gabi pleaded, struggling in vain.

"I've heard enough," Orlov said. "It's time to end this charade once and for all."

"Karl!"

"Gabrielle de Mar, you have been accused and found guilty of the crime of murdering innocent humans," Orlov pronounced loudly.

"Karl, please, you can stop this, tell them," Gabi begged, one last time, before turning her attention to Orlov. "Michael, I am innocent. I demand to be taken before the council."

"There's no need for that," he replied. "The council doesn't need a show trial, just an end to this unseemly episode."

Gabi felt her legs buckle beneath her.

Orlov turned to look back at Sigurdsson. "Any last words you'd like to say?"

Sigurdsson raised his head and stared at Gabi. He drew one final breath and whispered, "Die."

Gabi's eyes went wide in panic as she felt a pair of hands grab her head tightly.

"No!" she screamed as she felt her head jerk violently.

Gabi awoke from the nightmare, her scream filling the compact room and startling a pair of birds, who had taken refuge in the rafters, and sent them flying off through a hole in the roof.

For a brief moment, she was caught in that weird realm between dream and reality.

An eerie stillness gripped the empty room, as tiny flakes of snow flitted in through the broken window.

She peered around the abandoned cabin she had sought refuge in the previous evening. The dream had been so real, so visceral, and she couldn't help but wonder if it was a bad omen.

She pulled her knees up to her chest, wrapping her arms around them tightly, as she did her best to push away the images.

It can't end this way, she thought. *Not like this.*

Gabi knew what she needed to do; now she just had to find the courage inside her to do it.

CHAPTER TWENTY-FIVE

Sigurdsson sat on his balcony; staring down at the photo of them on his phone.

He studied every line on her face, every feature; from the way her hair hung over her shoulder to the gleam in her eye. Her beauty captivated him, but it was her smile that haunted him. It was a smile which had both captured his heart and terrified him.

He closed out the photo and chose a number from his contacts list, hearing it ring several times before going to voicemail.

"Gabi, call me, please," he implored and ended the call.

He tossed the cellphone onto the table next to the chair and picked up the glass tumbler.

How many messages have I left? he wondered. *Ten? Twenty?*

He'd honestly lost count of them all, but they had all ended the same way; with the call going to voice mail.

Sigurdsson took a sip of his whiskey as he stared at the twinkling lights of the city below him. Despite the frigid temperature this evening, he needed the fresh air to think clearly.

Seventy-Two hours ago his entire worldview had changed in an instant. Everything he thought he had *known* had been stripped away and pronounced a lie. Yet, through it all, he desperately fought to hold on to it, hoping that it was all just some terrible nightmare he would eventually wake from, but he hadn't.

What had started out purely as a punishment, in the assignment of the homicide investigations, had ended with his entire belief system in tatters.

Yes, there was a time in his life when he embraced the notion of myths and fantasy, but they were nothing more than folklore; tales passed along by generation after generation of parents to amuse and occupy the minds of restless children. However, there came a point in every young man's life when you put away those fantasies; when the whimsical adolescent dreams of epic battles, and feasts in *Valhalla*, were replaced with the reality of adulthood. They were good memories, but they weren't real.

"What you're describing is impossible," the words of Carlos Vega repeating in his head.

Yes, it was impossible, but unlike Vega and Reynolds, he had seen it happen. Yet even being a witness to it didn't make it any more believable.

But it did happen, he thought.

He closed his eyes tightly, in a futile attempt to will away the images, but they remained; tormenting him. No matter what he tried, he couldn't *un-see* the carnage he had watched unfold before his very eyes.

The images and sounds came rushing back; things he had never seen or heard before and prayed he never would again. The sound the bodies made upon impact, the blood-curdling screams, and the blood on her teeth.

Sigurdsson's body shuddered and he gulped down the last of his drink, hoping the alcohol would numb him.

He stood up and walked over to the balcony railing, peering off in the night sky.

She was out there; somewhere. A woman who both terrified him and…

And what? he thought.

More than anything else, it was this question that troubled him the most. He struggled to come to reconcile the image of the woman in the alley with the one that gazed at him from across the table.

Her smile, her laughter, her eyes; the way she nervously twirled her hair when she was embarrassed or held his hand tightly. Sigurdsson couldn't deny the way his heart skip a beat every time she was near him. What had started out as a physical attraction had turned into something so much more; something he had never felt before and despite the haunting images he couldn't deny the feelings he had for her. The woman in the alley wasn't the Gabrielle he knew.

Or was she?

The sudden realization, that he might not really know her, hit him hard.

Despite their lengthy conversations, he knew very little about her background and less still about her sister or any other family member. He had chalked it up to some family tension and figured she would share with him when she was ready. But what if there was something more, something she was trying to hide?

"You idiot," he said as he turned and headed back inside; pulling up a seat at his desk and firing up his computer.

Sigurdsson found it more than a bit ironic that, considering he was a detective, he had not even bothered to look into who he had been dating.

"That's what happens when you think with your little brain," he grumbled as his fingers tapped the keys.

He spent the next hour scanning through the traditional *go to* search engines, websites, and social media platforms, all to no avail. These days everyone was *plugged in*, but it seemed that Gabrielle de Mar was the exception. It struck him as odd that someone as young and attractive as she was didn't have some form of internet presence, unless she really was trying to hide something.

Sigurdsson picked up his cellphone and placed a call.

"Molly, it's Karl, I need you to do me a favor."

"Didn't I just do you a favor not that long ago?" Police Officer Molly Shea replied.

"Yes, but I need another one," he replied.

"This *favor* isn't going to end up biting me in the ass, is it, Karl?"

"Molly, I'm hurt that you would even think I would do that to you. I just need you to run a name for me."

"Don't even try to play innocent with me," she said. "What's the name?"

"Gabrielle de Mar," he replied, "She's a female, white, blonde hair, blue eyes. Height is about 5'8" and weight is around 130ish. Not positive about the d.o.b., but I would guess around thirty."

Sigurdsson could hear the sound of keys tapping in the background.

"Not coming up with a match," she said. "Closest I'm coming up with is a Gabrielle Del Mar, but she's 5'1" and 63 years old."

"Yeah, that's not her," Sigurdsson said. "Can you run another name?"

"You're killing me, Karl," Shea replied. "I'd better get more out of this than another rain-check for dinner. What's the name?"

"Serena de Mar, she's a female, white, black hair, and dark eyes, probably brown. Height is about 5'10" and weight is around 140. Age should be around thirty as well."

"Sorry," she replied as she tapped away at her keyboard. "Negative results. You're batting oh-for-two."

"Okay, it was worth a try," he replied. "Thanks, Molly."

"We should do dinner some time, Karl."

"I thought you hated my guts?" he asked.

"I did, but I got over it," she replied. "Now I only mildly dislike you."

"I'll keep that in mind."

"You do that," she said, before hanging up.

Who the hell are you, Gabi? he wondered.

After exhausting all the traditional methods, he decided to try something new. He typed in the search and waited as the website for Leaf Spring loaded up.

Sigurdsson had toyed with it in the past, researching his family's linage, but he hadn't touched it in a while. He typed in Gabrielle's information and waited for the results. It wasn't long until a list of potential matches was generated by their algorithms. After looking at the list he was able to cull it down even further and then he began going through the ones that remained. It wasn't until page six that he found what he was looking for.

"Bingo," he said as he hit the icon and waited for the screen to load up.

The entry belonged to a larger family-tree created by someone named Pablo de Mar, who hailed from Miranda de Ebro, Spain. Sigurdsson scrolled through the list of the four hundred plus family members until he came upon the one for Gabrielle; all seventeen of them.

It's never easy, is it? he thought as he selected the first one and began reading the biography.

One by one he perused the entries until he found a disqualifier and moved on to the next. Somewhere around number eight he had refilled his drink and by number eleven he was on the verge of admitting that he had just wasted another hour of his day.

"Here goes nothing," he said, selecting Gabrielle *number fourteen*.

As the screen loaded up, his eyes were immediately drawn to the image displayed in the corner; it was her, but it wasn't.

Sigurdsson stared at the photo, trying to figure out what was amiss. He read the page and found an entry that showed the photo was from a secondary source. He clicked the link which took him to a museum website and watched as a much larger scan began to load. It didn't take long to realize that the picture in question was actually a painting and he read the caption that accompanied it.

17th Century Oil Painting, Gabrielle de Mar, Winchester, England.

He leaned back in his chair and stared at the image.

While the woman bore an uncanny resemblance to his Gabrielle, it was clearly from a much different time period.

A fifth or sixth generation great-aunt? he wondered.

Either way, it was clear that the de Mar's shared amazing genes. The woman was as enchanting as her modern-day namesake. Her long blonde hair was pulled up on her head, while two long, curly locks hung over her shoulders. She was wearing a bright yellow dress, with delicate white trim around the neck, and was draped in a blue pastel shawl. Even in a painting, the woman had an air of aristocracy about her.

"Well, you *almost* had her," he said as he felt a wave of exhaustion come over him.

He knew he was on the right track, but he didn't want to miss anything because he was tired. He bookmarked the page, so that he could come back to it in the morning when he felt more clearheaded, and shut the computer down. Then he headed off to the kitchen to refill his glass with ice and pour himself another drink.

Sigurdsson made his way into the living room and turned on the television. He wasn't interested in what was on the screen, he just needed background noise and yet he found no relief from the thoughts in his head.

How did he reconcile his feelings for her and, more importantly, how could he even begin to investigate this?

Fear gripped him, but it had nothing to do with what he had *seen*. He feared that after last night's incident they would be forced to put a task force together and he would be screwed. A task force would mean additional manpower and supervision, which would limit his ability to protect her. That a video might exist and might be found by someone else terrified him. He knew what it would show and that it would put a face to the killer; her face.

He didn't know how he could ever face her again, but he also knew that he couldn't live without her.

"Fuck me," he mumbled as he took a drink.

The buzzing of the cellphone jarred him from his thoughts.

Another murder? he thought wearily as he reached down and answered it. "Sigurdsson."

"Karl, it's Gabi," the voice said. "I need to see you."

CHAPTER TWENTY-SIX

It was just past 11 p.m. when Sigurdsson pulled into the deserted parking lot next to the Montauk Point Lighthouse.

Turning off the headlights, he was struck by the blackness that enveloped everything.

A fast-moving winter storm had passed through, but thick, heavy clouds blanketed the sky, blocking any ambient light the moon would normally provide. It just added another layer of eeriness to the scene.

"This is dumb," he said as he stared out the windshield and took a sip of coffee.

He'd spent the last four hours making the trek from Midtown Manhattan to the farthest point east on Long Island; a remote section of a state park that dropped off into the Atlantic Ocean. The long drive had left him alone with his thoughts and he was now questioning his sanity in agreeing to meet her in this desolate place.

His mind could not shake the visceral images that his eyes had witnessed, and yet he ignored his brain and held on to the feelings he had for her in his heart.

"That's great," he said sardonically. "It will make a catchy little ditty for your headstone, 'he gave her his heart and she took it... literally.'"

He took a sip of coffee as he glanced around the lot, but there was nothing to see, although he felt a growing uneasiness deep within.

Fuck it, he thought as he put the lid back on the coffee container and opened the car door. *No one lives forever.*

He adjusted the collar of his jacket, pulling it up to protect his neck from the fierce wind blowing in off of the ocean, and set off down a path that led toward the water's edge, listening as the new fallen snow crunched beneath his feet. Four hundred feet later he emerged onto the deserted, windswept beach. He walked over to where several large boulders rested near the tree line and sat down.

As the minutes ticked by, he felt himself growing restless. The black sky, coupled with the never ending roar of the waves, began playing tricks on him. His head snapped around several times, as he *sensed* movement around him, but there was nothing there, only the rhythmic pulsing of the lighthouse beacon. Off in the distance, he watched as a bolt of lightning flashed inside the clouds, sending a dramatic burst of light pulsing through it. If it had been any other time, he would have enjoyed the raw beauty of it, but now it just seemed ominous.

His body began to shiver and he looked down at his watch; he'd been there for almost an hour.

Just leave, he thought.

The frigid temps were becoming increasingly unbearable and he wondered how much longer he could wait.

Then he felt it; a tingling sensation that raised the hairs on the back of his neck and foretold of impending danger.

Sigurdsson's head snapped up and he saw Gabrielle standing between him and the water, a dispirited smile on her face. She was wearing the same clothes that she had worn at dinner.

"Hello, Karl," she said weakly.

"Gabi,…" he replied, feeling confused. "Where did you come from?"

"You wouldn't understand if I told you," she said as she sat down on one of the adjacent rocks.

"Do you mind telling me what the hell is going on?" he asked.

"I'm in trouble."

"You don't say?" he declared. "Although I think *trouble* is probably a gross understatement."

Gabi stared off in the ocean's direction, not saying anything. In stark contrast to the last time he'd seen her, she now looked scared and vulnerable.

Sigurdsson sat there, giving her time to think as he struggled with his own thoughts. Any apprehension he may have felt about meeting her was gone and in its place was the unmistakable feeling of deep affection he held for her. He knew that he was in uncharted waters and he did not know how to proceed.

Suddenly, the clouds above them broke and the light from the full moon lit up the beach. It was as if a million diamonds had been scattered across the dark waters of the Atlantic.

He looked over at her, the moonlight radiating off her skin, and found himself transfixed. Even after everything they had been through, he knew he couldn't deny his feelings.

"Gabi, I can't help you if you won't let me," he whispered.

"That's very sweet, Karl, but I'm not sure if anyone can help me now," she said forlornly. "I just needed to see you."

"I *can't* help you or you *won't* let me help you?"

"You don't understand; it's complicated."

Sigurdsson felt an unexpected wave of anger boil up inside him at her rebuff.

"Complicated?" he barked as he got up from the boulder and took several steps toward the water before turning back around. "Is that what you think this is, Gabi? Complicated?"

"Karl—" she began to interject as she lowered her head.

"No!" Sigurdsson snapped. "No, Gabi, this isn't *complicated*. You know what's complicated? I'll tell you. Complicated is three bodies in the morgue. Complicated is a cop being a witness to their murders. Complicated is the prime suspect in those murders being the woman he loves…"

The spontaneous admission caught both of them by surprise.

For a moment, everything went silent; even the crashing of the waves abated, as Gabi slowly raised her head up and looked him in the eyes.

"What did you say?" she asked as her shock began to wear off.

"I.... Uhm...." Sigurdsson stumbled.

He hadn't intended to say it, he had just gotten caught up in the moment, but in his heart he knew it was true and there was no sense in trying to deny it.

"I said I love you, Gabi."

She continued to stare at him, for what seemed like an eternity, and for a moment he wished he could have taken the words back, but then he watched as her body began to tremble.

"Gabi, I'm sor—"

He never had a chance to finish the sentence.

Sigurdsson didn't see her move as much as he felt it. A blur and a sudden rush of wind, and then she was standing in front of him. He flinched, imagining the worst, until he felt her arms wrap around him. For a moment, he didn't know how to react, until he felt her quivering body pressing against his and he hugged her tightly.

"Oh, Karl, I love you too," she said, her voice muffled, as she buried her face against his shoulder. "I'm so scared."

"I know, babe," he replied, trying his best to comfort her, "but I can't help you if you won't let me."

"You don't know what you're asking."

"All I am asking you for is the truth," he replied. "I think I've earned that."

Gabrielle let go of him and took a step back as she looked into his eyes.

"It's not a question of whether you earned it, Karl," Gabi said. "It's a question of whether you can handle the truth."

"You asked me to meet you here and I did; even after what I saw the other night."

"I just wanted to see you one last time," she said. "I needed to know that you didn't hate me."

The finality of what she had said left him feeling as if he had just been sucker-punched. His head was spinning and the thought of losing her felt like a crushing weight on his chest; taking away the air he needed to breathe.

"Gabi, I could never hate you. I came here tonight because I can't deny my feelings for you. I don't understand what is going on, so you're going to have to help me make sense of all of this."

"Karl, once you open this door, you will never be able to go back," she said resolutely.

"What choice do I have?" he asked.

"You can walk away," Gabi replied. "Leave here and don't look back. I'll face the consequences of my actions."

"You're in trouble," he said. "I'm not going anywhere. Besides, I couldn't bear the thought of losing you. Damn the consequences, I won't leave you."

Gabi's eyes locked onto his.

The unselfish part of her wanted to push him away, to scare him off in order to save him, and yet she couldn't. She had asked him to meet her, partly because she didn't expect him to show, but he did and she didn't want to let him go. For the first time in her life she had something, *someone*, she didn't want to lose.

She reached out, taking his hand in hers.

"Karl, I'm warning you, what I tell you next will mean the world as you know it will no longer exist."

"You don't get it, Gabi," he replied. "Without you in my world, it won't matter."

She took a deep breath and resolved her mind to let him in.

"Okay," she replied. "I'll tell you everything, but not here."

CHAPTER TWENTY-SEVEN

Sigurdsson sat in a chair, inside the cozy bedroom of the hotel they had checked into, cradling a glass of wine in his hands, as he listened to the steady sound of running water coming from the shower.

Gabrielle had looked weary as they drove back from the lighthouse, so he suggested they find a place to rest. This area of Long Island was a seasonal hotspot, catering to the rich and famous during the summer months, but this late in the year they were lucky to find a place that was still open.

The clerk had eyed them suspiciously when they checked in after midnight, but Sigurdsson's credit card and police ID seemed to assuage his fears. He even provided a complimentary bottle of wine for the couple.

Now, as he waited for her to finish, he couldn't help but wonder about the conversation that would soon take place. He knew that he was in a precarious place; caught somewhere between reality and…

And what?

He let the thought slip away unanswered as he heard the water turn off.

A few minutes later Gabrielle emerged from the bathroom wearing a long white terry-cloth robe and a towel wrapped around her head.

"Feeling better?" he asked.

"Much," she said as she collapsed onto the couch across from him.

He reached over and poured her a glass of wine.

"You look like you could use this," he said as he handed her the glass. "So, are you ready to tell me what's going on?"

"It's a long story, Karl," she said as she took a sip.

"We have the room till noon, Gabi," he replied, "and I have nothing but time."

Gabrielle took a deep breath as she faced her inner fears. These were completely unchartered waters; something she had never had to confront before. She also understood that once she began, there would be no turning back. It terrified her to think what would happen at the end and whether they would even make it to the check-out time.

"Are you sure you want to know *everything*?" she asked one last time.

"I wouldn't be here if I didn't want to know," he replied. "I need to know, all of it, if this relationship is to survive."

"The truth is, I haven't been entirely honest with you," she replied. "My story is long, but in order for you to understand who I am, you must hear it from the beginning. Only then will what you witnessed make any sense."

"I'm ready," Sigurdsson said. "I can handle it."

Gabi took one more sip and then set the glass down on the table, "I hope you are right, Karl."

As he watched, Gabi's entire demeanor changed. It was as if a switch had been flipped and the girl he had known vanished; replaced by a woman whose appearance seemed almost regal.

There were a million things that he had envisioned her confessing, but none of them came even remotely close to what came out of her mouth next.

"I am the Countess Gabrielle de Mar. I was born in Navarre in 1671, and died in England in 1694, at the ripe old age of twenty-three."

The soberness of her statement only underscored the gravity of what she was saying.

What the fuck? he wondered as he stared at her, completely blown away by her admission. *That's great; you're locked in a room with a homicidal nut job.*

"My father, Alejandro de Mar, was a nobleman and came from a well-respected house in the Kingdom of Navarre," she continued. "My family were *Huguenots*, members of the Protestant faith, which was not a popular religious position to take at that time. As the Huguenots began to gain more power and influence in the region, they found themselves at bitter odds with Catholics, both in Spain and in France. In 1547, Henry II ascended to the French throne and under his reign the persecution of Protestants grew. They even established special courts in Paris for the trial of heretics. These courts had a reputation of issuing death penalties that were carried out on burning gallows. Despite increased prosecution, Protestantism continued to flourish and became a political movement; after more and more nobles converted.

"In 1555, Jeanne d'Albret became the queen regnant of the independent Kingdom of Navarre and she converted to Protestantism in 1560. Queen Jeanne became the movement's spiritual and political leader, as well as the highest ranking protestant in France. As a result, she earned the designation as an *enemy of the Catholic Church*. The power struggle between Catholics and Protestants led to the outbreak of the French Wars of Religion in 1562. At one point there was a plot led by Pope Pius IV to have the Queen kidnapped. If successful, they would have imprisoned her in Madrid and turned her over to the Spanish Inquisition. With her removed, the rulers of both France and Spain would have then had the ability to annex Navarre to their crowns. They summoned Queen Jeanne to appear in Rome, in order to put her under examination for heresy. The potential penalty she was facing was excommunication, the confiscation of her property, and a declaration that her kingdom was available to any ruler who wished to invade it. Ironically, it was the latter threat that incensed both the thrones of France and Spain. Each of whom viewed it as an example of the Papacy interfering in the affairs of sovereign states. Looking to appease the predominantly Catholic countries, the Pope backed off and the threat never materialized; effectively bringing the matter to a close.

"In 1570, The Queen pushed for a peace agreement to end the conflict with France. Part of the agreement called for a marriage of convenience, one that she reluctantly agreed to, between her son, Henry de Bourbon, and King Charles IX's sister Marguerite. This was in exchange for the right of Huguenots to hold public office in France; a privilege which they had previously been denied. Upon her death in 1572, Henry ascended to the throne as King Henry III of Navarre. When his brother-in-law, King Henry III of France, was assassinated, King Henry of Navarre ascended the throne and became known as Henry IV, King of France. He kept his Protestant faith initially, the only French king to do so, but soon found himself in a tenuous position with the Catholic League, which claimed that he could not wear France's crown as a Protestant. To get full control of his kingdom, he converted to Catholicism. Yet despite this conversion he issued the *Edict of Nantes* which guaranteed religious liberties to Protestants. This edict brought an end to the Wars of Religion. Unfortunately, rather than being seen as a moderate by both groups, he was reviled. The Catholics considered him a usurper, while the Protestants labeled him a traitor, and he became the target of many assassination attempts. They finally killed him in Paris in 1610 when a Catholic fanatic stabbed him. The independence of Navarre ended in 1620 when Louis XIII officially merged it into the Kingdom of France.

"Over the years my family grew tired of the endless wars, driven by religion and conquest. They were deeply troubled by the close relationship that the Pope had with both France and Spain. While the two countries often fought against each other, their strong Catholic ties still made them enemies toward Protestants. When Louis XIV ascended to the throne, he increased the persecution of Protestants and issued the *Edict of Fontainebleau*, which ended the legal recognition of Protestantism in France. They forced the remaining Huguenots to either convert to Catholicism or flee the country as refugees. Any who remained were subject to the *Dragonnades*, a policy which allowed for the billeting of ill-mannered soldiers in Protestant homes, with implied permission to abuse, bully, and plunder from the occupants."

Sigurdsson caught himself staring at her in utter amazement.

During his career, he had interviewed thousands of people and it had taught him to pick up on *tells*; those little giveaways that show a person was either lying or being misleading, but to his shock there were none. Gabrielle wasn't trying to create details, she was reliving them. She spoke with an air of authority in her voice that made her statements ring true; as implausible as they might seem. She was either delusional or she was telling the truth.

"After I was born," Gabi continued, "my father opted to leave Navarre, deciding that it would be wise for his family to find favor in a country more inclined with our religious beliefs. In 1681, Charles II of England had offered sanctuary to the Huguenots. My father's nobility, and position within the Protestant faith, allowed for a pleasant life and he soon found favor in the court of King William III and Queen Mary II. In her role, as Supreme Governor of the Church of England, the Queen would often seek my father's theological counsel. Eventually, I was bethroed to Robert, the Earl of Wessex.

"Robert was a caring boyish man, but his eyes never fell upon me in the way others thought. It was during that time that I became close to my sister-in-law. She was a few years older, but we were both young and we developed a bond. It didn't take long for her to confess to me that my husband was smitten with another. At first I felt betrayed, believing he loved another noble woman, but I was unprepared for the news that his attraction lay in the eyes of a young servant; a male servant. Once the initial shock subsided, I concluded that my life was what I chose to make it. I confronted Robert and told him I knew, but that I would stand by him. My life was there now and it was a good life. In return he treated me well and I played the part of the loving wife. It was a role that I was so good at that we became the envy of the other royal couples. In the fall of 1694, we were invited to meet with Queen Mary. What should have been a joyous event was soon revealed to be a deadly fate. Unbeknownst to anyone, the Queen had contracted smallpox, which we were also exposed to during our visit.

"Robert showed the symptoms first and the doctor quarantined him. Listening to him was heart wrenching, but I grieved twice as hard for his servant who had to listen to his anguished cries. His condition progressed rather quickly and he died within a week. When I began experiencing symptoms, I knew that my time was not long for this Earth. Word had already reached us that the Queen had died just after Christmas. I was lying in bed one night when his sister came to visit me; despite the order that I was infected and no one could come in. At first I thought it was a fever dream; I didn't know how she could have gotten past the guards, but there she was. I begged her to leave, to get far away, but she sat on my bed and held my hand. I remember vividly how she stroked it gently and said that she would help me. At that time, I was lapsing in and out of consciousness, but for a brief moment I saw it happen. It seemed like a nightmare. Her face transformed and then I saw them… her teeth, but they weren't teeth, they were like an animal's fangs. When she bit me, it was like liquid fire was coursing through my veins. I screamed, I pleaded for help, but no one came to my rescue. The virus was the perfect cover. My mind reeled as my body thrashed violently in bed. Then everything went still and darkness engulfed me. For a moment I thought I had died, but I still had a sense of consciousness. Indescribable pain racked my body, but I couldn't speak and there was no sense of time. I begged for death, wishing it would take me, but it only tormented me."

"It was Serena, wasn't it?" Sigurdsson asked.

Gabi nodded her head.

"When I woke, the fever and malaise were gone, but my bedroom was in shambles," she said. "I sat there in bed; my eye's darting back and forth, feeling like a caged animal, until I saw Serena sitting in the corner smiling. Instinctively, I knew something had happened, but I just didn't know what. Then the memories came flooding back and I looked down at my arm. It was then that I realized it wasn't all just a bad dream. I screamed at her, asking her what she had done to me. She told me she had *saved me*. I remember having an almost primal hunger, beyond anything I had ever felt before. Serena calmed me down and then gave me her arm and showed me how to feed. I remember biting her and being filled with a sense of euphoria; it was like a drug was coursing through my veins."

"Why did you bite her?" he asked in confusion.

"Turning someone isn't like the movies, Karl," Gabi said with a sheepish smile. "You don't just get bit and become a vampire. It's actually a virus that attacks the body and everyone is different. Some can withstand the transformation, but most don't, and we don't know why. Taking in the blood of the one who infected you is necessary to halt the virus' progression. Think of it like venom and anti-venom, but, as in the case with anti-venom, there are no guarantees."

"What happens if you don't get it?"

"If you receive only a small dose, just enough to bring about transformation, there is a lull," she said. "You wake up feeling hungrier than you can ever possibly imagine. It's at that point you need to take in the host vampire's blood. Without it, the virus will start to attack the body aggressively, turning it against itself, and you will begin to feel endless waves of excruciating pain. Eventually it drives a person insane before killing them. It's almost merciful to take enough blood right away to kill them."

"Couldn't you just feed off another vampire?" he asked.

"No," she replied. "Just like humans, no two vampires are the same. Our bodies process the virus in different ways; it would be like giving the wrong blood type during a transfusion. They've tried to do research, to see if the virus can be controlled or even modified, but they haven't come up with anything conclusive."

Sigurdsson nodded his head.

"While the feeding may have stopped the progression, it did nothing for the hunger I felt. Serena told me she would return shortly. I don't know how long I waited; I just paced the room, wrestling with feelings of intense hunger and rage. When Serena returned to my room, she had a *guest*; my husband's servant. She was holding him by the scruff of his neck and the look of terror on that man's face is something I will never forget. Serena threw the man to the ground and he landed at my feet with a loud thud. For a moment I stared at him, wishing I could feel compassion, but the moment was fleeting. I descended upon him and what I did next haunts me till this day. It was my first kill and you never forget that."

Sigurdsson swallowed hard, feeling a growing sense of uneasiness, as he had a flashback to the man in the alley.

"After killing the servant, Serena informed the staff I had died. Then she wrapped the body up in heavy linens and had it removed for immediate burning. No one wanted to expose themselves unnecessarily, so no one looked to make sure it was me they were hauling away. When night came, she took me to one of Robert's hunting cottages and kept me there; as she taught me how to control myself. Game was plentiful, at least for a while, but it was never enough. There is a big difference in the composition of animal and human blood. It was like trying to live off soy, when all you crave is steak. Eventually I could control the anger and she took me out, far away from the cottage, and we began to hunt humans. In those days, it was easy to find travelers and no one looked for them when they *disappeared*.

"What you go through that first year of transformation is almost indescribable; you're neither human nor animal. You are driven by an insatiable blood lust. It's not just that you want to feed, but that you want to destroy. At times I felt like I wanted to kill the entirety of humanity for what I had become, but yet I knew it was Serena who had created me and not them. Over time she had shared her turning at the hands of *Romanies*; gypsies who'd been given special privileges not afforded to other wanderers in England. She was thirteen at the time and her parents had sent her to visit her aunt and uncle. When her carriage was descended upon, the guards were quickly dispatched and then she was taken. Whether they had been sated by the blood of the guards, or moved by her youth, the one who'd taken her had stopped short of killing Serena. Instead, he had destined her to the brutal life of immortality. They found her wandering in the forest six months later in an *animalistic* state. They excused the behavior, as resulting from the trauma she had experienced, and locked her away for her own protection. In time she gained enough control and was eventually released.

"With my past now dead, we began wandering ourselves. We moved from town to town and eventually headed west through Europe. Fearing that someone might make the connection to her family name, Serena adopted mine and we passed ourselves off as biological sisters. We used the epidemics that gripped Europe to our advantage. It seems almost comical now, but you can't imagine the hysteria that was prevalent in those days. Fortunately for us, at least in the beginning, feminism wasn't a big thing, so the blame was mostly directed at men. That began to change in the east, where I guess some of our sisters weren't as careful, and quickly spread throughout all of Europe. So we decided to head to America and ended up in New York."

"How many of you are there?" he asked as he poured the last remnants of the wine into his glass and gulped it down.

"It's really hard to say," Gabi replied. "The legend of vampires dates back millennia, but little is actually known about our past or even our origins; it's more speculation than fact. There are established covens throughout the world, but there are also *nomads*, those who don't fall under the jurisdiction of a coven. Some are respectful as they pass through areas, others are not."

"So you even have *assholes* in the vampire world," he replied. "That's so reassuring."

Gabi smiled and nodded her head. "The truth is, vampires are very territorially. Unfortunately, our reasons for that have to do with hunting. So, in order to preserve the balance, we have carved out areas where we enforce our own laws."

"You have laws?" he asked.

"Yes, Karl, we do," she laughed. "Just because we are immortal doesn't mean that we still don't have the same *issues*. Fundamentally, we are still humans, but just like the rest of humanity, our laws are not universal. They change from location to location. Each coven is controlled by a council that establishes the law for the area they control. These laws are enforced by *sentries*, who function as a quasi-police force. Some covens have lax laws, others, like ours, have stricter laws. One of our most fundamental is that we do not kill humans."

"Uhm, yeah, well that hasn't been working out well now, has it?"

"No, it hasn't," Gabi admitted. "It's Serena; she's always pushed the boundaries. Like I said, the overwhelming majority of us do not kill humans, unless there is no other choice. Most of us rely on game animals to satisfy our needs, but some have access to other methods, like blood banks and even blood slaves."

"Blood slaves, what the hell is that?" he asked.

"Believe it or not there is an underground community that worships the *idea* of vampirism and they are willing to offer up their blood, as part of their service to someone they view as being a *vampire*. For these slaves it is part of the fantasy of a vampire *experience*, but some of us have learned to exploit it and use it to our benefit."

"It's not the craziest thing I've heard of, but it sure comes close," he replied. "So what happened to Serena?"

"Serena has always been a free spirit, so to speak. Mostly, the laws are like a guideline to her. She follows them, to a certain degree, but she has a tendency to grow bored with the status quo. In the past, she limited her prey to just criminals. I reconciled it in my mind that these were bad people who got what they deserved. I guess I was blinded by my *sisterly affection* for her. I didn't participate, and I even tried to talk her out of it, but she just has this thing about human blood. When she would start wreaking havoc in a particular area, we would simply relocate, but now things have changed."

"What's changed?" he asked.

"There was a recent vacancy on the council and Serena thought she deserved the spot, but she lost the vote and it didn't sit well with her. I have a feeling she is just lashing out in anger. Positions on the council are usually a lifetime appointment, but, just like in the natural world, you can make the wrong choices and *accidents* can happen from time to time. Even in the immortal world you can make enemies and one thing we vampires have is a long memory."

"I'm curious," Sigurdsson said. "How do you keep from being outed? I mean, you're telling me you're over three hundred years old, yet you don't look a day older than thirty. And you certainly don't fit the part of the classic *sun-fearing* vampire."

"Do you honestly think Hollywood came up with the concept of how vampires look on its own?" she laughed. "In the past, we would be forced to leave an area once others around us began to age beyond our own. It became too suspicious and, as I said, in the 17th and 18th centuries people were looking for any reason to hunt down supposed vampires. So it made no sense to give them an excuse; not that it would have ended well for them if they had tried. But we decided that it was just easier for us to roam. Because of our age, Serena and I had it pretty well, but others realized that if we wanted to have some type of normalcy in our lives, we would need to adapt. A decision was made to *fictionalize* the concept of vampires, so we created a period of romance. Books came first and then movies. Once people were told that vampires were only figments of someone's literary imagination, they accepted that it was all make-believe and enjoyed the theatrics. The movie industry provided an opportunity to test and improve. If you want to know how successful this campaign was, we now have people *rooting* for us in the theaters."

"Wait, does that make me part of *Team Gabi*?" he asked.

"You can be the club president if you like," Gabi replied mischievously.

"How often do you interact with people?" he asked. "I mean I honestly thought vampires didn't come out in the daylight."

"There's a bit of truth to that," she replied. "The sun has *some* effect on us, but not as much as has been made of it. We have slightly diminished strength during the day, as our bodies have to fight against the sun's effect, but I doubt a human would notice. As far as our interaction goes, you might be surprised. Some of us realized that you could do more from the inside than just depending on luck. Our ranks include many in the medical field, and we have pioneered a lot of new treatments in the search for a cure to our affliction. We are also heavily involved in entertainment, media, even politics, but we usually keep human interaction on the professional level."

"You said it was an *affliction*, but I would argue that there are some who would give anything for a shot at immortality."

"Only someone who hasn't lived it would think of it as a gift," she lamented. "However, the reality sets in very quickly as you watch everyone you have ever known or loved be put into the ground. It's the reason we keep to ourselves and why personal involvement is generally frowned upon."

"Personal involvement?" he asked. "Like in you and me *personal*?"

"Yes," Gabi replied, "but beyond the obvious reason, there is also a certain level of danger that is always present."

"Oh, you mean like taking your girlfriend out to dinner and then she saves your ass by decimating three dangerous criminals?"

"That's not funny, but yes," Gabi conceded as she sipped the last of her wine. "Or, you get your girlfriend angry and she—"

"So what do you do, when you're not with me?" he asked, quickly changing the subject.

"I write books," she replied, "about vampires."

"You're kidding me?"

"No, I always enjoyed writing, ever since I was a little girl, so I saw a niche and exploited it. They say write what you know, so it made sense. I guess I got in at the right time, because people love it."

"Well, what do you do when you're not writing about vampires?" he asked.

Gabrielle's mood became serious. "I'm the newest member of the council."

"Wait, you got the vacant spot?" he asked.

"Yes," she replied, "but I didn't want it. I told them that, but the community makes its decisions based on needs and not wants. Ever since then, Serena's attitude changed."

"Why didn't you out her for what she was doing?"

"She's my sister," Gabi replied. "How could I betray her?"

"Well I have a feeling that's gonna come back and bite you, no pun intended."

"I think it already has, Karl. One of those men said something before he died. He said, 'she made us do it.' When I asked him who he was talking about, he said, 'the woman with the black hair.' If Serena is behind this, then it changes everything."

"I guess sisterly love is a one-way street for her," Sigurdsson replied. "Didn't you think it might have been a better idea not to tear his throat out?"

"I told you, the rage is always there, you only learn to control it better, but once it is unleashed, stopping is almost impossible. Once that happens, the only way to have it subside is to force yourself to get away from humans."

"What happens if you don't get away?" he asked.

"There are tales of entire villages being wiped out in one fell swoop. Most believe they were crushed by an invading army, but the reality is that it was probably just one vampire that was consumed by blood lust."

"Yeah, I was kind of curious about that. The M.E. said she had never seen anything like that before. She said it looked like one of the bodies had fallen from a ten story building."

"The easiest way to explain it is to consider the difference between humans and primates," Gabi replied. "Think of the incredible strength an ape has compared to a human, even though they may weigh the same. The main difference between primate and human muscle is in fiber distribution, with primates having a much higher fraction of fast fibers than humans, but we have even more than apes. What works against the primate is that they lack finer motor skills; a problem we do not have. So in effect, we have it all; the strength, the speed, and the dexterity. The only time we seem to be grossly out of control is during the first year of transformation or when we are threatened. Even vampires have a fight-or-flight response, but rarely do we exercise the latter. Remember, under normal conditions we don't tire, we don't fatigue, and we have unlimited strength."

"So how exactly do you stop a one-person wrecking crew that doesn't want to be stopped?"

Gabrielle paused for a moment, staring at Karl, her face an impassive mask. It was a question she had never given much consideration to and one that she never imagined answering for a human.

Hey, I'm curious, how do I kill you? Oh, no problem, let me give you a step-by-step... Even the very thought seemed ludicrous to her.

"Very, *very*, carefully," she replied, a discernable edge to her voice, as she decided to share the deeply held secret. "In all seriousness, it can be done, but there are extremely limited means. Under our laws, decapitation is reserved for the most heinous of crimes, but that is something best left to other vampires, given our inherent strength. For a human that would mean you would have to be close enough and no mortal being could accomplish that. Something you witnessed in the alley. Once that is done, the body then has to be incinerated."

"Wait, why do you have to burn the body?"

"Because our bodies can regenerate," she replied. "We cannot be hurt in the same way a human is. Depending on the severity of the wound, our bodies can repair any damage within seconds or, in a worst-case scenario, hours."

"Whoa, whoa, hold the phone!" Sigurdsson exclaimed. "You're telling me that if you lost an arm it would grow back?"

"Yes, it would."

He stared at her, unable to process what she was sharing with him.

"Are you okay?" she asked.

Sigurdsson nodded his head, but he really wasn't. "So, *hypothetically speaking*, if I unloaded an entire magazine from my gun into you—"

"I'd be healed before you could change magazines."

"Gabi, I don't—"

Before he could finish the sentence, there was a blur of motion and the next thing he saw was the knife that he kept clipped to his belt in her hand. Without saying a word, she drew the blade deeply across her forearm. As the blade pulled free of her skin, the wound closed up leaving behind no trace.

"That's... No..." he stammered. "That can't,... How?"

"Sorry for the graphic example, Karl," she said as she closed the blade and handed it back to him, "but it was the easiest way to show you what I mean. It's not just our speed that is accelerated, but our body's ability to recover."

"If you can heal that way, I'm at a loss as to what a human could do."

"As I said before, it would have to be done very carefully. A vampire who feeds on human blood will be much stronger than one who relies only on an animal's blood. For a human to have any chance it would have to be through blood poisoning."

"What do you mean by blood poisoning?" Sigurdsson asked curiously. "I thought you were immortal?"

"We are, too a certain extent," she replied. "There are a lot of myths surrounding vampire lore, some we have created to mislead you, and others have some foundation in truth. The transformation affects us physically; we need blood because we cannot create enough of our own to sustain us. But the infection changes things at a molecular level. When we feed, our bodies alter the makeup to keep us alive, but it also exposes us to danger, specifically silver. Something in the chemical composition interacts with our modified blood and effectively poisons us. There are vampires who have walked the Earth since long before the time of Jesus, but there comes a time when we hit a point of diminishing returns, when we cannot consume enough blood to keep our bodies going. We don't know why, maybe it is a slow exposure to the chemical elements in our surroundings, like silver, which gradually attacks us or something else. No one knows. When that happens, we are vulnerable. Imagine a sailor, lost at sea, completely surrounded by an ocean, yet dying from a lack of drinkable water. The inability to find enough blood to satiate you can drive you to insanity or worse. Most who reach this point opt for a mercy killing, even though it forces us to confront our greatest fear."

"What's that?" he asked.

"Where do we go from here?" she replied.

Sigurdsson saw the immediate change in her demeanor, like a sense of despondency had taken hold of her.

"It's a theological question many of us struggle with," she continued. "They have portrayed us as monsters and evil, but, while there may be some truth to that, the reality is we are still human. Our physiology may have changed, but who we are has not. We still have desires, bonds, relationships, some even have faith, but one question always remains. Has what we become irrevocably altered us spiritually in a way that is beyond redemption?"

It was a thought he didn't want to consider; not about her.

"I don't think so," he said after a few seconds.

Gabrielle smiled. "You're being kind, Karl, but the reality is we don't know."

Sigurdsson got up and moved over to the couch, sitting down beside her. He took her hand in his and kissed her gently on the head.

"I may not know everything, Gabi, but I know that I love you. What happened to you was not something you chose and I can't imagine God blaming an innocent victim."

"Thank you," she said, squeezing his hand.

"So, getting back to the original question, how could a human kill a vampire with silver?" he asked.

"It would have to be a concentrated amount," she said. "I mean, you could always lock them in a silver room, but they'd probably outlive you anyway. For something to be immediately effective, it would have to be introduced directly into the blood stream so it would prevent the healing process from kicking in or at least slow it down so you could decapitate them."

"To be honest, I'm having a hard time wrapping my own head around the fact that I'd have to remove someone else's."

"There is also something else you need to know," Gabi said. "Not every vampire is the same. Even with our enhanced speed and strength, some are faster or stronger than others. Additionally, each of us has what you would call attributes or liabilities. For example, one might be capable of mental telepathy, reading minds, while another might have the ability to project their own thoughts onto someone else, to get them to do their bidding."

Sigurdsson eyed Gabi suspiciously. "And what abilities do you have?"

"Nothing like that, I promise," she said with a laugh. "Until now I felt as if my ability fell into the *meh* category, but I basically have no mental footprint."

"What's a *mental footprint*?" he asked curiously.

"Some of us can track others," she explained. "They can pick up an individual vampire's mental signature and hunt them down like a bloodhound; a particularly handy attribute for our sentries, but I seem to be invisible."

"So you're like a stealth fighter?" he asked.

"I'd argue that I am more stealth and less fight," Gabi replied, "but yes, although I prefer to avoid problems when I can."

"Changing subjects," he said, choosing to ignore her performance in the alley the other night. "If Serena is behind this, what can we do?"

"*We* can't," she replied. "This is something the coven needs to handle. You're going to have to go and talk to Janus; he's the head of the council."

"Me?" Sigurdsson asked, a shocked look on his face, as he felt a wave of panic set in. "Why me? I mean, why don't *you* just talk to him? You are a member of the council."

"Yes, but I broke the law."

"You didn't kill them," he argued. "Well, at least not *all* of them."

"No, but I didn't report it either," she said. "That makes me an accessory to her crimes. I can deal with the ramifications of my actions, but if Serena has turned against me and gone to the council, then I have to believe they are already looking for me."

"Isn't there anyone you can talk to?"

"No, anyone I come in contact with is bound by law to bring me before the council immediately. I need you to find him and let him know that I am not behind the killings. He needs to know that if Serena is behind this, then she probably has ulterior motives that could be aimed directly at the council."

"Why me?"

Gabi looked at him in confusion. "I already told you why."

"No, why did you choose me?" he asked. "You already said that personal interactions are frowned upon. You don't live anywhere near me, but you want me to believe that you just happened to walk into my local bar? C'mon, if we are being honest, then let's be honest."

"I... I... Uhm... I've never had..." Gabi stammered.

"Tell me."

"I've never had an *attraction* to anyone before, Karl. I saw you that night at the park and it was like nothing I'd ever felt before. So I followed you just to see who you were, where you lived,..... I wanted to know if there was anyone else."

A devilish smile grew on Sigurdsson's face as he leaned back against the couch's arm.

"What?" Gabi protested, pivoting in her seat to face him. "What are you smiling for?"

"So you were stalking me?" he asked.

They looked at each other for a moment, before the realization of what he had said hit them and they both began laughing.

"Yes, Karl, I guess I did," she replied, "but only in a good way."

"And what if there had been someone else?"

"I don't know," she said earnestly. "I can't explain this feeling."

"And now?" he asked.

Gabi moved closer as he leaned forward, their bodies near enough to feel the heat from each other's breath.

"Now we need to—" Gabi whispered softly.

"Yes," he replied. "Yes we do."

And then she felt the warmth of his lips on hers.

CHAPTER TWENTY-EIGHT

Sigurdsson awoke to brilliant rays of sunlight streaming in through the hotel room's patio door and it took a moment to orient himself to his present surroundings.

He rolled over and was dismayed to find the bed empty.

"Gabi?" he called out, but got no response. *"Damnit."*

He slid his legs over the side of the bed and sat there for a moment, as he rubbed at his face. It felt as if he had been hit by a train. For someone who worked out regularly, he felt as weak as a kitten.

Her kind of love might just be the death of me.

He stood up gingerly and made his way into the small kitchenette; thrilled beyond words to find she'd already made the coffee.

Is it possible to love someone even more than you already do? he thought as he filled the coffee mug she had left on the counter.

A smile grew on his face when he spotted the three Ibuprofen pills next to the mug. On a sheet of hotel stationary she had written a note.

I love you, Karl – This is who you need to speak to:

Jack Smith (real name: Janus Graf Schmidt)

Smith-Cabott Pharmaceuticals

297 Park Avenue

"Shit," he exclaimed as he glanced down at his watch and saw that it was almost seven thirty. He grabbed his cellphone from his jacket and placed a call.

The phone rang several times before he heard the gruff voice of Avery White come on the line.

"Fifteenth Squad, Sergeant White."

"Boss, it's Karl," Sigurdsson said.

"Well good morning, sleeping beauty," White grumbled. "Did you forget where you were supposed to be today?"

"Honestly, it was a rough night. Something's come up and I need to take the day off."

"Do I want to know why?" the man asked.

"I just need to help a friend with something," he replied.

"Make sure your ass is back to work tomorrow, Karl, or you're the first name on my list when the Chief is looking for *volunteers* for the New Year's Eve detail. Are we clear?"

"Crystal clear, boss," Sigurdsson replied. "Thanks."

He ended the call and picked up the coffee mug, before heading back into the bedroom. Along the way, he snatched up the robe Gabi had discarded the previous evening and put it on. He opened the patio door and stepped outside, feeling the sting of the cold, salty air rolling in off the Atlantic.

Sigurdsson sat down on one of the chairs and took a sip of coffee, as he did his best to reconcile the events of the previous evening. Despite the audacity of her confession, in his heart he knew every word she spoke had been the truth. What shocked him even more was the understanding that none of it mattered to him. He would do anything for her; risk everything, as long as it meant having her in his life for however long that might be.

Even if that means going into the lion's den? he wondered.

He knew what they shared, but he was under no illusion as to what she had asked him to do. The idea of coming face-to-face with the head vampire was not something that appealed to him on any level, but it was something he knew he had to do for her sake.

If he didn't take the risk, then the odds of them sharing any type of life together would be fleeting; not that it made things any easier.

He knew Gabi, but the others remained a mystery and he couldn't be sure how well this *Jack Smith* would handle the revelation that he *knew* about them.

It just might end up being the shortest conversation of your life, he thought.

Sigurdsson took a sip of coffee, wishing he had something a bit stronger, as he chased the thoughts from his mind.

What troubled him more than the impending meeting was coming to terms with their relationship. There were no words to describe the intensity of their passion; it was simply beyond anything he had ever felt before. In his arms, it felt as if she was making up for a lifetime spent alone. Even though he knew she was being *gentle* with him physically, he knew she had held nothing back emotionally. They'd given each other every part that made them who they were, mind, soul, and body.

As he laid in bed, physically exhausted, he held her close; gently caressing her arm. He loved her and he had wanted to promise her he would always be there for her, but he came to understand that it was a promise he knew he couldn't keep. In that moment, the weight of what she had previously said hit him hard.

"...*reality sets in very quickly as you watch everyone you have ever known or loved be put into the ground*."

"Don't think about it," he said as he got up and headed off to the shower. "Just take it one day at a time."

It was just after one o'clock when he made the trek from Montauk back to Manhattan. He grabbed a cup of coffee from one of the nearby shops and found a seat on one of the granite benches that lined the front of 297 Park Avenue.

Thanks to the Smith-Cabott Pharmaceutical's website, he had a face to go along with the name Gabi had given him. At around three o'clock he spotted a black Mercedes Benz G-Class SUV pull up to the front of the building and a rather large security man stepped out.

Showtime, he thought as he positioned himself to watch the front door.

About five minutes later he spotted *Jack Smith* exit the building, with another security man in tow, and head toward the vehicle.

Sigurdsson noted that the photo had not done the man justice. The studio photo on the website gave the impression of a warm, congenial man who appeared more like your average father than a corporate hawk; a smart move for a company looking to gain the public's trust, but the man walking across the courtyard was much different.

Even next to the burly security man, Jack Smith was no slouch. He was well over six feet tall and the way he carried himself left no question that he could handle any threat that came his way. His wavy brown hair was speckled with gray at the temples and Sigurdsson couldn't help but notice the resemblance to a young Christopher Plummer.

He got up and made a bee-line toward him.

"Excuse me, Mr. Smith," Sigurdsson called out, when he was about a dozen feet from the man.

Immediately the security man took up a defensive posture, putting himself between him and Smith.

"Take it easy, big guy," he said to the man as he held up his detective shield. "NYPD, I just need to talk to Mr. Smith."

"What's this about?" Janus asked, clearly annoyed at the intrusion.

"I'm Detective Karl Sigurdsson, Fifteenth Squad. I wanted to talk to you about a *personnel* issue, if you don't mind."

"If it's a personnel issue, then I suggest you speak with Ms. Baines in Human Resources," Janus replied dismissively as he turned and headed toward the waiting vehicle.

"Okay," Sigurdsson said, raising his hands in mock surrender. "I will pass along the word that you didn't want to help, *Graf Schmidt*."

The man's head snapped around, just as he was about to enter the SUV, and he glared at Sigurdsson. "What did you just say?"

"Just that you didn't want to help with a *sensitive* personnel issue," Sigurdsson replied.

Janus turned and walked toward him, the two bodyguards at his side.

"What did you call *me*?" Janus asked menacingly.

"Is this really a matter you want to discuss out here?" Sigurdsson asked as he motioned toward the number of people passing by on the sidewalk.

"After you, *detective*," Janus said, motioning him toward the Mercedes.

Sigurdsson got into the rear passenger seat, behind the driver, as Janus took the seat next to him. It was at that moment that he finally realized what it meant to go from the frying pan and into the fire. He could feel the penetrating stare of Janus' cold blue eyes on him as the vehicle pulled away from the curb.

"Now what did you need to ask me?"

"I'm willing to go out on a limb here and bet that this isn't the type of conversation you want to have in front of the hired help?" Sigurdsson said, pointing to the security men in the front seat.

"Understand that my graciousness has its limits, detective," Janus replied. "So I suggest that you tell me what this is all about or your ride will end on the corner and the next conversation I have will be with your commissioner."

"That's odd. Gabi told me you would be much more accommodating."

Janus stared at Sigurdsson for several moments without saying a word.

"Do you want us to stop, sir?" the man in the driver's seat asked.

"No, keep driving, Reinhard," Janus replied as he pressed a button that raised the up the partition, cutting off sound between the front and back. "So what is this all about and what does it have to do with Gabrielle?"

"Gabi is in trouble," Sigurdsson replied, "and she thinks her sister, Serena, may be behind it."

"You're the policeman she is *involved* with?"

"I'd ask you how you knew, but I guess good news travels fast, which lends support to Gabi's belief that Serena is behind this."

"Regardless of who is behind the accusation, the fact remains that Gabrielle is charged with a serious crime, not to mention her involvement with *you*."

Whether or not Janus had intended the last word to be a character indictment, it had the effect. His career had made him become immune to the slurs and snide remarks associated with being a cop, but that was all professional. Janus' remark had the air of being a personal attack.

Remember where you are and who you're with, he told himself.

"I must admit that I am fascinated at how a detective can be so dismissive of the charges," Janus continued. "I thought the police believed in pursuing justice."

"We do," Sigurdsson replied. "I do, but I also believe that people are innocent until proven guilty."

"Three bodies in an alleyway, one of whom had their throat ripped out, seems like it would be compelling evidence to even the most *incompetent* of detectives."

"Yes, it would be," Sigurdsson replied, ignoring the barb. "But then again most detectives would not have been witnesses to the act that led to their demise."

A perplexed look came over Janus' face. "You were there?"

"Yes, I was, and it might sound like evidence of a crime, but I can tell you, as a *veteran* detective, that not everything you are told is as it appears."

"Then tell me what happened."

"I picked Gabi up and took her out to dinner," Sigurdsson said. "We were there for several hours. As we were leaving through the back door, we were attacked by the now deceased men. They were armed and it was a worst-case scenario for me. Understand, at the time I did not know who, or should I say what, Gabi was. My only concern at the moment was protecting her from the three of them. It was they who instigated things, not her."

"She killed them," Janus remarked.

"Yes, but I can tell you it was in self-defense, or rather in defense of me."

"Those haven't been the only killings," Janus replied. "There have been several over the last few days, including the one at the zoo and Serena blames that one on Gabrielle."

"But that wasn't Gabi," Sigurdsson replied. "I know that for a fact."

"How can you be so sure?"

"Because the security guard at the zoo was killed around 10:00 p.m. and Gabi wasn't there."

"How can you be so sure?" Janus asked.

"Because at the time of his death we were having coffee downtown," Sigurdsson replied. "I know you folks have this speed thing going for you, but unless you can travel eight miles round-trip, stalk and kill your prey, and then return to continue your conversation mid-sentence, you might have another *problem* on your hands."

Janus desperately wanted to believe the man, but he found himself caught in the middle. On one hand he had the accusations of Serena, and the detective had even confirmed he was there for the latest deaths, but at the same time there was no possible way for Gabrielle to have killed the guard.

Could that have been a nomad? he wondered. *Or is the detective lying to protect her*?

"Look," Sigurdsson said. "If Serena is trying to pin these attacks on Gabi, especially the zoo one that I *know* she wasn't involved in, you have to ask why? On top of that, prior to his death in the alley, one of the victims made a spontaneous admission, he said, 'She made us do it.' When Gabi asked him who *she* was, he replied, 'The woman with the black hair.' If that isn't evidence enough to cast doubt on Serena's claims then I don't know what is."

"Yet he is dead."

"Unfortunately, he is," Sigurdsson replied.

"You've raised some important issues," Janus said. "And I want to believe you, detective, but I also have to make sure I do not allow my closeness with Gabrielle to cloud my judgment. Do you understand?"

"Do I understand?" Sigurdsson asked, a shocked look on his face. "You can't be serious? Look, less than forty-eight hours ago I was living in my own little screwed-up world, thinking everything they had ever taught me to believe in was real and the rest was the product of an overactive imagination. Now here I am trying to come to terms with me not knowing what to believe in anymore. The only thing I know is that Gabi did not kill the guy at the zoo and the three she did kill deserved it. Now you're telling me you have a hard time believing this? How the hell do you expect me to make sense of all of it?"

Janus suppressed a laugh as he nodded in understanding, "I guess we are both faced with a dilemma."

"Yeah, I just have to accept it all, but you're the one with the real problem."

"Why do you say that?"

"Gabi shared a lot with me," Sigurdsson said. "I know it probably wasn't right, but that's water under the bridge now. She said that Serena has been bending your rules for a while now, but in the past she limited her hunting to criminals and that does line up with the findings of my criminal investigation."

"Then why didn't she come forward?" Janus asked.

"Haven't you guys ever heard the line, 'never take sides with anyone against the family'?" Sigurdsson asked. "Gabi didn't come forward, because she didn't want to betray her sister. So she might have been wrong, under the letter of your laws, but her intentions were good. Clearly Serena doesn't have that same concern. From the look of things, it seems to me that she may be pissed that Gabi got the seat on the council and now she's inclined to terminate those familial bonds. The only question that remains is whether you folks will go along with her plan?"

"If what you are telling me is true, then Gabrielle is in serious danger," Janus replied. "Where is she now?"

"I don't know."

Janus smiled, but it wasn't one of benevolence, "I could make you talk."

"I have no doubt that you could," Sigurdsson replied, "but it still wouldn't do you any good, because I don't know. She left in the middle of the night. She has my number and I am assuming she will call me when she is ready."

Janus stared at the man; a deep intense look that sent a cold chill down Sigurdsson's spine. An unpleasant silence hung in the air, as the car continued through the steel and concrete canyons of the city.

"I believe you," Janus said, after an interminably long time. "If or when you speak to her, tell her that I will talk to the council on her behalf, but I cannot make any promises. They were split on Serena's accusation and I believe, without compelling evidence, they will be split on Gabrielle's as well."

"Then what?"

"I am afraid that there will be *no* winners in this matter, young man," Janus said glumly.

CHAPTER TWENTY-NINE

"It looks like you might have a problem on your hands," Michael Orlov said, on the other end of the cellphone.

"What kind of problem?" Serena asked as she sat in the living room smoking a cigarette.

"Have you ever heard the old saying, 'three can keep a secret, if two are dead'?"

"Spare me the philosophy lesson, Michael, I'm in no mood. Just spit it out."

"It looks like someone whispered in Janus' ear and gave him an *alternate* account of recent events."

"*Sonofabitch*," Serena retorted. "When did this happen?"

"If I had to take a guess, I would say sometime over the last few days," Orlov replied. "I just had it whispered in my ear."

"What exactly does he know?"

"According to my source, Janus claims he was approached by some detective, named Sigurdsson, who claimed that you're behind the killings and that Gabrielle was covering for you," Orlov replied, "at least the ones that pre-date her little homicidal rampage in the alley; although you're being accused of setting that one up. Supposedly one of them said, 'she made us do it,' before he was killed. It's not direct evidence of your complicity, but it raises the question of who this *she* was that he was referring to."

Serena stared silently out the window.

Her mind was racing, as she tried to come to terms with what Orlov was telling her. This had gone on far too long. She knew that she couldn't control everything, but she hadn't counted on Gabi letting one of them live long enough to squeal like a stuck pig.

"What is Janus' position?" she asked.

"My contact feels as if Janus believes the detective's account, although he has conceded that without definitive proof it is still up in the air."

"Why is Gabrielle still on the loose?" she asked accusatorily. "If this doesn't get resolved quickly, then the odds grow stronger that the Grand Council will get wind of it."

"Because she has *disappeared*, Serena," Orlov shot back. "She's become a ghost. There is no trace of her."

"I was led to believe that your people had a reputation for getting things done."

"You know her abilities make things harder for us," Orlov replied. "On top of that, no one has seen or heard from her."

"No one except this detective, apparently."

"Give it a rest, Serena. I don't need your attitude; I'm getting enough grief from the council. I just found out about this myself. As I am sure you are well aware of, this isn't a matter that I can entrust to everyone, so I am rather limited in the amount of sentries I can have pursuing this. The last thing anyone needs is to have someone bring her in alive. I have someone watching the detective now."

"We can't just fade into the woodwork, Michael. We're not like them. It's not like we can waltz into the blood bank and order a *happy bag* to go. She has to be feeding somewhere."

"That's just it, Serena, there are no tracks or at least none that have surfaced. All the usual places are silent. I've even had my people reach out to their folks in the conservation department to see if there have been any unusual animal kills reported, but there's nothing. At this point we need to consider that she may have left the country."

"Perhaps," Serena replied, even though she had already dismissed the scenario in her mind. "Pull your person off the detective."

"Pull them off?" Orlov asked. "Why?"

"Because there's no point wasting time if she has fled," she said. "It's more prudent to have them focus on whether she could have left the country. I'll monitor the detective myself."

"Are you sure?"

"Positive," she replied. "I know what he looks like and he'll be easy to track."

"As you wish," Orlov replied.

"I don't have to remind you of the precarious position we have created for ourselves. We might enjoy some small measure of favor from a minority of the council members, but that will evaporate rather quickly the longer this goes on. There can be no change if we end up with the spotlight shining down on us and the last thing any of us need is for the Grand Council to stick their collective nose where it does not belong. Your heavy-handedness pales in comparison to what they will do."

"I'll have my sentries double their efforts."

"Perhaps they should have been doing that from the beginning," she snapped, before ending the call.

Serena crushed the cigarette out and got up from the couch.

"Imbecile!" she screamed as she began pacing back and forth.

Her mistake had been to assume that Gabi would immediately come back home and beg for her help. It was at that point that Serena would have been forced to *defend* herself against the violent criminal. With only one side of the story being told, and the accused dead, the matter would have been put to rest. Sure it would be viewed as rather unseemly to most, but there were those on the council who would be more than happy to take the spotlight off of her and put it squarely on Janus; for his failure to take immediate action when the accusation had first been raised.

It had been a simple enough plan and yet it all seemed to be unraveling because some useful idiot just couldn't die *quietly*.

You need to figure a way to salvage all of this and do it quickly, she thought.

Serena knew that getting rid of Gabi now wouldn't remove the cloud of suspicion off of her, at least not in the eyes of Janus and his lot, but it would put the matter to rest for the council at large. Her name, at least not her *actual* name, was not associated with the killing, so the argument could be made about who this *she* really was. A technicality to be sure, but enough that would establish a reasonable doubt.

Now she just needed to formulate a plan which would draw Gabi out so that she could finish this once and for all.

Despite what Orlov believed, she had a hard time accepting the idea that Gabi would leave her new *friend* so soon. Regardless of the way she felt about humans, Gabi clearly had a different opinion. It was also clear to her that she had to have had some form of contact with him already, if she had convinced him to see Janus on her behalf; someone had to have given the detective his name. So it made sense that she was still around; somewhere.

Three can keep a secret, if two are dead, she thought. *Orlov might have been on to something.*

CHAPTER THIRTY

"Paging, Dr. Reynolds. Dr. Reynolds please contact the security desk immediately."

She glared at the speaker, hanging above the autopsy room door, as she withdrew the dissection scissors from the body she was working on. Reynolds laid the instrument down on the table next to her, and began removing her rubber exam gloves, irritated at the interruption.

"Don't go anywhere, *Mr. Doe*. I'll be right back," she said to the body before making her way over to the desk to pick up the phone.

"The building better be on fire, Ronnie," she said, when the security officer's voice came on the line.

"Dr. Reynolds, you need to come up here *right now*," Officer Ronald Kushner said curtly.

Normally, the staff at the medical examiner's office was professional, but friendly to one another, even during traumatic events. Something in Kushner's voice told her that something wasn't right.

"I'm on my way," she said, before hanging up the phone.

This had better not be bullshit, she thought as she walked out into the hallway and stripped out of her examination gown.

She made her way up the long corridor and turned left at the landing, heading in the direction of the security desk. As she drew closer, she could hear a loud conversation that was getting out of control. As she rounded the corner, the scene began to devolve into chaos.

She could see Kushner standing in the middle of corridor, blocking a group of people in front of him. Suddenly, a man in a black suit grabbed him, jerking him out of the way, and the group moved toward her direction.

"Whoa, whoa, whoa," she said, raising up her hands. "Let him go."

"Who are you?" another man in a suit asked tersely.

"I'm Dr. Andrea Reynolds, the Chief Medical Examiner," she announced, standing her ground. "Who the hell are you?"

"I'm FBI Special Agent Dominick Nostromo," the man said, holding up his credentials. "I'm the head of the Joint Terrorism Task Force."

Reynolds looked around and realized that several in the group were wearing military fatigues.

"What the hell is going on here?" she asked.

"We have a national security matter," the man replied. "We need to speak *privately*."

"I don't care who you are or what this is about," she replied. "You let my officer go first and then we'll speak."

Nostromo frowned, but he turned around and motioned for his agent to release the man.

"Happy?" he said.

"*Overjoyed*," she retorted. "Follow me."

Reynolds led them back down the corridor to her office and opened the door.

Nostromo walked in first, followed by a military officer.

"Dr. Reynolds, this is Major Caroline Madison, she's from the New York National Guard's 24th Civil Support Team."

"Ma'am," the woman said crisply.

"Major," Reynolds replied, acknowledging the woman, before looking back at the agent. "So Agent Nostromo, would you mind telling me what this is about?"

The man reached into his pocket, removing a piece of paper, and handed it to her.

"Dr. Reynolds, did you contact the Centers for Disease Control about this case?"

It took her a moment, as she examined the document, to make the connection.

"Yes, we sent them a blood sample that contained an unknown organism, why?"

"Is that body still here?" the man asked.

"Yes, he's in the freezer."

"Have you been able to identify him yet?"

"Not that I am aware of," Reynolds replied. "It's a triple homicide investigation."

"Triple?"

"Yes, three men were killed in an alley last week."

"Who's investigating this?" he asked.

"The NYPD," Reynolds said. "Det. Karl Sigurdsson is the investigator; he's from the Fifteenth Squad."

The man removed a note pad from his jacket pocket and began taking notes. "We're taking all the bodies and we'll also need all your post-mortem reports."

"Excuse me?" Reynolds asked in disbelief.

"We need everything related to this case," he replied as he looked up from the notepad.

"Uh, no, but nice try, I'm the Medical Examiner and I alone...

Nostromo reached into his pocket and removed a letter which he handed to her.

Reynolds took it and began reading it. She made it about halfway through before she looked up at him with a stunned expression.

"That's a *national security letter*, Dr. Reynolds," he replied. "I assure you that I can, and will, leave here with everything related to this investigation, with or without your help. As far as you are concerned, this crime never occurred."

"You can't be serious," Reynolds replied. "You just don't make a triple homicide go *away*."

"Dr. Reynolds, I can do anything I want," Nostromo said. "This is a matter of national security and deals with a *clear and present danger* to this country. I am authorized to take *any* action that I deem appropriate."

"I have to call—"

"No, you won't," he declared. "If you continue reading you will see that there is also a *non-disclosure provision*. It outlines your responsibilities in this matter, but, in a nutshell, this case no longer exists. You will take all necessary measures to conceal any aspect of your involvement from your colleagues, your family, and any other persons, beyond the fact that this was a planned government exercise."

Reynolds eyes darted back and forth between Nostromo and the military officer who just stared back with no sign of emotion.

"Dr. Reynolds, I understand your confusion," he said, "but the best thing you can do right now, for yourself and your staff, is to make this go as quickly and as smoothly as possible."

"*Fine*," she said in frustration. "Follow me."

Reynolds opened the door and immediately stopped dead in her tracks. The hallway was now lined with soldiers wearing Level A hazmat suits.

"Dr. Reynolds, perhaps it would be better if you just provided me the location of the bodies and allow my people to handle the removal," Major Madison said.

Reynolds stepped back inside the office and went to her desk. She rummaged through several folders until she found the ones she was looking for.

She wrote down the drawer numbers and handed them to the woman. "The freezer is down the hallway, it's the first door on the right. The bodies will be in these three drawers."

"Thank you, ma'am," she replied, before leaving the office.

"Are those the autopsy reports?" Nostromo asked.

"Yes," Reynolds replied.

"I'll take them now."

"Can I at least make copies?" she asked.

"No, doc, you can't," he replied. "Like I told you, you will never see this case again; there is no need to keep anything on file."

"Can you at least tell me what this is all about?"

"I wish I could, but it's too far above my pay grade," Nostromo replied.

"You can tell me not to talk all you want, but people here will ask questions about what went on and, if I can't explain it, I would imagine some might even go to the media."

"We're not going to let that happen," Nostromo said matter-of-factly. "So let me tell you what we *are* going to do."

A half-hour later all three bodies had been removed from the medical examiner's office and a motorcade was in route to the downtown heliport; where an Army National Guard Ch-47 Chinook helicopter was waiting for their cargo.

Reynolds and Nostromo left her office and entered a large conference room which was filled to capacity with employees.

Reynolds made her way up to the podium, with Nostromo in tow, and stepped in front of the microphone.

"Thank you everyone, I'll make this brief," she said. "I know you are all busy and probably very confused. What happened today was a joint training exercise between the Medical Examiner's Office, the Federal Bureau of Investigation, and the

Department of Defense. I will let Special Agent Dominick Nostromo explain the details to you."

"Thank you, Dr. Reynolds," he said as he stepped up to the podium. "And thank you to all of you for your patience. I would like to extend my sincere apologies for the sudden disruption you had to deal with today. What you just experienced was part of *Operation Game-Day*, a real-world law enforcement and military exercise that deals with a sudden notification that a person, infected with a biological threat, has come into the custody of law enforcement or medical staff. The purpose of the exercise is to gauge the response time and deficiencies we will have to deal with on short notice when we are alerted to a potential outbreak threat. Unfortunately, we find that we get the most actionable feedback when we do these scenarios *unannounced*. Today's event underscores the need for a comprehensive *memorandum of understanding* between first responders and medical staff, so we don't have a repeat of the conflict we experienced today with Officer Kushner."

The man, seated in the front row, had an embarrassed look on his face and gave a half-hearted wave.

"No, seriously, you did a great job, officer," Nostromo emphasized. "It is through interactions like this where we learn that we need to temper our emergency response mindset with those who may not know of the exigent circumstances under which we are operating. To ensure the highest levels of realism in these scenarios, we use bodies that have been donated for scientific purposes. The bodies are tagged and prompt a notification, by the medical examiner, to the CDC who in-turn alerts us. It isn't a perfect scenario, but it provides a foundation for which we can build on. Because these drills deal with the government's response to potential terror threats, I must caution you as to the need for secrecy in protecting our response capabilities. Prior to leaving, you will all be asked to sign non-disclosure letters. In this fight, even the slightest slip of the tongue risks the safety of all of us. We do not want to alert our enemies to our methods, lest they find a way to exploit them. Once again, thank you for your cooperation and your invaluable assistance in this training endeavor."

Reynolds and Nostromo walked off and exited the room.

"You really think that will work?"

"People believe what they want to believe, Dr. Reynolds. You have a good day."

Reynolds watched as Nostromo made his way down the corridor.

"Fucking government," she whispered in disgust.

At the same time, Operation Game-Day was being conducted in three major cities and four rural counties throughout the country. A Friday night Department of Justice press release would include the benign details of a successful exercise aimed at the ongoing efforts to keep America safe from the threat of a chemical, biological, radiological, or nuclear attack. If any of the news outlets bothered to cover it over the weekend, it would be a non-issue by the time the Monday morning news cycle came around.

CHAPTER THIRTY-ONE

The ringing of the telephone jarred Sigurdsson from his thoughts and he instinctively reached for his cellphone. It took a second for him to process that the sound was actually coming from the phone on his desk.

"Fifteenth Squad, Det. Sigurdsson," he said as he answered the call.

Immediately, an irate sounding woman began yelling on the other end of the line.

"Ma'am, is this an emergency?" Sigurdsson asked as he attempted to figure out what the woman was shouting about.

"No, Det. Janovic is not in the office today, it's his day off. Is there something that I can help you with?"

He listened as the woman continued to prattle on for several more minutes, ignoring every attempt he made to interject.

Sigurdsson reached over and picked up his coffee mug, taking a sip as he waited for her to come up for air.

"Yes, I do appreciate that your apartment was burglarized Tuesday night," he replied. "It must have been a very traumatic experience, but I can promise you that the police lab will not have the results back this quickly. It's only been three days."

Sigurdsson held the phone away from his ear as another round of angry yelling emanated from the phone.

"Yes, ma'am, I understand that *CSI: Las Vegas* gets them back much quicker, but I think they received a federal grant for better equipment than we have."

He closed his eyes, feeling the headache that was already beginning to develop. "No, you're right, ma'am, I'm not very funny.

I'm a cop, not a comedian, but I will be sure to give Det. Janovic your number and ask that he call you back as soon as possible."

Sigurdsson endured another fifteen second salvo of anger before he heard the line go dead.

"Another happy customer?"

He looked up to see Sergeant White walking through the squad room.

"I'm not a betting man, but I'm pretty sure Janovic can cross her off his Christmas card list," Sigurdsson replied as he wrote a note to leave on the other detective's desk.

"What did they want?" White asked curiously.

"Best I can make out is she was unsatisfied with the speed in which our lab processes things."

"Well, next time tell her to move her little *hippy-happy* ass out to Vegas."

"Can I use you as a reference when I get called down to Internal Affairs?"

"Son, when I was a young bull like you, I had my own damn chair at I.A.B.," White said with a laugh as he refilled his coffee mug.

"Then why are you always riding my ass, sarge?"

"Because, you're supposed to work smarter, not harder, Karl," he replied, before heading back to his office.

"If I was smarter I wouldn't be working," Sigurdsson mumbled as he turned back toward the paperwork on his desk.

It had been several days since he had last seen Gabi and the lack of contact was messing with his head. It felt as if he had been pulled into some foreign movie, without the benefit of subtitles, and he had no idea what the hell was supposed to be going on. A part of him understood the reason for her absence, but he couldn't help but wonder if something had happened to her. The not knowing was the worst and he highly doubted that the coven had a policy covering death notifications.

He picked up the cellphone and sent a text: *Are you all right? Please call.*

It matched the previous twenty that he had already sent her, which had also gone unanswered, but he felt that he needed to be doing something; anything.

He got the feeling that if he could put his thoughts and emotions into a picture, it would look like some really screwed-up Rorschach ink blot. He had gone from the highest of highs to the lowest of lows and now he found himself waiting.

But what are you waiting for? he thought.

He stared down at the reports on his desk, but they could have just as easily been written in *Sanskrit*, for all the good it was doing him. He was supposed to be investigating something that made little sense and that was after being a witness to it.

Sigurdsson leaned back in his chair, rubbing his eyes.

He had at least eight victims, but he was between a rock and a hard place. How was he supposed to investigate this? He knew who, or at least had a strong gut feeling, was behind the murders, but how long would his career last if he walked into Vega's office and proclaimed that vampires were behind the killings?

About as long as it took for White to cuff you and haul your ass down to psych services, he chided himself.

But could he even do it if he wanted to?

Sigurdsson found himself in a dilemma that now seemed to eclipse even a moral one.

He'd spent the last week trying to come to terms with everything he knew, but he kept coming back to the fact that he was madly in love with Gabi. Despite her shocking revelation, it still didn't matter to him. He was drawn to her, like the proverbial moth to the flame, and if she was dangerous, he would risk it;

because he couldn't imagine his life without her. Even what happened in the alley couldn't shake the feelings he had for her; after all, she was just being protective.

The night at the hotel proved to him that there was a much different side to Gabi. He remembered holding her close, not sure if he was trying to comfort her or find comfort in her embrace. He wanted that moment back, when they were lost in their own little world; safe from everything except each other.

It sounded cliché to say she had given *all of herself* to him, but she had. She had shared everything with him, even the least desirable parts of what she was, which was precisely why this last week had been so painful. Without any contact from her he felt lost and unable to concentrate on anything, especially his job.

How this would all work out was anyone's guess, but he couldn't walk away from her, and he couldn't let her take the fall for her sister's crimes.

"Wake up, Karl," Sigurdsson heard White bellow from his doorway.

"Sorry, sarge, I guess I zoned out."

"Yeah, well you can do that on your own time," the man replied as he walked over to the desk, "but right now you're on the department's time and you got work to do."

"What's up?" Sigurdsson asked.

"I just got a call from a guy named Cosmo Rivera," White replied. "He owns an art studio over on W. 47th."

"What did he want?"

"He said he just got back from vacation and was looking through some surveillance video footage. One of his interior cameras was aimed at the back door and he thinks he might have picked up some activity from your alley homicide the other night."

Sigurdsson felt his stomach drop, "Video?"

"Yeah, apparently he had some break-ins a while back, so he had an interior security camera system installed," White replied as he handed him a piece of paper with the address. "Hopefully you can find something useful."

Not only was the idea of a video with Gabi's image on it, the last thing he wanted to think about, but it was the last thing he wanted anyone in the department to see, especially Vega.

"I'll go and take a look," he replied, taking the paper from White.

CHAPTER THIRTY-TWO

Sigurdsson pulled his car into a parking spot in front of the Gallery 47 studio and got out.

As he entered through the front door a sing-song chime announced his arrival.

The glitzy interior of the storefront gallery was filled with a large variety of pieces that pushed the limits of what he considered art. More than a dozen large statues, of naked men and women in suggestive poses, dominated the center of the open plan layout, while abstract art and wire sculptures lined the walls. Sigurdsson took in the pieces with a bemused look on his face.

There's no accounting for taste, he thought as he examined an alabaster sculpture that depicted a couple with reversed genitalia.

He made his way deeper into the showroom, looking for his complainant.

"Hello?" he called out. "Mr. Rivera?"

"I'm upstairs," he heard a man's voice shout back. "There's a staircase in the back."

Sigurdsson made his way into the rear of the studio where he found a wrought-iron staircase leading to the second floor. He paused for a moment, spying the familiar dome shaped surveillance camera perched on the ceiling, its unblinking eye facing the back door.

"Fuck me," he whispered as he peered out the back door.

The door's large glass panel had security bars on it, but it still provided an unobstructed view to the alley behind the restaurant.

This can't be good, he thought as he turned and made his way up the stairs.

The second floor mirrored the first floor layout, with the exception that there were at least double the number of unfinished pieces scattered about. One colossal statue stood in the center of the room and nearly reached the fifteen foot ceiling above.

How the hell does he move these downstairs? he wondered as he meandered through the maze of artwork.

"Mr. Rivera?" he called out, before spotting the man sitting in a chair at the far end of the room, working on an ornate wire sculpture of a rampant horse.

"Mr. Rivera, I'm Detective Sigurdsson from the Fifteenth Squad," he said as he walked up to the man. "You called about a video you have?"

The man didn't respond.

"Mr. Rivera?" he asked again as he drew abreast of him and tapped him on the shoulder.

The man crumbled forward, crashing into the sculpture and knocking it to the floor. As his body rolled onto the floor he stared up at Sigurdsson with lifeless eyes. Two telltale bite marks on the man's neck removed all doubt as to the cause of his sudden demise.

"*Sonofabitch*," Sigurdsson muttered.

"Tsk, tsk, such language coming from a policeman," a voice resembling Rivera's said from across the room.

As Sigurdsson watched, Serena emerged from behind one of the statues, her tongue dabbing an errant drop of blood from her lips.

"You?"

"Yes, me," she replied, maintaining the dead man's voice.

Sigurdsson reached for his gun, barely getting his hand around to his hip before he felt an intense pain in the center of his chest, which lifted him off the floor and sent him flying across the room.

He hit the ground with a resounding thud, his body sliding several more feet until it came to a stop against the far wall. He struggled to breathe as he tried to shake off the blow.

"Ooh, that's going to leave a mark," Serena said with feigned concern, her voice changing back to her own.

Sigurdsson rolled over onto his hands and knees as he struggled to get up.

"Here, let me help you," Serena said, grabbing him by the scruff of the neck and tossing him back in the opposite direction like a rag doll.

A moment later he felt his body impact one of the statues, caroming off of it and into another, sending them toppling over.

"I'm so sorry," she purred. "Sometimes I don't even know my own strength."

Sigurdsson could hear the click of her boot heels as she strolled over to him. Pain was coursing through his body and he could feel himself getting lightheaded.

Serena squatted down in front of him; grabbing him hard by the chin and jerking his head up to face her. "I just realized that we've not been formally introduced. My name's Serena and I hear you've been spreading nasty rumors about me."

"I know who you are," he said tersely, "and what you are."

Serena's cruel laughter echoed off the walls. "Oh, has my dear, sweet sister been filling your head with scary stories?"

"You don't scare me," he replied, jerking his head as he tried to free himself of her grasp.

Serena held firm, her warm chestnut brown eyes transforming into orbs of polished onyx. She fixed her cold hard stare on him. "Then my sister did you a grave disservice."

Sigurdsson used the woman's distracted state to ease his right hand into position to draw his pistol and bring it around, but before he could get off a shot, she swatted it from his hand, sending it clattering across the floor.

"Nice try, sport," Serena said sarcastically as she released his jaw and grabbed him by the neck. "Now it's my turn."

He felt his body leave the floor, suspended in the air by one hand, as she walked him over to one of the exposed steel support beams that held up the roof and pinned him against. His head snapped back and hit the beam with enough force to daze him.

"I'm growing weary of playing these foolish games with you, *human*," she sneered, the last word coming out with loathing. "So perhaps I need to give you an example of just how one-sided this situation is for you."

Sigurdsson felt his vision begin to narrow as he struggled for breath. Soon the edges began to darken and close in and he felt himself drift off into unconsciousness. The last thing he saw, before he blacked-out, was Serena smile to reveal two large white fangs.

CHAPTER THIRTY-THREE

"Where's Karl?"

White looked up from the complaint report he had been reviewing to see Vega standing in the doorway. "He went out to interview a store owner regarding the alley murders. Guy said he might have a video from the incident."

"When did he leave?"

"He left about an hour ago, why?" White asked.

"I just got a report on one of the victims," Vega replied, holding a paper up in his hand.

"Is it anything good?"

"Oh no, not at all," Vega said as he closed the door behind him and sat down. "In fact, it just opened up a whole new can of worms."

"What do you mean?" White asked curiously.

"This little *chat* we're about to have never happened, Avery," Vega replied. "Do you understand?"

The serious look on Vega's face told White he wasn't going to enjoy this conversation. He nodded his head.

"Look at this," Vega said, sliding the paper across the desk for White to read.

The man spent several minutes scanning the familiar document, but paused midway through the findings and raised his head to look at Vega. "What the hell is an unidentified organism?"

"That's the million dollar question. I stopped by the morgue on my way into work this morning, to see if there were any updates on our victims, and had an interesting hypothetical conversation with Dr. Reynolds."

"A *hypothetical* conversation?" White asked with a puzzled look on his face.

"Yes, hypothetical, because we no longer have any victims."

White leaned back in his chair as he stared at Vega. He'd been his executive officer for three years now and, while they had not always seen eye-to-eye on all matters, he'd never known him to be *flakey*. So this conversation was baffling to him.

"Carlos, I'm a simple man," White said. "I think and speak in simple terms. If it makes you feel better, I'll swear that the only conversation we had this morning was the latest valiant attempt by my beloved Giants to once again snatch defeat from the jaws of victory, but don't make me play twenty questions."

Vega inhaled deeply as he contemplated what he was about to tell White. He knew the implications, but took refuge in the fact that he hadn't been interviewed *yet* and was under no official obligation not to speak about the incident.

"When I got to the morgue, Andrea Reynolds appeared shaken up. When I tried to press her about the victims, she clammed up and told me I was mistaken; that there were no victims in the morgue. For obvious reasons you might say that I was a bit puzzled by the exchange. When I asked what happened to the bodies, she introduced me to one of their security officers, who explained that the FBI's JTTF and National Guard showed up this morning for a CBRN exercise."

"A CBRN exercise?"

Vega nodded.

"That would be the Civil Support Team's bailiwick," White replied. "Probably the 24th."

"You know about them?"

"Yeah, I was a master sergeant in the 69th Infantry Division," White replied. "CST is the unit that handle's the weapons of mass destruction stuff."

"Well, according to the security guy, they were wearing bio suits and removed prop cadavers."

"What the hell is a *prop* cadaver?"

"A body donated for medical research that they are supposedly being used to stage events to test the response to active crisis situations."

"You buy that bullshit?" White asked.

"I want to," Vega replied, "but it seems entirely too convenient."

"Every time I've had to work with the feds, I've always found myself needing to take a second shower," White replied. "I don't have a problem with the street level guys, but those D.C. folks calling the shots are some nefarious fuckers."

"I agree, not that any of what I think makes a difference."

"Why is that?"

"I got a call from the Chief's office on my way back to the office," Vega replied. "She told me that the special agent in charge of the New York Field Office had called and briefed her on their exercise. They also requested the names of everyone who was involved, so they can conduct a debriefing."

"What?" White asked sharply.

"They're playing the *post-exercise assessment* card; claiming they want to know if there is anything from a patrol or investigative standpoint that could have made things go smoother."

"I ain't buying any of what they're selling," White replied. "We're told to believe that they just happened to pick a deserted alley, with an unmarked car parked there, to run their little exercise and no one saw them staging it?"

"I know and I agree with you," Vega said, "but at least Karl will be happy."

"Why?"

"Because they have also requested that we forward them all the case folders and reports associated with the incident."

"Are you serious?"

"Well, since they have come out and said it was an exercise, it is no longer considered a homicide investigation. So they want to secure the folders so it will not inadvertently compromise any other cases."

"And you're telling me that the chief buys that?" White asked suspiciously.

"What choice does she have, Avery?" Vega asked. "The police commissioner is a former fed, so he's not going to push back. I guess she figures that if the P.C. isn't going to make waves, neither is she. It looks like she has adopted the whole *don't ask, don't tell* philosophy."

"Do you think there's any chance of getting some *hypothetical feedback* from the Bureau people?"

"Well, according to Reynolds they were less than forthcoming with information; so I wouldn't expect too much from our federal brethren."

"Is it just the alley investigation or are they looking into Sigurdsson's theory that these may all be related?"

"That's a good question," Vega replied. "We'll probably know more after he and I pay a visit to 26 Fed."

"Why are you going down there?"

"They want to interview us about what happened that night and since Karl's the investigator, and I am overseeing the investigation, we get to go first." Vega replied. "So see if you can get him on the horn and let him know to go directly there when he finishes his interview. I'm heading down there right now."

"Are you taking a union rep with you?" White asked.

Vega shook his head. "For what purpose? It's not a criminal investigation anymore; it's a debrief."

"Yeah, right until it isn't," White replied. "The feds have a way of being all chummy when they want something."

"Then I'll have to find a way to give them what they want so they quit asking questions."

"Good luck with that," White said, "but if I were you I wouldn't give away any information on anything beyond the alley investigation."

"I'll do my best," Vega replied.

CHAPTER THIRTY-FOUR

"**W**akey, wakey," a muffled voice said.

Sigurdsson felt his head snap to the side, followed by a stinging sensation on his cheek, as his body slumped over.

He was fighting for consciousness and was keenly aware that he was losing the battle.

"Come on," Serena said as she lifted him off the floor and unceremoniously dumped him onto an old couch. "You didn't think you would get off that easy, did you?"

He fought back, forcing his eyes open and tried to focus on what she was doing.

Never give up, he challenged himself. *Stay in the fight.*

With one hand, he pushed himself up into a seated position.

Serena had walked over to the chair that Rivera had been sitting in and dragged it back toward him. She dropped it onto the floor directly in front of the couch and sat down.

As he stared at her, he was struck by the absurdness of the situation. Serena was wearing a black leather jacket, zipped up to the neck, and a pair of denim jeans with thigh-high black leather boots. He wasn't sure whether she would be more at home on a fashion runway in Milan or playing the evil villain in a Bond movie.

Serena leaned in, resting her forearms on her thighs, and grinned. Under any other circumstance it would have been a dream come true for any man, but her smile was more sinister than sexy and he knew his nightmare was only just beginning.

"You and I are going to have a little chat," she said. "I'm going to ask you some questions and I strongly suggest you tell me the truth; because I'll know if you're lying."

"I won't tell you anything," he said tersely.

"Sure you will," she replied. "We just have gotten to that point yet, but trust me, you will. So let's begin. Make this easy on yourself and tell me what my sister instructed you to tell Janus."

"Who?"

Serena reached out, her movement so fast that he never had a chance to move out of the way, and grabbed his face tightly, pulling him closer. An intense pain radiated through his jaw as her fingers squeezed against the bone, threatening to break it. He reached up to pry them free, but it was like trying to undo a steel trap.

Serena ignored his clawing fingers as her eyes darkened. She turned his face sharply, first to the left and then to the right, as if she was a scientist examining some alien specimen.

"I never understood my kind's affinity toward some humans," she said matter-of-factly. "In fact, I'm amazed at how long the human race has managed to survive, being as inferior as it is."

Serena pushed him backward, releasing her grip.

Sigurdsson rubbed at his bruised face, doing his best not to reveal the pain he was in.

"Well, your sister seems to appreciate me," he said defiantly.

"Please, don't flatter yourself, *Karl*," she said derisively. "Gabi's always been a sucker for the downtrodden of society. You could easily be replaced tomorrow by a puppy dog."

"Then why are you so scared of me?"

Serena's head flung backward and her laugh reverberated through the loft.

"Oh, that's absolutely precious," she replied. "Perhaps I was wrong; maybe Gabi keeps you around because you're funny."

"Go ahead and laugh," he said, "but something has you worried or we wouldn't be having this conversation."

The amused look left her face.

"Did you honestly think I wouldn't find out you talked to Janus?" she asked. "He might be the head of the council, but he is far from being in control of it."

"That's what really pisses you off, Serena," Sigurdsson said, "the fact that Gabi is on the council and you're not."

"It was Janus' vote that put her there," she replied. "It's too bad for him that she turned out to be a murderer."

"We both know that's a lie. You've been behind all the murders, not Gabi, and you were the one that staged the attack in the alley."

"You're right, *we* do know it's a lie, but *they* don't. Nor will they ever find out."

"Janus knows," he replied.

"No, Janus *suspects*," she corrected him. "His downfall will be his blind obedience to the law. Even if he believes you, in our world you have no standing. The word of a human won't sway him without evidence. If you had gone to any other council member, you would have had a fifty-fifty chance of finding a compassionate ear, but you chose the poster child for rules and regulations."

"Regardless, the seed has been planted," Sigurdsson replied. "And maybe when I appear before the council I will sway enough of those *compassionate ears* to change their minds."

"Perhaps," she noted. "It's just too bad that you'll never make it out of here to find out."

"Because killing me is going to make you look even more innocent."

"Don't kid yourself, I've never been *innocent*," she declared, "but with you gone, things become less complicated for me."

"You're still going to have a target on your back," Sigurdsson said. "Janus doesn't believe you and I am sure there are others on the council who don't buy your lies."

"Maybe, maybe not," Serena replied. "Janus might *think* the council is split, but there are a few who are just waiting for the right person to make their move. Sorry to inform you and the rest of humanity, but most of us think it's time to change the rules."

"Then just get it over with," he said. "If you're going to kill me, why prolong this?"

"Because you're going to tell me what my sister told you and what exactly you told Janus."

"Bite me, Serena!" Sigurdsson hissed and instantly regretted his poor choice of words.

She smiled sinisterly. "Soon, but not quite yet."

"Then I guess we're done talking."

She leaped up from the chair, knocking it over, as she grabbed him and lifted him off the couch. "Okay, have it your way."

Sigurdsson felt his body sail through the air effortlessly, like a leaf picked up by the wind. A moment later he crashed into a large oil painting, sending it, and the easel it rested on, toppling to the ground. His body carried for several more feet until it struck a pillar and he crumpled to the ground.

He doubled over, groaning in pain, and fought the urge to vomit. It felt like the entire right side of his torso was on fire and it was obvious that he had broken several ribs. Each raspy breath he took felt as if razor blades were cutting him from the inside out.

"Still feeling *spunky*, Karl?" Serena called out.

The rhythmic tip-tap of her heels, against the hard wood floor, sent a chill through his body, as she slowly walked toward him. It was like being in a horror movie where you knew the monster was getting closer, but you couldn't run away.

She kneeled down next to him and dabbed her finger at the blood dripping from his lips. He watched as she raised it to her mouth and licked it seductively.

"Mmmm, I was wrong, apparently my sister has good taste," she purred. "I just may have to rethink my whole approach to this; perhaps I should take my time and enjoy you. You're a scrapper, Karl, and I like that."

Sigurdsson wanted to fight back, even though he knew it was pointless, but the pain coursing through his body was growing more intense with each passing second.

"You know, you can put an end to all of this by telling me what I want to know," she said cheerfully. "I promise, it will be our little secret."

"And miss out on our little bonding moment?" he said, before a coughing fit doubled him over in agony.

Serena sighed dramatically. "I'm impressed by your tenacity. I guess that means you're ready for round three?"

"Do what you gotta do, bitch."

Once again he felt his body take flight, tumbling through the air until it struck a large alabaster statue of the Greek goddess, Aphrodite. Sigurdsson plummeted to the ground and then watched in horror as the looming sculpture pitched back and forth several times. Before he could muster the strength to crawl out its way, it toppled down on top of him and shattered.

His scream filled the room as his body was pinned down under the tremendous weight of the piece. He desperately tried to move his right arm, but there was no feeling in it.

"Aw, poor baby," Serena said as she casually strolled over to him. "That looked like it hurt like hell."

Darkness gripped his peripheral vision and it felt as if he was being drawn deeper into a black abyss.

So much for the light they told me about, he thought.

"You're very brave, Karl, but what's the point?" she asked as she crouched down next to him. "You're here, all alone, and for what? I admire your desire to protect my sister, and I am sure you think you have some weird feelings for her, but she's abandoned you."

Sigurdsson gritted his teeth as he stared up at her in silence.

A part of him felt angry, not about what Serena said, but because he was already thinking it. This was *their* world, and he had been thrust into it. He hadn't asked to be, but here he was. He was nothing more than a lowly pawn, drawn into the middle of some unholy chess game, and about to be sacrificed for some greater good.

Serena's words echoed in his mind, "*And for what*?"

She could see the conflict through the silence, knew that there was a battle going on inside him.

"You know I'm right, don't you," she whispered as she reached over and gingerly brushed an errant strand of blonde hair from his face. "Perhaps I misjudged you, Karl. You're not like the rest of them; you're a fighter. The average human would have caved fifteen minutes ago and spilled their guts. Hell, they would have given up things I didn't even ask for, but not you. No, you're a different breed, aren't you? It has to be tough, being a cop; hated by half the population, feared by the other half, and doing a thankless job that no one cares about. Why?"

"Because I'm not like them," Sigurdsson said angrily. "I do it despite them; someone has to stand against *evil*."

Serena's eyes twinkled and she smiled. "Is that what you think I am, evil? Well, guess what? You're right, I am, but I'm not without some virtue. I'm here, Gabrielle isn't, and I'm extending you an olive branch. There's no need for it to end this way. Give in and I'll give you a life you never dreamed of."

"And be like you? No thanks."

"You make it sound like it's a dreadful thing, Karl, but is it?" she asked. "The world is changing, whether you or anyone else wants to believe it. The status quo never lasts. No matter how hard Janus and his ilk try, they cannot stop what is coming, no one can, so choose wisely. I see something in you; something that could be an asset to me. I'm offering you a place at my side."

"Just because you dress it up and make it sound good, you're still asking me to take sides with evil and the answer is still no."

Serena gave him an exasperated look as she lifted up a large section of the broken statue like it was a child's toy.

"That's a pity," she lamented as she examined the shattered artwork. "I can play this game with you all day, but I have a feeling you won't last quite as long."

"You can do whatever you want, but I still won't betray Gabi."

"I hate to break the news to you, but you will," she said brusquely. "The only remaining question is how much pain you are willing to put your body through before your mind gives in?"

"Then I guess it's time to change the rules."

Serena stared blankly at him, trying to figure out what he meant.

It was all the opportunity he needed.

With his last remaining ounce of strength, he brought up his left arm and drove a shard of alabaster into her cheek, leaving a jagged, gaping hole in its wake.

For a moment, the two of them stared at each other and Sigurdsson wondered if he had actually hurt her. Then, to his shock, the wound began to close and within seconds there was no sign that it had ever existed.

Then Serena's face changed.

As he watched, her eyes darkened until they appeared to be nothing more than two obsidian orbs. Rage took hold and he felt his heart stop when her lips parted to reveal her fangs.

"Game over," she snarled, and drove her face into his neck.

The pain was immediate and beyond anything he had experienced before; it dwarfed all the other injuries she'd previously inflicted on him.

It radiated throughout his entire body in an instant; like a lightning strike that coursed through an electrical line, short-circuiting anything that was connected to it. He wanted to scream, wanted to lash out, but his body had already begun to shut down.

As the darkness enveloped him, he surrendered to it; accepting the fate he had apparently been destined for.

So this is it? he thought. *This is how it ends? Not heroically, in a hail of bullets, but on the floor, in some dingy loft, all alone?*

A second later, he felt his body contort violently, as if something had been ripped away. As he lay there motionless, he felt a soothing warmth course through his body.

Well, this isn't so bad, he thought as he felt the pain start to subside.

He took one last breath and, just before everything went pitch black, he saw two dark figures battling in the distance.

CHAPTER THIRTY-FIVE

Gabrielle's body slammed into Serena with enough force that it knocked her off of Sigurdsson and sent the two of them tumbling half way across the loft.

A second later they collided into the brick wall, sending a cascade of stone and mortar crashing to the floor below. In an instant the two women were back on their feet, squaring off against one another like two Roman gladiators.

"What did you do to him?" Gabi screamed.

"I put an end to your pathetic plans once and for all," Serena said sharply as she moved around the room cautiously, sizing up the fight in her sister.

Gabi's arrival hadn't been unexpected; in fact, it had been part of Serena's plan all along. Serena knew that her sister would never abandon her new plaything; she just needed to figure out how to draw her in to spring her trap.

She had been toying with Sigurdsson, hoping that Gabi would sense his pain and come to his rescue. What she hadn't planned for was that he would put up as much of a fight. Killing him this early could have easily screwed everything up and she was grateful that Gabi had finally come to his defense. Although she was too late to save him, she had arrived in time to salvage Serena's plan.

"I've never hurt you!" Gabi said angrily. "I've never betrayed you. Why would you do this to me? Why would you take this one thing from me?"

"Because you're like the rest of them, Gabi; pathetic and weak," Serena sneered. "Consider it my wake-up call."

"I loved him," Gabi said.

"Loved him?" Serena asked, her voice dripping with contempt. "God, you make me sick. How can you love something like that?"

Serena's arm swung wide as she pointed toward Sigurdsson's body.

The moment Serena's attention was diverted from her, Gabi went on the attack, lurching forward, but she was a split-second too late. Her sister swatted her away, like an annoying gnat, sending her tumbling to the ground.

"What's wrong, sister? Are you weak?"

Gabi jumped to her feet and faced her, "Don't worry about me, I'm fine."

"No, you're not," Serena countered. "You're weak; I can tell you haven't been feeding. When are you going to accept that we are different? You're like Janus and the rest of them, pretending we can be something we are not. You make rules to protect them and they aren't even worthy of it."

"And what is your answer? To kill them all?"

"No, at least not all of them," Serena said, shrugging her shoulders. "Just the ones who refuse to bend the knee."

"You're insane."

"And you're an idiot," Serena declared as she rushed forward, seizing Gabi by the throat and pinning her to the support pillar a few feet from Sigurdsson's body. "Look at him! Look at your hero!"

Gabi stared down at him; her face a mix of pain and suffering.

"You and your precious council make rules to protect them and they can't even protect themselves," Serena said angrily, "It's not altruistic, it's cruel. It goes against the natural order; the strong are supposed to thrive, while the weak fall and perish. You're saving them through some misguided sense of charity, yet at the same time our kind suffer and for what?"

"We're not animals!" Gabi screamed as she brought her arms up, breaking Serena's hold on her, and drove her body into hers.

The two women fell to the ground, bearing their fangs and flailing wildly as they struggled for dominance. Gabi felt a searing pain course through her body as Serena raked her fangs over her right shoulder. She jerked hard, preventing Serena from getting a hold on her as they rolled across the floor.

Gabi knew she was in a dangerous position and she could feel it. Despite her protestations, Serena was right about her being weak; she hadn't fed in days. She was in the fight of her life and it felt as if Serena was just toying with her.

"No, we are not animals," Serena replied as she gained control and pinned Gabi to the floor. "We are better. There was a time when this world embraced the notion of gods and that time has come again."

"The council will never let you get away with this," Gabi said as her body thrashed about wildly, doing her best to knock Serena off of her.

"You fool, the council can't stop me," Serena said. "You've spent so much time listening to that rubbish Janus has been spewing that you stopped listening to the others. Change is coming to the Crystal Coven and I am it. With you gone, the rest will turn against him."

"I hate to tell you this, but I'm not going anywhere," Gabi said in disgust.

"I beg to differ, *sister*," Serena replied as she reached over and picked up one of the painting easel's broken wooden legs.

In a sudden moment of clarity, Gabi realized that her sister's plans had taken a dark turn.

She struggled violently as she tried to get out from under Serena's body, but it was no use.

"Don't do this," Gabi pleaded.

"Every rebellion needs a sacrifice and you're it," Serena said as she held her down with one arm and raised the stake over her head.

"You're my sister. I love you."

"No, I'm not, and it's time to put an end to your misplaced affection once and for all."

Gabi could see the hatred in Serena's face; the bond they had once shared was forever broken.

"Goodbye," Serena said grimly.

As the stake started to drive downward toward her chest, Gabi heard a thunderous roar fill the room. A split-second later Serena's chest exploded, sending the stake flying across the room, as her body collapsed onto Gabi, who let out a scream.

A moment later, Sigurdsson's knees buckled and his body began to drop to the floor, still clutching the pistol in his left hand.

CHAPTER THIRTY-SIX

Gabi pushed Serena's body off of her and dashed toward Sigurdsson, catching him before he fell to the ground.

"I never thought those weak-hand shooting drills would ever come in handy," he said weakly as she cradled him in her arms and lowered him gently to the floor.

"But... Karl,... you're alive?" she asked with confusion.

"If you say so," he replied, leaning back against the pillar and keeping a watchful eye on Serena.

"No, you don't understand, she bit you."

"Yeah and she didn't even ask my permission," he smiled weakly.

"Stop joking around, this is serious," Gabi said.

She had sensed the attack, but by the time she got there Serena had already gone in for the kill. A split second later she had crashed through one of the loft's large windows, but she knew in her heart that she was too late; seeing his lifeless body sprawled out on the floor had only confirmed that fact. Now she was amazed and confused that he was even alert.

"How serious?" he asked.

"I don't know," she said earnestly. "You shouldn't even be talking right now, but you are. I guess it depends on how much went into your system. It could kill you today or in days."

"Can I take her blood?" he asked, recalling Gabi's confession in the hotel room.

"How do you feel?" she asked.

"Like I got hit by a train," he said.

Gabi stared at him, unable to make sense of what she was seeing.

Everything she knew about the transformation process had just gone out the window. No one simply *got up* after being bitten like this. If a vampire didn't kill their victim straight away, then the virus attacked their body with a vengeance, but he showed no signs.

"No," she replied. "It doesn't work that way. The transformation has to start before you can feed on the host."

"Maybe she didn't infect me," he replied.

Gabi shook her head, "I'm sorry, but it transferred the moment her fangs drew blood."

Sigurdsson raised his hand up, running his fingers across his neck, and examined them. Fresh blood dripped from his fingertips.

For a moment Gabi felt herself go weak; the intoxicating scent of his blood beckoning to her. She bit her lip as she watched the twin liquid crimson trails disappear under his collar.

"Gabi!"

His cry startled her and she jumped back, her eyes a mix of terror and longing. Her weakened state was clouding her judgment.

"Snap out of it," Sigurdsson said.

"I'm….. I'm…. sorry."

"Stop," he said. "Right now we've got bigger issues that we need to deal with."

Gabi looked back over her shoulder at Serena and then back at him, as the sudden realization of what he had done hit her.

"Karl, how did you?"

"I took your warning about vampires to heart," he replied. "I had a friend make up some bullets with silver heads."

Gabi cautiously made her way over to the body and examined it. There was a gapping exit wound in the center of her chest, but even now she could see it was trying to repair itself. The silver had struck her down, but it hadn't been enough to kill her and the clock was ticking.

She looked at her sister's face, but she couldn't get past the image that had unnerved her moments before. Something had changed in Serena, something that was both dark and terrifying. She had become a threat to their existence and Gabi knew that if she recovered, the danger would not go away.

In her hubris, Serena had shown her hand and it chilled her to the core. There were others in the coven that supported her, and a power struggle, with Serena at the center of it, would put all of them at risk; human and vampire.

Sigurdsson struggled to his feet and made his way over to her.

"What do we do?" he asked.

"She'll recover," Gabi said somberly as she stood up.

"That's excellent news, isn't it?" he asked. "I mean that will clear you with the council, right?"

"Karl, if she lives, we will be in even worse danger."

"Why do you say that?"

"What do you do with a serial killer that you catch?"

"Put them in prison," he replied. "And then throw away the key."

"What happens if someone finds the key and releases them?"

"You're not suggesting—"

"She will not stop killing," she replied. "The balance of power within the coven is at a tipping point. She will become the force that galvanizes them and if they seize control more will die."

"What about me?" he asked. "With her gone, my fate will be sealed."

"As is mine," Gabi replied.

They stared at one another as each wrestled with the dire implications they were facing.

"This is your world," he finally said, breaking the silence. "Just promise me that when the time comes, you won't let me suffer."

"Never," she said as she took him in her arms and hugged him gently. "I promise."

"Never forget how much I love you, Gabrielle," he whispered, kissing her head softly.

Her body quivered in agony and she cursed her eyes that could not weep.

"I love you too, Karl," she said, choking on the words.

It seemed like such a cruel end to something that was so profoundly beautiful.

"You need to get the bodies out of here and do whatever you need to do," he said.

"What about you?" Gabi asked.

"I'll make sure there's no incriminating evidence left behind."

"I'll find you when I'm done," she said.

Sigurdsson nodded, forcing a smile on his face. "I know you will. Just make it quick."

A moment later she was gone and he slumped to the floor, a searing pain radiating through his chest.

CHAPTER THIRTY-SEVEN

Death came for Sigurdsson, not with fear, but with the warm embrace of an old friend.

He had been much too young to concern himself with thoughts of his own mortality, but now, as he felt the shadows fall upon the room, he couldn't help wonder why so many feared its touch.

He'd kept his promise to her and wiped all of the surveillance video files off the gallery's computer hard drive. There was little he could do about the mess they had left, but without a body and no evidence there would be little to go on; not that it would be *his* problem.

The pain had only grown in intensity since he'd left the gallery and he had barely made it back to the apartment. White wasn't happy when he called in and said he was going sick, saying that the feds wanted to speak with him right away, but something about the sound of his violent retching had convinced his sergeant that he wasn't trying to pull one over on him.

The last thing Sigurdsson did was to open the patio door for her, before collapsing onto the bed. He hadn't known what to expect, so he had placed his pistol on the bed next to him, just in case, but now he found himself too weak to lift the gun up, let alone pull the trigger.

He had held out for as long as he could, hoping she'd come as promised, but the fight finally left him.

"I love you, Gabrielle," he whispered, just as the room went dark.

Walk toward the light.

He'd heard the joke a million times, but there was no light here.

Death was like a sleep deprivation tank.

There was no sound, no pain, no time, no movement; just him alone with his thoughts.

Please don't tell me this is it, he thought.

All at once the fables he had been raised on flooded back.

He was supposed to go to Valhalla, the majestic hall located in Asgard, which was ruled over by Odin, but there were no Valkyries to guide him, no warriors to greet him.

Was my death not honorable? he wondered.

He wanted to scream, to lash out in anger, but there was nothing. It felt as if he had become nothing more than a disembodied thought.

A profound sadness gripped his heart as he faced the possibility that there was nothing.

In an instant, an intense bright light split the blackness and then even his thoughts were gone.

CHAPTER THIRTY-EIGHT

Gabrielle's head hung low, her hands clasped in front of her, as she sat on a wooden bench a damp holding cell next to the council chamber.

She wasn't sure how long she had been held there, certainly hours, but more likely days, as they had assembled the tribunal. Not that it mattered; at this point she had nowhere else to go.

She wore no restraints, because there was no need. There were two members of the sentry who flanked her and they would not hesitate to tear her apart if she offered even the slightest resistance; not that she could muster much of a fight at this point.

After leaving the gallery, she had gotten rid of the bodies. The gallery owner had been easy, but she wasn't willing to take the chance with Serena. Gabi knew that Sigurdsson was suffering; she could feel his pain tearing away at whatever was left of her soul. Every ounce of her being wanted to rush back to him, to be there for him, but her sister was much too powerful and she wasn't willing to leave anything to chance.

Once she had gotten to a desolate area in upstate New York, she had decapitated her and burned Serena's body. Despite what her sister had become, it didn't make the task any easier and she struggled with what she had done. Serena had created her and nothing could ever take that away.

Unfortunately, she had allowed herself to mourn a moment longer than she should have; her emotions clouding her thoughts and her judgment. While her own abilities hindered the sentries' ability to track her, that didn't apply to their ability to track Serena. As she stood mourning her loss, they caught her off-guard.

She expected that her own death would come swiftly, when Michael Orlov arrived, but there seemed to be confusion. After several heated phone calls, a decision was made to remove her back to the council to face a formal tribunal.

At first, she embraced the opportunity to speak in her defense, but along the way something had changed.

Gabi had lost her will to fight because she knew that she had lost him.

The feeling of pain and suffering had been a constant companion since she had left the gallery, but in a flash it was suddenly gone. Now, she faced the grim reality that, on this day, she had not only lost her sister, but the only man she had ever truly loved. Now she waited for them to pass judgement and seal her fate. Her only hope, slim as it might be, was that maybe Karl had been right and she could join him on the other side.

The sound of the door opening interrupted her thoughts. Gabi raised her head as Roderick Luther entered the room.

"I am truly sorry for everything, Ms. de Mar," he said earnestly. "The council is ready to hear your case."

"Thank you, Mr. Luther," she replied as she stood up.

A hush fell over the assembled council members as Gabi entered the room.

There were twelve of them, with the only empty chair being hers.

She could feel their eyes on her, a mix of contempt and compassion from her peers.

But how will you vote? she wondered.

Gabi took her place at the podium, in the center of the room, and waited for it to begin; she didn't have to wait long.

"Mr. Luther, will you please read the charges against the defendant," Janus said.

"Gabrielle de Mar, you stand accused of the gross and willful violations of the sacred laws of this coven," Luther said, in a firm and measured voice. "To wit, on the night of December 7th, you knowingly, and intentionally, caused the deaths of three humans. You are further charged with the intentional murder of a member of this coven, Serena de Mar, who was a witness in these proceedings against you. How do you plead?"

Gabi paused for a moment, considering her response, as she took the opportunity to stare each of them in the eye.

"Guilty as charged," she said defiantly.

The chamber erupted in clamor as Janus banged his gavel.

"Silence," he roared, his voice echoing off the stone walls, as he tried to restore order to the chamber.

After several seconds, and several more falls of the gavel, the conversations abated.

"Ms. de Mar," Janus said, clearly shaken. "Do you understand the severity of the charges and the penalty they carry?"

"I do, sir," she replied, "and my plea stands, with the proviso that I be allowed to explain my actions to the council."

In the coven's history, no member accused of killing another vampire had ever pled guilty; they were in unchartered territory.

"That is a highly unusual request," Janus said.

"I am prepared to accept my fate," she replied, "but I believe the council deserves to hear all the details surrounding my charges."

"I object," Sophie Janssen said. "The defendant has already pled guilty to the charges against her; to what purpose should we continue this case?"

"You object?" Logan Tremblay asked. "If I recall correctly, you were one of the votes for bringing Gabrielle before this court. I'm shocked that you wouldn't like the opportunity to hear her story. Would you care to comment?"

"I'm not the one who is on trial for murder," Janssen shot back.

"It must be nice to be in your position," Logan replied smugly. "To be so flippant while someone else is facing death."

Janssen held his gaze, seething with anger.

"I voted once to stray from the rules," Abigail Kensington said, "but I won't do it a second time. The defendant is either guilty or innocent, and in this case she has made her choice clear."

Charles Heroux stood up from his seat. "Janus, if I may address the council?"

"You may, Charles."

"There are several of us here tonight that did not have the opportunity to attend the council meeting that has led us to this predicament," Heroux said accusatorily. "While I agree that this is unusual, I believe it is in the full council's best interests to shine as much light on these unfortunate events as is possible. I will accept her guilty plea, but I would also like to know what she has to say."

"You make a convincing argument, Charles," Janus replied. "Under the circumstances, and considering the gravity of the charges, I think the council will be best served by hearing all the available information. I will allow it."

Murmurs filled the room, as like-minded council members shared their views on what was transpiring.

"If we are to break with the rules, then I demand that the full council have a say," Zoë Bathory stated. "I call for a vote."

"This is absurd," Trembley interjected. "She's facing death and you're carping about the legality of a statement?"

"Enough," Janus declared. The tribunal was starting to spin out of control and he needed to do everything in his power to keep it from fracturing further. "Mr. Orlov, please have the sentries remove the defendant."

"Yes, sir," Orlov replied, motioning for the two guards to remove her from the room.

When Gabi had been taken out, and the doors closed, Janus turned to the council members and glared. "I will not have a mockery made of these proceedings! Remember, a life is on the line."

"There is no precedence for this, Janus," Kensington interjected. "If Gabrielle wanted to speak in her defense, then she should have pled not guilty."

"I have to agree with Abigail," Pavel Reznik replied. "Despite your fears, Janus, I'm inclined to believe that it is she who will use this opportunity to make a mockery of the tribunal."

"As much as I would like to hear what Gabrielle has to say," Winston McFarlane added, "I believe there is some merit to Zoë's suggestion. I'm not against you, Janus, but we all serve our members. All I am saying is that I agree that the council should vote on the matter, so that the record reflects their position."

CHAPTER THIRTY-NINE

The door to the chamber opened and Gabrielle was led back inside.

She did her best to gauge the outcome of the meeting, but their faces were impassive and she couldn't get a read on where she stood.

"Ms. de Mar," Janus said. "The council has taken your request under vote. They have accepted your guilty plea, but you will be afforded the opportunity to present your case. However, I must warn you that I will not have these proceedings turned into a travesty. Is that understood?"

"I do, sir," she replied.

"The council has agreed to this, but they also have their own stipulation," he continued. "They reserve the right to question you regarding any statements you make. Do you accept this?"

"I do," she answered.

"Then please proceed."

Gabrielle took a moment to look each member in the eye before she began. She knew she was in a nest of vipers; the only question was who *looked* deadly and who *was* deadly.

"I stand before you accused of the crime of murder," she said, "and it is a charge for which I readily admit my guilt. But while I intended to kill them, I want the record to show that this was not a case of premeditation, but a matter of self-defense and in the defense of another."

Once again, murmurs erupted in the hall.

"Silence," Janus said, banging his gavel. "If you have questions, please direct them to the defendant, otherwise keep them to yourself."

"Ms. de Mar, please explain to us how you acted in self-defense on the night of December 7th," Jeremiah Blackstone asked.

"On that night I was having dinner—"

"Excuse me; did you say you were having *dinner*?" Kensington asked.

"I did," Gabi replied. "I was out with a friend that evening. We were leaving the restaurant when we were attacked by three men. The actions I took that evening were strictly out of defense for him."

"And does this person have a name?" Heroux asked.

"He does," Gabi replied, "but it's not important; he died."

There were exchanges of curious looks among the council members.

"What is important is the fact that this attack was not random," Gabi continued. "The presence of those men in the alley was not accidental, but intentional. They were sent there for the sole purpose of instigating a confrontation."

"By whom?" Blackstone asked.

"By my sister, Serena," Gabi said.

"I object to this charade," Janssen cried out. "The defendant has the audacity to lay the blame for her actions on her victim? How are we to take this seriously?"

"Silence," Janus ordered. "Ms. de Mar, what evidence do you have to support this accusation?"

"An admission, made by one of the men, that they were forced to attack us by a woman with black hair."

"I have black hair," Bathory replied. "Does that make me a suspect also?"

"I don't know *your* history, Zoë," Gabi said pointedly, "but I know my sister's and the truth is she has been breaking our laws, by engaging in the unsanctioned murder of humans, for some time."

"And you know this how?" Trembley asked.

"Because I was present for several them," Gabi replied.

Kensington slammed the pen she'd been holding onto the table. "Janus, will you please put an end to this charade? How long must we listen to these baseless accusations against a woman whom the defendant has admitted to killing?"

Loud arguing erupted among the council members.

At the far end of the table, Brixton Nash stood up and cleared his throat.

Nash was one of the oldest members of the coven and had held his seat ever since he was first appointed to the council by Pier Gerritse. In many ways he was an enigma. There was very little that was known about him, a mystery he maintained by living a rather reclusive life, but there were *stories* from the old country and they weren't pleasant.

He was afforded the highest level of respect by the others, the result of his status as the council's elder statesmen along with a healthy dose of fear, even though he rarely spoke at meetings. This sudden change caught them by surprise and a hush fell over the assemblage.

"Why did you not report this to the council, when it first happened, little one?" he asked.

"Because she was my sister, sir," Gabi replied, "and I loved her. I could not betray that."

"Yet, if we are to believe what you say, she was willing to betray you and you were ultimately willing to kill her."

"My reasons for telling you this was not to establish my innocence, but to warn the council," Gabi said.

"About what?" Nash asked.

"That Serena was not acting alone," Gabi exclaimed.

Gabi could see that several members of the council were enraged, but as long as Nash was asking the questions, they held their tongue.

"Then why didn't you bring her here?" he asked. "She was willing to accuse you, why not make her answer the accusations you have brought against her?"

There was no simple answer to his question.

She had lost everything and she had no desire to live, but she wanted them to know the threat that lurked among them.

The look on Serena's face her told everything she needed to know, but how could she explain her sense of betrayal or, for that matter, that there were others who supported Serena's cause?

Which one of you is complicit? she wondered.

Before she could formulate her reply, the door to the tribunal opened and Luther walked in; a harried look on his face.

The man quickly approached Janus and leaned over, whispering in his ear.

Whatever Luther had said caused an immediate response.

Janus' expression was a mix of confusion and alarm as he stood up.

"We have another *witness*," he said.

"A witness?" Reznik asked.

"Apparently," Janus replied. "Mr. Luther, please bring them before the tribunal."

All eyes were on the door as Luther left the room and returned a moment later accompanied by another.

"I present the witness, Detective Karl Sigurdsson."

Gabi's head snapped around, her eyes wide in amazement, as she watched him walk up to the podium.

"Karl!" she exclaimed, trying to rush toward him before being grabbed by a sentry.

Sigurdsson approached her, taking her hand in his.

"It's okay, everything will be all right," he said calmly, before taking his place at the podium.

"I'm sorry, Janus," Abigail Kensington said as she stood up. "I have put up with this charade long enough. I entertained your nonsense, by allowing *her* to speak ill of the dead, but I draw the line at allowing a *human*."

Before Janus could reply, Sigurdsson said, "I'm not."

"What did you say?" Blackstone asked.

"I'm not human," he replied, "at least not anymore."

Whispers and sideways glances were exchanged among the council members.

"Not human?" Pavel Reznik asked as he got up from his chair and made his way over to Sigurdsson.

"No."

Reznik smiled and extended his hand. "Then allow me to welcome you, *friend*."

Sigurdsson took the man's hand in his, as they locked eyes, and he immediately felt Reznik begin to exert extreme pressure.

Seconds ticked by as the man continued to squeeze even harder, his face transforming from one of bemusement to shock.

"My turn," Sigurdsson said, returning the favor and causing the man to grimace in agony.

"Stop!" Reznik cried out as pain radiated through his arm.

"Satisfied?" Sigurdsson asked, releasing the man's hand.

There was confusion and fear in the man's eyes as he rubbed his aching hand, "Yes."

Janus eyed Sigurdsson suspiciously as Reznik quickly returned to his seat. He did his best to reconcile the man before the council with the one he'd met a few days earlier. There was no physical change, but there was something noticeably *different* about him.

"For the sake of determining all of the facts, I will allow you to address the council," Janus said, "but I will remind you that this is *our* court, Detective Sigurdsson, and Ms. de Mar faces very serious charges. I expect you to act accordingly."

"Thank you."

"I still strenuously object to this," Kensington said.

"This council is supposed to be about finding out the truth, Abigail," Janus declared. "Are you telling me you are willing to suppress testimony simply because it does not conform neatly to your interpretation of the rules?"

Abigail glared at Janus, knowing he'd successfully backed her into a corner.

"Why pick a fight with me, Janus, simply because I disagree?" she asked. "I'm just a council member and you're the doyen. Do what you want, because this trial rests on your shoulders and you will be judged accordingly."

Janus turned to face Sigurdsson. "The witness may make an opening statement, but you will also answer the questions directed to you by the members of this tribunal."

"Understood," Sigurdsson replied. "My reason for coming here today is simple; I was murdered by Serena de Mar."

A palpable uneasiness gripped the hall at his accusation.

"I'm aware of the accusations Serena made against Gabrielle," he continued, "but they are lies."

"I take it you are the one who was with Gabrielle the night she killed those men?" Charles Heroux asked.

"Yes, I was," Sigurdsson said, "but she didn't kill them out of malice, but out of self-defense. It was Serena who sent them to attack us."

"Here we go again," Zoë Bathory said with an air of exasperation, "more unfounded accusations against a dead woman, by a man who is a convenient witness for the accused."

"It has nothing to do with convenience," Sigurdsson replied. "Serena admitted to me that she was behind the attack in the alley."

"She admitted this to you?" Brixton Nash asked. "How? Where?"

"I'd been assigned to investigate the recent unexplained murders, including the ones in the alley. A lead was called in and I was sent to interview someone who had potential evidence about the alley attack, but it was an ambush. When I arrived I found Serena there; she'd already killed the gallery owner. Serena attacked me, wanting to know what I had told Janus."

"You knew about this man, Janus?" Nash asked.

"I did," Janus replied. "I met with him after we made the decision to bring Gabrielle in, but I was convinced that he had no knowledge of her whereabouts."

"And I didn't," Sigurdsson replied. "Not until the day I was attacked."

"And she admitted to you that she sent the men to attack you in the alley?" Nash asked.

"She did," Sigurdsson replied, "but I don't think she anticipated things turning out the way they did."

"And how exactly did things turn out, detective?" Sophie Janssen asked.

"Like I said, it was a set-up. Serena had questions and she had no qualms about being the *bad cop* to get her answers," Sigurdsson replied.

"And yet you're here and she's not," Janssen said.

"Yes, but it wasn't for a lack of trying on her part," Sigurdsson shot back. "Somewhere between being thrown across the room and into a statute I reached the conclusion that my chances for making it out alive were somewhere between slim and none, so I fought back."

"You're not suggesting that you killed Serena, are you?" Logan Trembley asked.

"No, not at all," Sigurdsson said. "In fact, it ended rather badly for me."

"How so?" Kensington inquired.

Sigurdsson removed his tie and opened the collar of his shirt to reveal the scars on his neck.

"She bit you?" Nash asked.

"Yes."

"When?"

"Friday afternoon," Sigurdsson replied.

Murmurs of disbelief filled the room.

"You're telling me,... This council,... That you were bitten three days ago?" Nash asked.

"Yes," Sigurdsson said, nodding his head. "I'd been thrown into a statue which toppled down on me and pinned me to the ground. I'm pretty sure it shattered the bones in my right arm as well. Serena came over to continue her *chat* and I realized then that she would eventually kill me. So I grabbed a piece of the statue with my left hand and slashed her face. That's when she bit me."

"How did Serena die?" Nash asked.

"After she bit me, things started to go downhill very quickly," Sigurdsson replied. "It wasn't a horrible feeling, but my sight began to darken and I felt myself slipping away. Then, rather suddenly, it was over. I remember laying there wondering if I had died, but my vision began returning. At first, I wasn't sure if I was hallucinating or in hell. I could make out the hazy image of two figures fighting. Eventually I realized that it was Gabi fighting with Serena and she was losing. Any concern I had for myself was gone and I pulled my arm free from beneath the statue. At the time, I thought it was an adrenaline surge, even though I still felt as if I was dying. I watched Serena pin Gabi to the floor and grab a busted piece of a wood easel. About that time I was able to retrieve my weapon and I shot her."

"You think shooting her killed her?" Nash asked skeptically.

"Permanently? No, but it was certainly my intent and the silver bullets I used took the wind out of her sails. I was in too much pain to do anything at that point, so I let Gabi deal with her. It took everything I had left in me to clean up the mess for you folks, but don't feel as if you're under any obligation to thank me."

"Excuse me for questioning your veracity, detective, but you must admit that this all sounds conveniently self-serving," Kensington said, with a raised eyebrow. "Serena comes before the council with some serious accusations against Gabrielle, who then kills her, and suddenly her boyfriend appears as a witness who accuses the deceased of the crimes."

"It seems to me that Serena was a problem for some on this council, but perhaps not all," Sigurdsson said accusatorily. "That being said, I don't care whether it sounds convenient or not and I'm not asking you to take my word for it."

He reached into his jacket pocket, removing a USB drive, and motioned toward Janus. "May I?"

Janus got up and walked over to him. "What is this?"

"A gift," Sigurdsson replied. "It's the surveillance video from inside the gallery, during my little *bonding moment* with Serena. I downloaded it before I wiped out the hard drive. Not only does it confirm everything I just told the council, but it also shows Serena's murder of the gallery owner."

Janus reached out his hand to accept the drive, but Sigurdsson held it tightly. For a moment the two men locked eyes.

"There's more," Sigurdsson whispered, as he released his hold on the drive, "much more, but that's your problem, not mine."

"Thank you," Janus replied.

"Don't thank me until after you watch it."

Janus looked at him for several seconds, before nodding his head and returning to his seat.

"Excuse me, but am I missing something here?" Nicolaus Mavros asked. "Does anyone else here share my concerns that Detective Sigurdsson was not only bitten and is still alive, but that he doesn't seem any worse for wear?"

"Can we even be sure he was infected?" Kensington asked.

"You didn't shake hands with the man, Abigail," Reznik scoffed. "If you did, then I think you would have reached a different conclusion."

"Whatever is going on here, it is beyond anything we have encountered before," Heroux said. "I believe it is this council's obligation to find out exactly what we are dealing with and to identify any potential risk."

"What the hell does that mean?" Sigurdsson asked.

"I'm sorry, detective," Heroux replied, "but until we know more about your *condition*, I'm afraid you're going to have to remain with us."

"Thanks, but no thanks," Sigurdsson said, "I've given you everything you need and now we're done."

He turned around, taking Gabi's hand in his, and headed toward the door.

"Stop them!" Kensington cried out.

Marcus Dräger was the closest sentry, and he seized Sigurdsson by his left arm, just before they made it to the door. "You're not going anywhere."

Sigurdsson looked over his shoulder, his jaw clenching tightly.

"Let go of me," he growled menacingly.

"Or what?" Dräger asked, laughing contemptuously.

Sigurdsson glanced down at Dräger's hand and then looked back up, locking eyes with the man.

"Karl, trust me, this isn't a fight you can win," Gabi whispered.

An odd look appeared on Dräger's face, as he watched Sigurdsson's eyes transform. Starting from the edges of the sclera, the white in his eyes receded, replaced by a growing deep yellow topaz color that quickly engulfed the blue iris, until only the black of his pupils showed.

"Or *this*," he snarled, releasing Gabi's hand and driving it into Dräger's chest. The sentry sailed across the room and into the stone wall.

The next closest sentry sprinted forward, but Sigurdsson spun around, catching him in mid-stride, and snatched him up effortlessly by the neck, until he was two feet off the ground. Beyond them, the council members were frozen in shock, but Michael Orlov rushed forward to help his sentry.

He'd only taken a few steps when Sigurdsson's head snapped around and he glared at Orlov; rage in his eyes. Orlov's body stopped abruptly, but it wasn't by choice; something kept him from moving. It was as if his body had been taken hold of by an unseen specter and prevented him from reaching his prey. He struggled to break free, but it was no use.

"I didn't start this," Sigurdsson raged, "but if you force me to, I swear I will *finish* it."

Orlov watched helplessly as Sigurdsson's hand tighten around the sentry's throat. The man's hands clawed at Sigurdsson's, but he couldn't break the grip.

"Karl, stop," Gabi pleaded, taking his free hand in hers. "For *me*, please."

Sigurdsson's head pivoted around angrily, but upon seeing her the color began to drain from his eyes, returning to the blue ones that had captivated her.

He released his grip and the sentry fell to the floor, gasping, as Orlov stumbled forward and fought to regain his footing.

"Enough," Janus cried out. "Sentries stand down, that's an order."

"Janus, are you insane?" Bathory cried out. "Can you not see the *threat* before your very eyes?"

"This man has done nothing wrong," Janus exclaimed. "He has not violated one of our laws and I will not have him treated as a criminal or an experiment."

"What are you suggesting we do, Janus?" Kensington asked. "Are we to just let him leave?"

"Would you like to try to stop him, Abigail? Would any of you?"

The members of the council appeared stunned at his rebuke. They looked to Sigurdsson, then at Orlov, before exchanging uneasy glances with one another. As much as they didn't want to admit it, they knew Janus was right.

"That's what I thought," Janus said scornfully. "This man is not a member of this coven and he is not governed by our laws. I don't know what is going on here, but I know that this is not the way to handle it. Under the rules governing nomadic members, I am declaring him a guest in this territory and he will be treated as such."

"And what about Gabrielle?" Nash asked.

A scowl grew on Janus' face as he considered the question.

Notwithstanding Sigurdsson's testimony, she had admitted to breaking the law. There were no exemptions for protecting family members, even those that ultimately betrayed you.

"Gabrielle has admitted that she violated the law by not informing the council of Serena's actions," Janus said, "but I also believe this tribunal needs to consider that there are mitigating factors at play, namely Serena's actions that have led us here."

"And what do you suggest, Janus?" Nash asked.

"I am recommending a one-year sanction be imposed on Gabrielle and that she be permanently removed from the council."

The members of the council shared glances with one another, and quiet whispers passed between some. A sanction would label her as *persona non grata* within their community. She would be isolated and would not be able to communicate with anyone, nor would they be able to communicate with her. It also removed her from any protection the coven normally provided for its members.

"I guess under the circumstances we don't really have much of a choice now, do we?" Logan Trembley asked.

"It would seem the most prudent thing to do at the moment," Janus replied. "All those in favor say 'aye'."

Gabi watched as several of the members immediately replied, and then one by one the others joined in until there was a majority approval. She felt Sigurdsson clasp her hand and she sighed as she felt the burden of the tribunal lift from her shoulders.

"I recognize that a majority of the members have affirmed my ruling and I am officially closing out this matter. The tribunal has concluded, thank you."

Without saying a word, the members of the council got up and streamed out of the hall, until all that remained were Janus, Gabi, and Sigurdsson.

When the doors were closed, Janus spoke. "I am truly sorry, Gabi, but it has to be this way."

"No, I was wrong and I bear the responsibility for that," she replied.

"You don't owe me anything, Detective Sigurdsson," Janus said. "In fact it is I that owe you for ensuring that justice was served, but I would ask for a moment of your time."

"Of course," Sigurdsson replied.

"Please, follow me," Janus said.

CHAPTER FORTY

Janus led them through the tunnel, back into the main house, and brought them to his study.

"Please have a seat," he said to Gabi and Sigurdsson, motioning them toward the chairs across from his desk.

"Will you be requiring anything else this evening, sir?" Roderick Luther asked from the doorway.

"No, Roderick, thank you."

"Have a good evening, sir."

Janus said, waiting until the man closed the door to speak. "I'm afraid I don't even know where to begin, since we are in uncharted waters. Gabrielle, were you aware of this?"

"No, sir," she replied. "I haven't seen Karl since I left with....."

"I understand," Janus said, turning his gaze to Sigurdsson. "Detective, would you mind answering a few questions?"

"No, not at all, but I think we can dispense with titles."

"Thank you, Karl. I am sure you can understand that we are all perplexed by what has happened with you. I'd like to know what occurred at the gallery between you and Serena. The details, as best you can remember."

"You mean beyond her using me as a human piñata?"

"Yes, if you could take me through it all, it might be helpful to discover what has changed about transformation from everything we previously knew."

"I'll tell you as much as I can remember," Sigurdsson said. "I passed out at least once and there were a few times where things got foggy."

"That's understandable," Janus said. "You said you had been pinned under a statue. What happened specifically?"

"Well, it was during one of her *question-and-answer* sessions with me. She sent me flying across the room and I hit this large statue, which ended up falling on me. One of the large pieces pinned my arm to the ground."

"And it was heavy enough that you couldn't move it?"

"Not on my life and that was exactly what was at stake," Sigurdsson replied. "I knew the damage had to be severe, because I had no feeling in my forearm and I couldn't move my fingers."

"And you obviously can now," Janus replied as he recalled the image of Marcus Dräger's body sailing across the hall.

"Obviously," Sigurdsson smiled.

"And that is when she bit you?"

"Yeah, she came over to gloat a bit more and try to convince me to join her. I knew there was no way she was going to let me go and I wasn't sure how much more I could withstand. So with all the strength I could muster, I stabbed her with a shard of the statue and that sent her into a rage."

Sigurdsson felt Gabi's hand take his and squeeze gently.

"What do you remember about Serena biting you?" Janus asked.

"I remember the searing pain. It started in my neck, but it quickly began to radiate throughout my entire body. It reminded me of being electrocuted, when your nerves are so out of whack that you lose the ability to control your body. I knew I was in trouble, but my body felt frozen; like there was a disconnect between my brain and the rest of me."

Janus nodded in understanding. The venom from their bite was not unlike electrocution; it had a paralysis effect designed to immobilize their victims, so they couldn't offer up any resistance while they fed.

"It felt like everything slowed down and my vision began to fade fairly quick, perhaps only a couple of seconds," Sigurdsson continued. "Just before everything went black, I felt this odd sensation. It was like someone covered me with a warm blanket and the pain was suddenly gone. I remember feeling incredibly relaxed, almost euphoric, and I embraced my fate."

"Then what happened?" Janus asked.

"It was like something pulled me back," Sigurdsson confessed. "The warmth was ripped away and the pain came rushing back, but I still felt paralyzed. When my sight returned I saw Gabi and Serena fighting; it was obvious to me that Gabi was losing. At the time, I still wasn't convinced that I wasn't dying, but it was like a cruel joke was being played on me; that I couldn't die until I saw the woman I love be killed. When I saw Serena get on top of Gabi, I knew what she was going to do. I ripped my arm free from the statue and managed to get hold of my pistol. I managed to get off the shot before Serena could kill Gabi. Initially, I just chalked it up to an adrenaline surge."

"When did you get your feeling back in your arm?" Janus asked.

"About an hour later; after Gabi left," Sigurdsson said. "I noticed it while I was cleaning up the mess. I could move my fingers, but the pain never went away. In fact, it just continued to get worse. By the time I made it back to my apartment, I could barely move. I knew something was wrong. It wasn't just a physical pain; it was like my body was shutting down. I could feel whatever it was coursing through my system, destroying everything from the inside and killing me. The last thing I did was open the patio door for Gabi and laid my pistol by my side in case she didn't get back in time."

"You were going to kill yourself?"

"That was the original plan, but when the time finally came I no longer had the strength left in me."

He felt Gabi grip his hand tightly.

"What happened next?" Janus asked.

"I woke up," Sigurdsson replied. "The pain was gone and I was alive."

"And you have no desire to feed?"

"Oh, I ate the hell out of everything in my kitchen like a ravenous animal, but if you mean did I have a desire to hunt someone down and drink their blood, then the answer is no."

"Please understand, I do not doubt anything you have said, but none of it makes sense," Janus replied. "What you are describing flies in the face of everything we know about vampirism since the beginning of time."

"If you're confused, then you can imagine how I feel."

Janus eyed Sigurdsson cautiously, trying to read the man's thoughts. Unlike their previous conversation, where he knew the man wasn't lying about knowing where Gabrielle was, this time his thoughts were opaque.

"Would you like a drink?" Janus asked.

"I would."

Janus walked over to the dry bar and poured three glasses of whiskey, handing one to each of them, before returning to his desk.

"Do you know the true extent of your strength, Karl?"

"No, I don't," Sigurdsson said earnestly, "and if you ask me, I couldn't even tell you if it is me."

"What do you mean?"

"Back in the hall, when the guard grabbed me, it was me, but it wasn't me. It's as if something else takes over inside, something that is almost beyond my control; a rage that is nearly all consuming and I'm in a struggle with myself."

"What did you do to Orlov?" Janus asked. "I have never seen him just *stop* an attack before."

"I wanted him to stop," Sigurdsson said.

"You thought it and it happened?" Janus asked.

"It's kind of hard for me to explain," Sigurdsson replied. "I'm still figuring this out myself."

"Do you mind if I try something?"

"No, but again, this is all new to me."

"I promise, Karl, I'll go easy on you," Janus said with a smile. "Please, follow me."

Gabi watched as the two men got up and walked to the other end of the study.

"Just stand here for a moment," Janus instructed.

Sigurdsson stood in place as Janus returned to the dry bar. "Pardon me, the night has been unusual, to say the least, and I think it requires a second—"

In mid-sentence, Janus pivoted sharply, a blur to the human eye, and sent the glass flying toward Sigurdsson at supernatural speed.

Time stopped.

Sigurdsson saw the glass track across the room in the same detached way a sports analyst watches frame-by-frame game footage. He saw Janus' arm out stretched, the shocked look on Gabi's face, even the tiny droplets of amber liquid that spilled from the glass and were caught up in the air.

Then time resumed, but the glass and whiskey remained frozen.

"Amazing," Janus muttered as he walked over to where it hung suspended in mid-air.

"I.... I don't.... Janus, how is this possible?" Gabi stammered.

"I don't know, child," he replied as he tapped his finger against one of the droplets and watched it spin. "Are you doing this?"

Sigurdsson nodded his head.

"Amazing," Janus repeated. "Can you control it, Karl?"

"Yes."

"I threw it at you, do something else with it."

Janus watched in stunned silence as the cup slowly rotated 180 degrees, scooping up the liquid that had spilled from it, and then shot past Janus' head before landing on the dry bar.

"Impressive, Karl," Janus whispered. "Very impressive indeed, but it is also very dangerous."

"What do you mean?" Sigurdsson asked.

"I would like to tell you that your secret is safe here, but I cannot tell you that in good faith."

"The council?" Gabi asked.

"It is well known that there are those on the council who do not share our views, but it is not the overt ones I fear, but those who hide in the shadows."

"I heard Serena tell Gabi, '*Every rebellion needs a sacrifice and you're it,*'" Sigurdsson said. "Obviously she has like-minded friends, or at least those who sympathize with her world view."

"So what do we do now?" Gabi asked.

"We?" Sigurdsson asked. "No, there's no we, I'm not dragging you into this, Gabi."

"She is already dragged in, Karl," Janus replied. "Like it or not, your relationship is known and the danger applies to both of you."

"Not if I walk away," he said. "Let her do her one-year penance, or whatever you guys call it, and let her get her life back to normal."

"Excuse me, I'm right here," Gabi exclaimed as she got up from the chair and into his face. "Don't I get a say in this matter?"

"Gabi, I almost lost you once before—"

She pressed her index finger to his lips with an angry look.

"Yes, and I almost lost *you* as well, Karl. I'm not going anywhere and if you think you can decide to walk away than the council will be the least of your problems."

"I just meant—"

"I know what you *meant*, but have you considered what a life without you would mean for me?" she asked. "You think you would be removing me from danger, but what would be the purpose? So I could just continue to exist; aware of what I had and what I lost?"

"She's right, Karl," Janus interjected. "My fear isn't the council so much, but those outside of it. There has always been a *status quo*, and as long as we held the upper hand there were no problems, but that no longer exists. Some will be threatened by you and fear can lead to irrational behavior. Having Gabrielle with you will give you an ally with insight and abilities."

Sigurdsson frowned. "But—."

"But nothing," she said. "You don't get to tell me you love me and walk away, Karl, no matter what your reasoning is. Is that understood?"

"Yes, ma'am," he replied.

"I'm glad you two have settled that," Janus laughed.

"There's something else you should know," Sigurdsson said, the tone of his voice becoming more serious as he looked over at Janus. "There's been some other *interest* in what's been going on."

"What kind of interest?" Janus asked.

"The federal kind," Sigurdsson replied. "After the gallery attack, I called my office to tell them there wasn't any evidence and that I was taking the rest of the day off. I was told that I needed to report to the F.B.I.'s office because they wanted to talk to me about what happened in the alley. I let them know I was too sick and it would have to wait, which didn't make my boss very happy, but he eventually relented. I had a little sit down with them this morning. Mostly they wanted to know what I saw and who I talked to. I played dumb and stick to the story that I stumbled on it after the fact. They seemed satisfied and went to get great lengths to assure me that the deaths in the alley were staged by them, a sort of *preparedness drill*, but we know that's a lie. To make matters worse, they have the bodies. Which begs the question, what do they know and what are they trying to hide?"

"That's not good," Gabi said.

"No, it's not," Janus replied. "If they have taken possession of the bodies, there's no telling what they may discover."

"Or what they may use that knowledge for," Gabi added.

"Karl, these threats are serious, for all of us," Janus said. "I will do what I can, to deal with things on my end and within the coven, but I'm afraid that it will take much more to find out what's really going on."

"What do you need me to do?"

"For now, nothing," Janus said. "You're our only inside source at the moment. I don't want to tip our hand that we know something is amiss. Just monitor things and let me know if there are any additional inquiries."

"I'll do my best."

"I am sorry for the penalty I had to impose on you, Gabrielle," Janus said, turning his attention toward her.

"No, I understand, you were right," she replied. "I broke the law; I deserved it."

"Well, I had ulterior motives for issuing the sanction."

"What do you mean?" she asked.

"Our system has worked for as long as it has because there has always been a majority consensus, but lately that has shifted," Janus replied, "and my control is being tested. I pushed for you to be on the council, because I believed you would bring a voice of measured reason, but it was a narrow vote."

"I'm sorry I failed you," Gabi said.

"Don't be, everything happens for a reason," he replied. "The vote shined a light on those willing to show their hand, but this hearing revealed that there are others who are hiding and waiting. If it weren't for Karl's testimony, I think your fate this evening would have been much dire. I imposed the penalty, because I wanted to insulate you from the council to take on a new role."

"What do you mean?" she asked.

"There are those who no longer believe in the path we have set for ourselves; who want to take things in a decidedly darker direction," Janus explained. "Karl's existence represents an existential threat to them; someone who can potentially stand against their machinations. He needs a guardian."

"I'm pretty sure I can take care of myself," Sigurdsson chimed in.

Janus turned to look at him. "Of that I have no doubt, Karl, but for how long?"

"What do you mean?"

"Will it last a day, a week, a year, forever?" Janus asked. "You haven't broken the rule of transformation, Karl, you've shattered it and with that comes many questions; questions that others will want to get answers to, by any means possible. As I said, the council is already fractured and I have little doubt that word of you is already being shared. It won't be long until the grand council knows of you. If your powers are fleeting, you will need someone who can protect you, because even though you may be defenseless, they will still come for you; they will still want answers."

Sigurdsson glanced over at Gabi, whose face was a mix of sadness and resignation.

He reached over and gently caressed her cheek with his hand. "It's going to be all right."

She nodded, not because she believed it, but because she wanted to.

Janus walked over to the desk and picked up a pen, writing something on a piece of paper. Then he walked over and handed it to Gabi.

"After tonight, I think it is best that we do not talk again until we figure out a resolution to all of this," he said. "If you need to get a message to me, reach out to this person. He knows how to contact me through secure channels."

"Understood," Gabi said.

"I wish you luck, Karl, and I will do my best to protect the two of you from the council, but from this point forward you are on your own; trust no one."

Janus extended his hand and Sigurdsson shook it.

"Good luck," Janus said, "to both of you."

Sigurdsson nodded as he took Gabi's hand and walked out the door. A moment later they slipped into the evening and were gone.

CHAPTER FORTY-ONE

Sigurdsson opened the door to the apartment, allowing Gabi to step inside, before closing and locking it. In retrospect, it seemed absurd to lock the door, or maybe he was just protecting the outside world from *them*.

Is that what I've become, a threat? he wondered. *And a threat to whom*?

"You want a drink?" he asked as he helped her remove her jacket and hung it on the coat rack.

"Sure," Gabi replied as she sat down on the couch.

"Coming right up," he replied as he hung his jacket next to hers.

"So tell me what you're thinking, Karl."

"Honestly, I'm trying to figure out where I go from here."

"What do you mean?"

"I'm not sure where I fit in anymore or whether I can even stay here," he replied as he handed her the drink and sat down next to her.

"Please don't shut me out, Karl," she said. "You're not going through this alone. I may not understand exactly what you went through, but I do understand the aftermath."

He took a sip of his drink and cradled the glass in his hands as he searched for answers.

"I guess I'm scared," he replied.

Gabi placed her hand on his knee. "It's okay; I'll be here."

Sigurdsson cocked his head and looked at her with a smile. "I know you will, but that's not what I meant."

"Then what is it?"

"I feel as if I don't belong anywhere," he replied. "I'm clearly not human, but I'm not a vampire either."

"We don't know that," Gabi replied. "Janus is right; this just could be a rare mutation of some type. We're just going to have to wait and see how it progresses."

Sigurdsson took a drink, but remained quiet.

"There's something you're not telling me, isn't there? Something you didn't tell Janus."

Sigurdsson swirled the whiskey around in his glass and then gulped it down. "I don't know what this is, but I don't think it's a mutation, Gabi."

"What do you mean?" she asked, her tone becoming serious.

"I died in that room, Gabi," he said, pointing toward the bedroom. "I waited for you, as long as I could, but I gave up. I lost my will to fight and I surrendered. There is no doubt in my mind that I died."

Gabi shook her head. "No, Karl, you don't know that. We don't know how your body processed the venom—"

"It wasn't the venom," he said, before getting up and refilling his drink.

"Tell me what happened, everything," Gabi said. "I can't help you if you hold anything back from me."

"There came a point where I couldn't take it anymore and I just wanted the pain to stop," he said as he rejoined her on the couch. "I wasn't scared to die, at least not at first, but then everything went black; as black as the darkest night. I couldn't hear anything, couldn't see anything, and I couldn't feel anything; there was nothing. That's when I became afraid. The prospect of spending eternity like that brought me to the point of madness, but the cruelty was only made worse because my mind knew everything."

"I don't know what to say, Karl. I've never heard of anything like that happening before, in any transformation."

"That was only the beginning," he replied. "I don't know how long I was like that, time had ceased to exist for me, but then there was this intense light that tore open the blackness, blinding me. The pain was unimaginable. All at once it felt as if my body was hurdling along at a speed my mind couldn't comprehend. It felt like it was tearing me apart. I wanted to scream for it to stop, but my mouth couldn't even form the words. A moment later my body collapsed onto a beach, naked and trembling."

Gabi's eyebrow arched upward in surprise as she stared at him. "Naked? On a beach?"

"Yes, but it wasn't a normal beach," he replied, taking a drink. "The sand was as black as finely crushed charcoal. To my right was a vast angry sea and to my left was a desolate range of jagged mountains, their peaks shrouded in an eerie mist. The sky above was gray and flashes of lighting coursed through the clouds. I looked behind me, but it was all the same, for as far as the eye could see."

"What did you do?"

Sigurdsson inhaled sharply as he relived the memory.

"I figured I only had two choices, either I went into the water or I climbed the mountains. So I headed to my left. I reached the base and realized the mountain was constructed of these hexagonal shaped rocks, each one of differing sizes, which formed stepping stones. I began to scale it, choosing my path carefully. Sometimes the rock crumbled under my weight and I would fall until I could get a handhold. Then I would start over. By the time I reached the summit, my body was battered and bloodied. As I climbed over the edge, the scenery changed. The sky was clear and lush green fields lay before me. Off in the distance I could make out another mountain range, which had massive water falls cascading over the top. I knew my only option was to head for them.

"I don't know how long I walked for, but it felt like I was walking for days. The sky never changed, it never grew dark, but I couldn't make out the source; it was just light. Eventually I was able to make out something in the distance. At first it just appeared to be a hill on the horizon, but as I drew closer, I realized it was a structure. It was a simple wooden home, with a thatched roof, and I could see the slightest hint of smoke wafting through the top. A fence of cobbled tree branches surrounded the outside. I called out several times, but there was no reply. I felt exhausted and just wanted to rest. So I climbed over the gate and made my way toward the door.

"I opened the door and peered inside, my eyes adjusting to the dimly lit interior. It seemed so much bigger than it did from the outside. In the center of the room I could make out a person sitting in front of a fire with their back turned toward me. They were wearing an old brown cloak and had a tan colored wolf pelt draped over their shoulders. The room was filled with the aroma of something being cooked over the fire. I kept calling out as I approached the figure, but I still didn't get a reply. As I made my way around to face the figure, my heart stopped, as they raised their hooded head and I saw the face of my mother."

"Your mother?"

Sigurdsson nodded. "But she wasn't as I remembered her; she was familiar, but different."

"How had she changed?"

"She stood up and removed the cloak she was wearing, allowing it to drop to the floor. I recognized that it was her, but she was young again and there was a fierceness about her that was unsettling. It was like being in the presence of a true warrior. On one side, her long blonde hair was draped over her shoulder, but the other side was shaved to just above the ear and the remaining hair was woven into tight braids that hung down. She was wearing the most amazing outfit I'd ever seen. It was blood red and was laced with woven gold braid. Her chest and forearms were banded in leather armor embossed with the images of wolves. On her hip was a

Carolingian sword and I could make out intricately carved runes on the pommel. She looked at me and asked, 'Why are you here, Karl?'"

"What did you say to her?" Gabi asked.

"At first I didn't know what to say," he replied. "Eventually, I just blurted out that I had died. She looked at me impassively, as if she was sizing me up. Then she shook her head and said, 'No, you haven't, not yet.' It must have been obvious that I didn't understand what she meant, because she pointed to a log seat across from her and told me to sit down.

"I asked her where I was and she told me I was nowhere. I remember this profound sense of sadness coming over me; as if I had failed her. She said to me, 'Karl, this wasn't your time and the gods are angry.' I asked if they were angry with me and she replied, 'Yes, they are, by the unholy act between man and the *undead*.'"

Gabi swallowed hard, understanding that the unholy act was them.

"She explained that she had appealed to the gods, Odin and Freyja on my behalf, but they were divided. Odin argued I had not died in battle, but through being cursed and that I was not welcome in Valhalla. Freyja argued that Odin himself had blessed his ward, Starkad, who'd been cursed by Thor simply for being beloved by Odin and that I deserved the same chance. She added that she would gladly welcome me into her hall, *Folkvang*. Odin dismissed the argument as pointless, since I was already dead. Freyja countered that she was entitled to half the dead and that she would raise me back up, through *seiðr*, to battle again. The two gods argued for and against, until the goddess Frigg, Odin's wife, interceded, aligning herself with Freyja. She said that only another mother could understand the grief of losing a child, as she had with her son, Baldr. Frigg said that there was great honor in saving a mother from the *first grief*.

"Odin agreed, but he countered that raising me back up from the dead would not alone determine whether I was worthy to dine with him in Valhalla. So he proposed a challenge and it was accepted."

"What kind of challenge?" Gabi asked.

"My mother reached her hand out and I took it. She led me outside and we began walking. She explained that there was more to fear than death. That death came to all man and beast in its own time, but that it was the period before that appointed time that determined whether the life was worth living. She said that a life of fear had killed more men than the blade of death itself. It seemed as if we had been walking for hours, but we finally reached a massive longhouse which had to be about thirty feet wide and at least two hundred feet long. She stopped outside the door and motioned with her hand for me to enter. I asked her what was inside and she replied, 'the fears you must face alone to prove you are worthy.'

"As I began to open the door, she put her hand on mine and stopped me. She kissed my cheek and said, 'Remember, Karl, you are never alone. You come from a bloodline of kings and great warriors and they are always at your side.' Then I watched as she reached down and unsheathed her sword and handed it to me. 'This sword is named *Tyrfingr,* and it belonged to King *Sigurðr*, of whom you are descended. Take it and carry on his legacy.' As I gripped the sword in my hands, the runes began to glow a warm orange color and it felt as if it were radiating energy. I nodded to her, then opened the door and stepped inside.

"The room was dark, except for a small amount of light that shined through the smoke holes in the roof, glistening off the dusty air inside. There were large timbers on either side of the room, which held up the roof and formed corridors to either end of the building before disappearing into darkness. I walked around the center of the room, toward the closest of the fire pits, eyeing the shadows, but there was nothing but blackness. At first I wasn't sure what was going on, but then I heard it; a low growl that emanated from the far reaches of the building. I raised the sword up, as my eyes struggled to identify the threat. Seconds ticked by, as I heard a faint *tip-tap* sound grow louder.

"A moment later my fear was realized when a large wolf emerged. It was massive, Gabi, bigger than any I have ever seen in my life. It had to be five feet at the shoulders and nearly ten feet long, with thick black fur and bright yellow eyes that pierced through darkness. My heart was racing as it stalked me around the room. It stayed just at the edge of the shadows as if it were taunting me. I could sense the anger in it and I remember walking around the fire, trying to keep it in front of me. I'd made my way halfway around the room, when it turned and started to come toward me. I could feel my heart thumping in my chest and my arms ached from holding the weight of the sword. It let out a deep roar that reverberated through my body. I waited for it to lunge at me, but then I was struck in the back and slammed to the ground. There was an intense pain radiating through my body, but I scrambled to my feet. At first I thought I'd hit my head and was suffering from double vision, but I soon realized that there were now two of them. They began stalking me from either side, and I found myself having to move deeper into the darkness. They split up, each on either side of the beams in the shadows, and followed me as I retreated. I did my best to try to stay near the light of the fire pits, but they slinked away into shadows. I pivoted from one to the other, holding out the sword to keep them at bay, watching as their eyes glowed in the blackness.

"The wolf on the left struck first, he turned his head for a moment and I lost him. Then my attention was diverted toward the other who'd growled, and a second later I felt the other wolf's jaw clamp down on my left shoulder. I swung the sword wildly, but missed. Then, the one on my right barreled into me, knocking me to the ground; the force of the blow dislodging the sword from my hand. Terror gripped me as I searched for the blade on my hands and knees. I could hear them pacing around, growling softly."

Gabi sat on the edge of the couch, hanging on every word he spoke.

"In the dim light I could see blood streaming down my arm and pooling onto the ground below me. With each beat of my heart, I waited for them to finish me off. In my mind I knew there was no way to defeat something I couldn't see. By sheer luck my hand struck the hilt of the sword and I seized it, before leaping to my feet. I began swinging it wildly from side to side, doing my best to keep them at bay. After a few minutes my back hit the wall of the building and I knew my luck had run out. I remember feeling this wave of rage boil up inside of me and the memories of the gallery, of Serena, came flooding back; the feeling of helplessness, as she sunk her teeth into me. I swore an oath that if I were to die there, that I would do it on my feet as a warrior. I screamed for them to come for me, daring them to attack. They howled in unison, and I braced myself, determined to do as much damage to them as I could before they tore me apart. Then, in an instant, the wall above me erupted inward and the room was flooded with light. Out of the corner of my eye I saw a gigantic, bluish-gray cat sail through the air and land about thirty feet away. The silence was ripped apart, as the wolves howled angrily, because they'd lost their advantage. Now that I could see them, they went on the attack. The one on the right leaped at me, but I had sensed it and swung the sword around, catching him in mid-air. The sword sliced cleanly through his neck, killing him before he hit the ground, but the momentum exposed me to the other one and he pounced. His weight sent me hurtling forward, jarring the sword from my grip, and I felt his claws rake my back.

"I remember feeling a sense of pride, as I tumbled to the ground, knowing that I had taken out the one beast. I could see the sword, mere inches beyond my grasp, and I struggled to reach it. Then I felt the wolf bite my shoulder; its teeth burying themselves deep into my flesh. I screamed out in pain as it thrashed about, my body limp as a rag doll in its mouth. But the ferocity of his attack had driven me forward and just when I thought the end had come, my fingers slid across the sword's hilt. With my last ounce of strength, I scooped it up in my right hand

and drove it backward, over my left shoulder, burying it in the beast's skull.

"For a moment I laid there, too exhausted to move. The dirt floor had turned to a crimson mud from the blood that poured from my wounds. I knew my injuries were severe and accepted the fact that I would probably not survive them, but I felt a peace about me, laying there on the battlefield. There was some measure of comfort in knowing that, even if I died, I had bested them. I cried out, 'I won,' but it was then that I noticed the cat. It approached me with its ears pinned back and its body low to the ground. I wondered if it was sizing me up to finish the attack. It seems weird, but at that moment I remembered the words of Marcus Aurelius, '*Death smiles at us all, all a man can do is smile back.*' So I made my peace with death and I smiled up at the cat, as it peered down at me, its eyes glowing brightly. Then it reached over and touched my hand with its paw. I felt a surge of heat pass between us. Not a burning heat, but one of warmth and soothing. I remember closing my eyes and feeling the pain slip away. When I came to, the cat was gone and everything was still. I stood up, grabbing the sword and scanned the room, but there were no more threats so I made my way back outside.

"When I emerged, my mother was sitting there by a small fire. She looked up and her face beamed with pride. The hardness I had previously seen was gone now and she ran over and hugged me. 'You have proven yourself in battle, Karl, and have been counted worthy,' she whispered in my ear. 'You can now take your rightful place in the great hall with your kin.' Her words caught me off-guard and I knew she could see the doubt in my eyes. I told her I wanted to stay with her, but that I didn't belong there; not now. She looked at me with her dark blue eyes and smiled; a smile that told me she knew my heart. 'Go to her, my son,' she said, 'and protect her.' Then she added that I needed to go home and find my Aunt Fritha. The next thing I knew I awoke in my bedroom."

"That's an amazing story, Karl," she said, "and I want you to know that I believe you felt it was real, but have you considered the possibility that it was just a fever induced dream, brought about by the venom?"

Sigurdsson nodded. "Yes, I did, at first, but it wasn't a dream."

"Are you sure?"

Sigurdsson got up and began unbuttoning his shirt. A moment later, Gabi's eyes went wide as he turned slowly and revealed the long jagged claw marks across his back.

"Still think it was all just a dream?" he asked.

"Karl… I… I don't know what to say," she stammered.

He turned around to face her, buttoning up his shirt. "It's okay, you were right to doubt; it seems all a bit fantastical. Trust me, I know the feeling."

Gabi laughed. "I'm sure you do."

"Let's just say it's been quite an *interesting* month for my belief systems," Sigurdsson said, "and I'm not sure if I can survive the New Year if this keeps up."

The smile on Gabi's face was soon replaced by a pensive look.

"What's wrong?" he asked.

"You left her, Karl," she said. "You left your rightful place, to be with me?"

"Yes."

"Why?"

"Because I knew you were in trouble and I couldn't bear the thought of being separated from you again," he replied as he sat down next to her.

"You gave it all up for me?" she asked, taking his hand in hers.

"Without you, there is nothing for me, Gabi," he said, squeezing her hand. "From the moment I first saw you on the news video I couldn't stop thinking about you. Without ever saying a word, you captivated me. Then, the night I met you in the bar, I was transfixed. I hung on every word you said and fought desperately not to look like an idiot."

She smiled. "You didn't look like an idiot, Karl."

"I realized that not only were you beautiful, but you were intelligent and funny. I could have stayed there forever with you. Even after the alley and your *confession,* I could never have walked away. When I saw Serena attacking you it felt like something was crushing my soul. For a moment, the thought of losing you..."

Gabi squeezed his hand. "You're not going to lose me."

"At that moment I thought I was and I accepted that I would rather be dead than live without you; that I'd roll the dice and take my chances in the afterlife, then to take one more breath without you. Now I am worried that by coming back, it is I who has put you in danger again."

"You haven't put me in danger."

"What if Janus is right; what if they are coming for me?" he asked. "We don't know what *this* is. What happens if I wake up tomorrow and I am *normal* again? Then you're left alone protecting me. There are too many unknowns."

"Then we will fight them together," she replied. "Because, just like you, I would rather fight and die by your side, than spend eternity with a hole in my heart."

"I don't want to be the one that puts your safety at risk."

"It's not my safety that I am concerned with," she said. "Things are changing and I'm afraid that the danger is something we will all have to confront."

"Like the danger from Serena?" he asked.

"Serena may have been the face, but I fear the tentacles run much deeper and are a lot less transparent. I've heard grumblings from others and not just from those within the Crystal Coven. There is a growing faction that resents any restriction on our kind; the whole *might over right* thing. While they appear to be a minority, that doesn't mean that others won't back them if their message gains momentum. It only takes one spark to turn a message into an angry mob. I don't even want to think of the potential ramifications of that."

"And now it looks like we have the feds involved in a cover-up," he said.

"Yes, but for what purpose?" she asked. "That's something we need to figure out quickly."

"So I'm going from the frying pan into the fire?"

"Hey, if it was easy anyone could do it."

"So I guess it's you and me against the world?" he asked.

"More like you and me trying to save the world," she replied.

"What happens if the world doesn't want to be saved?"

"The world doesn't know the threat they are facing, Karl, and maybe they shouldn't. Maybe the nicest thing would be to allow them to just stay in their blissfully ignorant little world."

Sigurdsson smiled warmly as he raised his hand and pointed in the direction of the coffee maker sitting on the kitchen counter, its blue LED display steadily flashing 12:00. "Gabi, I still haven't bothered to learn how to program the damn coffee pot yet, and I'm going to save the world?"

"Well, consider yourself lucky that you have me around now to help you."

"What if I can't do it?"

"You took on two sentries and stopped Michael Orlov in his tracks," Gabi replied, her tone becoming very serious. "Whatever interest in you they may have, that alone should give them a reason to question whether they want to tangle with you."

"And if it doesn't last?"

"They won't know that and I will always have your back."

"Now what?" he asked.

"Now we need to find your aunt. Maybe she can shed some light on what has happened."

"I love you, Gabi," he said.

"I love you too, Karl," she replied.

Sigurdsson leaned over and kissed her, feeling her arms wrap around him tightly, as she whispered in his ear, "Forever."

CHAPTER FORTY-TWO

Pier Gerritse sat in the Land Rover's backseat, staring out into the crystal blue waters of the Bay of Algehro, as the SUV made its way along the *Strada Provinciale* 105.

He had just been summoned from Zurich, where he was spending the Christmas holiday, to attend an emergency meeting of the Grand Council. The lengthy drive from *Alghero-Fertilia* Airport gave him ample time to ponder the urgency of the gathering.

Long before the Great Pyramid of Giza were constructed, and before the Sumerians and Akkadians dominated Mesopotamia, vampires had roamed the Earth.

There was no recorded history, no direct linage to the *first* vampire; they just existed.

Over time, folklore had been passed down from one generation to the next. Some believed that they were originally conceived through Lilith, who according to Hebrew mythology was Adam's first wife, born of the same clay as him, but who refused to bend the knee in subservience. The legend claimed that Lilith had left the Garden of Eden and had taken up with Samael, the fallen Archangel of Death.

Others believed that vampires were the offspring of Lamia, who was the secret lover of the Greek god Zeus. When Zeus' wife, Hera, discovered his infidelity she killed all of Lamia's children and afflicted her with sleeplessness so she would remain in constant anguish. In retaliation, Lamia swore her vengeance and preyed on young children in their beds at night. It was believed that those who did not die were turned.

There was also a belief among some that their origins reached far beyond the earthly realm; that they were the offspring of the *Watchers*, angels who'd been sent by God to watch over humanity. But the Watchers soon developed a lust for human women and began to have sexual relations with them. At the urging of their leader, Samyaza, they defected from God. The Watchers began to instruct humanity on illicit things and started to procreate with the women. This unholy union produced the *Nephilim*, a race of savage giants who pillaged the Earth and endangered humanity. Many believed that they were the Nephilim; neither human nor angelic. Through their supernatural abilities, it was believed that many had survived the great flood designed to destroy them. In their anger and resentment, they unleashed their lust and evil desires on humanity and laid the foundation for future generations of vampire.

In the beginning, their numbers were few and they lived a mostly nomadic lifestyle. Feeding along the established travel routes and moving on before they aroused suspicion. Over time, and conquest, their numbers began to swell, as did the risks.

Whatever the truth was about their origins, they existed, but throughout recorded time the process of transformation had remained the same.

That was until now.

Word had spread like wildfire through their community and within twenty-four hours it had shaken them to their core. Some viewed it as a positive; a possible breakthrough which might lead to a *cure*, but others saw it as a grave threat.

Gerritse found himself somewhere in the middle. There was so little information on this new fledgling, that he was doing his best to keep an open mind. He had reached out to Janus, the moment it had come to his attention, and he could sense the reluctance in the man's voice as he shared with him the details from the tribunal, but he also felt there was more to the story than was being told. He didn't blame Janus for being tightlipped; he was the doyen and he had a coven to protect.

Based upon what he had been told, he had to agree that it was best to let the man go on his own terms, in the hope that he would willingly agree to help them learn more about what had changed. Unfortunately, he also understood the risk involved with this.

Fledglings had a notorious reputation for being unpredictable. Their anger and insatiability for blood, especially in those early days, made them difficult to control. Without a strong master to take control, they could utterly decimate an area; which was precisely what made this case so unique. Here, the master was dead and the fledgling appeared to be in absolute control.

"Where almost there, sir," the driver said.

He watched as the SUV turned onto a winding access road made of hard packed dirt and rock. The area was in a rugged stretch of mountains dotted with the remnants of old stone buildings that had once been the homes of silver miners. The irony was not lost on him. This location was part of a larger area that the Sardinian government had designated as being off-limits to the public, to protect the pristine beauty of the area, but the true reason was that the government was obliged to protect the occupants of this particular place. There were so many marine protected areas, that no one questioned the government's decision to make this a sanctuary area. Its remoteness and rugged terrain ensured that its permanent resident was never disturbed.

The SUV made a right onto a service road and a moment later passed through a large stone gate that dated back to the Nuragic period. Two marked patrol cars from the *Polizia Locale* where parked just outside the entrance and the officers standing guard averted their eyes as the vehicle drove through.

Plausible deniability meant that if you didn't *see* anything, you couldn't *say* anything.

When the SUV pulled up at the mansion, Gerritse exited it and headed straight into the medieval building, listening to his footfalls on the cobble-stone walkway. He paused at the cloak room, to don the traditional black and gold robe of a council member. It was something that had always struck him as theatrical, but he knew there was a purpose behind everything. Within the walls of the council, individuality and allegiances were abandoned at the door; at least in theory.

"Pier," a voice called out from across the room.

Gerritse pivoted to see Remigius Pelletier standing near a large window overlooking the bay. Several other members of the council stood further down the hall talking with one another. He donned his robe as he made his way over to the man.

Pelletier represented the Western European covens and had always been a stalwart ally to him on the council.

"I'm glad you're here," Pelletier said softly. "Do you know what's going on?"

"Just the same rumors I am sure you have already heard," Gerritse replied.

"Do you think it could be true?" he asked. "That there has been a change?"

"I certainly believe that we have to take what we are being told seriously."

"Pier, you have always been a voice of reason. There are many who claim that this is a threat to us, but I want to know what you think?"

"Change scares all people, Rémy," Gerritse replied. "They fear what they don't know and it can cause them to overreact."

Just then their conversation was interrupted by the opening of two large wooden doors at the end of the hallway.

A man in a dark suit emerged and beckoned them forward. "They are ready to begin."

"Well, I guess we're about to find out more of the story," Gerritse said.

The members entered the council room and took their assigned seats.

The Grand Council was composed of representatives from covens around the globe; from the endless expanse of the Eurasian Steppe to the darkest reaches of the Amazon rainforest and everything in between. They were the old guard of the vampire world and their duty to protect their members was a solemn one. Most of the members, like Gerritse and Pelletier, had held their positions since the inception of the council, but they were not the oldest members.

Gerritse had been an adolescent man living in Nijmegen, a city in modern-day Netherlands, in 6 AD. He'd been forced into domestic servitude for Gaius Claudius Flavius, a Roman Governor in the region. Flavius' wife, Antonia, had taken a liking to the young Pier, which soon turned sexual. While Flavius marched down to his summer headquarters in Xanten, Antonia stayed behind to enjoy her stud. Their escapades lasted only as long as it took the *Batavi*, a Germanic tribe that lived along the Dutch Rhein delta, to overrun the Roman *castrum*.

Flavius had been tricked into believing that the Batavi posed no threat to the might of the Roman army, because their numbers had dwindled due to a harsh winter and famine, but it was all a lie. Within hours, they had decimated Flavius' security detachment and burned everything in the encampment to the ground. Bodies littered the smoldering battlefield, while the screams of the dying filled the night air. Gerritse had done his best to defend his lover, but he was no match for the brutality of tribal warriors. They had made it as far as the forest tree line before they fell. All he could do was stare at Antonia's body, back lit by the fires of the encampment, as he waited for death to join them in the afterlife.

Just before dawn, scavengers descended upon the battle field to loot what they could before the Romans returned. It was then that Gerritse met his future master, Brennus, who'd been a member of the Galic tribe known as the *Boii* before he had been turned. Over two thousand years had passed since that fateful night, but in the vampire's world, that was the blink of an eye.

Gerritse eyed the others assembled in the room. Even though the members of the council were considered equals, there was most definitely a caste system in place.

Under normal circumstances it was insignificant, as the council was generally of the same mindset regarding the governing of covens. Each member was here because they understood the fundamental need to maintain balance and order, but he also couldn't shake the feeling that this fragile system could now be in jeopardy.

Each of them took their seats as they awaited the arrival of the presiding chief of the council.

A hush soon fell over the room, as the doors opened at the far end, and they all stood as a cloaked figure entered, flanked on either side by two guards. Unlike the other members of the council, the presiding chief wore a gold robe, trimmed in black; a visible sign of his authority. The guards who accompanied him wore dark emerald green robes and their identities were hidden behind featureless alabaster masks.

Each of the members bowed their heads, as a sign of respect, as the man shuffled across the floor.

"Be seated, my friends," a soft, measured voice said as he took his place at the head of the table.

The members sat down, watching as he removed the hood of his robe to reveal a grotesque face.

He stood there for a moment, hunched over, as if he was barely clinging to life. His skin had an almost translucent appearance and it was pulled taut against his skull, giving him a malevolent look, while large black eyes peered out from recessed sockets.

Namtaru was believed to be the oldest vampire in existence, although no one knew what his actual age was; throughout recorded time he had just existed. The ancient world told stories of him and they revered him as the god of death. Folklore claimed that his father was the god of wind, air, and storms, while his mother was the goddess of Kur, the land of the dead. Regardless of his origins, one thing was for certain, for as long as Namtaru had walked the Earth he had brought immeasurable death upon the land.

It was Namtaru that had created the Grand Council; bringing an end to the warring factions that had plagued the vampire world for centuries. He formed the council with members from the original thirteen covens and it became the regional blueprint used by all covens to handle any issues internally.

Even though the head of the council was an elected position, this was not the case with the Grand Council. Namtaru had held the spot since its inception and there had never been a challenge to his leadership. Despite his frail looking appearance, he was still a vampire of considerable strength. Many believed that his pure-born lineage was the reason for his vitality and longevity, but whatever the reason, he was someone who was both respected and feared.

When next he spoke, the words came out crisp and with the strength of steel.

"I've summoned you here today because of a grave threat that we must confront," he said as he took his seat. "Word has reached me, as I am sure it has all of you, of a possible mutation in the transmission of the virus and we must take this threat seriously. I've gathered you here today in order to formulate our response."

The other members of the council shared wary glances with one another, but held their tongues."

Finally it was Gerritse who broke the silence. "Pardon me, sir, but why exactly are we viewing this as a *threat*? My understanding is that the transformation may have been unusual, but that the fledgling has not been identified as a threat to the coven."

"And what would you suggested we do, Pier?" Namtaru scolded. "Do nothing?"

"I'm just saying that perhaps we should see this as an opportunity and —"

"And what?" Namtaru snapped. "Wait until it is not and we are under attack?"

"I have spoken to Janus," Gerritse said. "He has assured me that he perceives no threat from this evolving situation."

"Well if this *thing* intends no ill-will toward us, then it should have no problem appearing before this council."

"Janus says that he has no idea where the fledgling is," Gerritse advised. "Perhaps it is best to give this matter some time and just monitor the situation."

"We have already lost enough time," Namtaru said dismissively. "I will not wait for this problem to appear on our doorstep before taking action. Which is why, as of this moment, I am issuing a warrant to all covens directing them to bring this *abomination* before this council."

Namtaru's order shocked the entire council.

"I vehemently protest this action," Luciano Toscani said as he stood up from his chair. "It is *contra legem*; it flies in the face of our laws. What crime has been committed against us to merit the issuance of a warrant? What threat does this man present? Before we consider what action to take, wouldn't it be more prudent to have all the facts made available to us first?"

"Sir, the Crystal Coven has granted him nomadic status," Gerritse quickly interjected. "If they found no grounds for concern, then why are we considering taking such a drastic measure to bring him before this council against his will? A decision, which I would respectfully like to point out, that the council has neither been consulted on nor approved."

Namtaru leaped to his feet, slamming his fist into the table hard enough to split it and sending wood shards flying across the room. "I *am* the council!"

The words reverberated like a shockwave through the hall, causing almost every member to avert their eyes. If they had any inclination to protest Namtaru's order, most kept it to themselves.

Toscani swallowed hard as he stared at the shattered table for a moment before nervously sitting back down.

"I still believe this to be a grave mistake," Gerritse protested, before taking his seat.

"Your concern is duly noted, Pier, and overruled," Namtaru continued, "but my order has been given and I expect you all to ensure that it is fulfilled without delay. This meeting is adjourned."

They watched as Namtaru walked around the table and left the room with his guards in tow.

Once the doors had closed, the assemblage shared uneasy glances with one another.

"This is absolutely wrong," Gerritse said. "If the law can be abused like this, to suit any one individual's personal needs, then we no longer have a rule of law, we have a dictatorship."

"I agree with you, Pier," Jennifer Usher said, "but it seems the council's opinion on this matter has been rendered moot."

"And what about the next time, Jenny?" he asked incredulously, looking first at her and then scanning the room. "If we turn our backs on our laws, what will be the next one we break?"

"I understand your frustration," Li Wei Zhao, said. "This is your coven, but what if Namtaru is right? What if this fledgling is a threat? Shouldn't we at least know what we are dealing with?"

"You can choose to play devil's advocate, Li Wei, but I won't," Gerritse replied angrily. "We formed this council to put an end to hostilities and to codify a standard of laws within our community.

Let me remind all of you that not all of those laws were well-received, but they were obeyed in large part due to this council's unflinching resolve to enforce them to the letter. What do you think will happen when word spreads, and we all know that it will, that this council has chosen to break its own laws? On what authority will we be able to stand, when handing down punishment in the future? What other laws will be subject to revision on a whim?"

"I agree with Pier," Rémy said. "This is not something I can go along with. From what I have been told, there is not one law that this man has broken. I will not be part of an *abduction* just to satisfy a curiosity. Who else will take a stand?"

Gerritse watched as Rémy and Jenny raised their hands, joined a moment later by Evgeni Kuznetsov, Jacinda Suarez, and Amal Rajpal. The others lowered their heads, signaling their decision.

He shook his head in disapproval. "Mark my words, *friends*, you have just crossed a line that leads down a very slippery slope."

"Let's be intellectually honest here for a moment, Pier," Kwame Mobutu said. "We are a council in name only. This is not the first decision that we have had *an issue* with, but we have made our choices for the greater good."

"Those choices did not involve taking action against an innocent man!"

"Pier, the lot has been cast," Jacob Gal said. "What is done is done, but when he comes before the council we can get our answers and stand united."

"United?" Gerritse scoffed. "No, Jacob, if this is the stand you choose to make then it is not unity you are talking about. It is complicity and I will not be a party to it."

"What will you do?" Zhao asked.

"I won't be a member of a witch-hunt, if that is what you're asking me," Gerritse replied. "I fear the choice this *council* has made today will be a cross it has to bear in the future.

Remember this, without the rule of law, there is only the *rule of man* left and you've all just been put on notice today as to who that man is."

The members watched as Gerritse left his place at the table and strode out of the room. He was just hanging up his robe, for what he believed to be the final time, when Rémy and Jenny caught up with him.

"Pier, wait," Rémy said. "What are we going to do?"

"I can't answer that for you, my friend," he replied. "It seems that each of us is at a crossroad and we must make our own decision."

"What about the council?"

"Rémy, the council is dead," Gerritse replied. "It's been dying for a long time; we've just been ignoring the signs. I can't do that anymore."

"What do you mean?" Jenny asked.

"I mean that I'm done."

"Done with what?" Rémy asked, his voice a mix of concern and confusion.

"All of it," he replied, gesturing back toward the council chamber they had just departed. "You know that what I am saying is the truth. This place was built on a common goal, but it has become corrupted. Today a majority turned a blind eye to justice, not on reasoned principal, but out of fear. Fear of losing their precious power as members of the council."

Gerritse turned and made his way out the door with Usher and Pelletier following close behind. He walked over to the stone patio, which sat on the precipice overlooking the bay, and stared out. The water was still and bathed in a majestic purple color reflecting off the evening sky, while traces of gold and orange streaked across the horizon, as the last rays of the sun faded from view.

"I understand your anger, Pier" Jenny said, "but you must realize that they are afraid."

"Fear doesn't justify an *injustice*," Gerritse replied. "We've all been around long enough to have seen this scenario played out countless times in *their* world and now it is here in ours. If it forces us to make decisions based upon the whims of one man, then there is no longer any point in maintaining this façade. When our history is told, it will not count me among the collaborators."

"Where will you go, Pier?" Jenny asked.

"Home," he replied. "To take a stand."

CHAPTER FORTY-THREE

"**G**ood morning, Madame President."

President Karoline Richmond sat up in bed as the Navy steward brought a mug of black coffee over and set it down on the nightstand.

"Is it really a *good* morning, Michelle?" Richmond asked as she picked up the mug and took her first sip of coffee.

"We woke up in the greatest country in the world, ma'am," she replied as she opened the drapes. Sunrise was still over two hours away, but Richmond was a habitual early riser who liked alone time before the hustle and bustle of the White House's West Wing kicked into high-gear. "Besides, Congress is still on recess."

"I'd get more done if they stayed on vacation, Michelle."

"Where's the fun in that?"

"Some days I wish I was still flying *plastic bugs* off the USS *Hairy Ass*."

"Well, I think it's safe to say that your F/A-18 flying days are over and you know that the admirals hate when you call the Truman that."

"I know," Richmond smiled, "and I also know that they work for *me* now."

"Rank does have its privileges," Michelle laughed.

"Indeed, it does," Richmond replied. "I wonder how many coronaries I would cause by telling them I wanted to fire up the afterburners one more time."

"I'd say about half the folks in the five-sided foxhole across the river and most of your Secret Service detail."

"What's life without a few thrills?"

"You're the President, ma'am."

"Here's to another fine Navy day," Richmond joked as she raised her mug in a toast.

Twenty minutes later she made her way down to the Oval Office with her security detail in tow.

"Can I get you anything, Madame President?" Special Agent Thomas Shea asked.

"Coffee, from the Navy Mess," she whispered conspiratorially. "I have a feeling it's going to be one of those days."

"Yes, ma'am," She smiled.

Richmond entered the office, closing the door behind her, and sat down at her desk. She went through the stack of papers, filtering through them by importance and making notes to address with the various cabinet secretaries. To the curious outsider, the reports would have seemed Earth shattering, but she had long ago grown accustomed to the fact that the world was a dumpster fire at any given time. Most of the time it was all just theatrical saber rattling, but occasionally things would threaten to go *hot* and then the adults would have to enter the picture. Nothing says, 'maybe we should talk,' than waking up to 100,000 tons of diplomacy floating off your coastline in the form of an aircraft carrier battle group. Fortunately, none of today's problems merited that kind of response.

She got up and walked over to one of the couches, just as Shea returned with her coffee.

"Here you go, ma'am," he said, setting the mug down on one of the coffee table coasters.

"Thank you, Thomas," she replied. "Are there any movements on today's schedule?"

"We're all clear, ma'am," he replied. "Vice President Jackson is coming back from Aspen with his family. They'll touch down at Andrews at 1300."

"I bet you boys are glad I have no family commitments that drag me across the country for holidays."

"It does help out the ones who have kids, especially during Christmas," Shea said.

"To bad the media and those clowns down the street don't hold me in such high regard," Richmond joked. "They think I'm the personification of the Grinch."

"I believe it was Sir Winston Churchill who sad, *'You have enemies? Good. That means you've stood up for something, sometime in your life.'*"

"It's not my enemies that concern me, Thomas. It's the ones that pretend to be my friend."

"That's what you have us for, ma'am," he smiled. "Is there anything else you need?"

"No, I'm fine, thank you."

Richmond picked up the remote, as the man left the room, and turned on the television. Even though she would get the *news* before it hit the airwaves, there was something comfortable about having the background noise as she drank her coffee and did her morning crossword puzzle. There were still some habits that she couldn't shake.

Thirty-Six down, justifying God, she mused as she tapped the end of her pen on the arm of the couch.

"Theodicy!" she declared triumphantly as she filled in the boxes.

Her celebration was cut short by the chirping of the phone on the coffee table.

"Really?" she groused as she set the paper down and picked up the phone. "Yes?"

"Madame President, I have Major General Nakagama on the line for you."

"Put him through on the secure line," she said curtly. "This is a private call. Notify the Situation Room; no monitoring or transcriptions."

"Yes, ma'am,"

Richmond got up from the couch and made her way over to the desk.

She'd handpicked Reid Nakagama to lead the Army's Chemical Corps, which was tasked with defending the nation against chemical, biological, radiological, and nuclear weapons, but the military had a chain of command and generals didn't just call the White House to have a chit-chat with the *boss*. That he was calling her directly at this time of the morning told her something was wrong.

A moment later the phone chirped and she pressed the button to connect the call. "Good morning, general."

"I'm sorry to disturb you, Madame President, but we have a problem."

"How big of a problem, general?" she asked.

"*Primal Fear*," he replied.

"How? When?"

"This isn't a discussion we should have over the phone, ma'am, even a secure line," he replied.

Richmond leaned back in her chair, exhaling deeply, as she scanned the interior of her office, her eyes coming to rest on the portrait of George Washington, which hung above the fireplace.

The world was filled with politicians, pundits, and arm-chair poly-sci experts, who liked to tell you that they *fundamentally understood* the problems that this country faced, along with how to fix them, but the truth was that they were clueless. Even the

Capitol Hill idiots, two miles down the road, only knew half the story, sometimes even less. The only ones who knew *everything* were the ones that called this place *home*, and it was one of the principal reasons her predecessors had aged so quickly during their tenure. Ironically, Washington was probably saved from the curse because he was the only President who had not lived here.

The threats the country faced were many, but they were not always man-made ones, and from the tone of Nakagama's voice, it appeared one had just shown up on her doorstep.

"I'll plan to be there this morning," she said.

"Do you think that's wise, ma'am?" he asked. "Not that I don't think the fine folks here at Ft. Leonard Wood wouldn't love a visit from their Commander-in-Chief, but do you really want to take the chance that someone in the press might start asking some inconvenient questions."

"You raise a valid point."

"I can travel private and be at Reagan by noon if you can arrange for a pickup. I think it's best if we keep things *close hold* at the moment."

"Agreed," she replied. "Someone from my detail will be in contact with you shortly to make arrangements to pick you up."

"Yes, ma'am."

Richmond hung up the phone and pressed the red button on the presidential call box on her desk. Seconds later Shea came through the door, his eyes scanning the room for threats.

"Is everything okay, ma'am?"

"No," she replied, as she wrote down a phone number onto a piece of paper. "I need you to handle a highly sensitive matter for me, Thomas."

"Yes, ma'am, what do you need?"

"I want you to meet General Nakagama at Reagan and bring him to the residence," she replied, handing him the number. "This is a private visit and I don't want there to be a record."

"I'll take care of it."

CHAPTER FORTY-FOUR

"**G**ood morning, sleepyhead," Gabi said cheerfully as she set the mug of coffee onto the night table.

Sigurdsson squinted as he leaned up in bed and took a sip. "Is that my shirt?"

Gabi popped the collar of the white linen dress shirt that was only partially buttoned up. "You know what they say, 'what's yours is mine.'"

"Girl's say that," he muttered, taking another sip. "Besides, it's still dark out, so I don't think that really qualifies as *morning* or even good for that matter."

"Well, until you figure out what you're doing with your life, you still have a job to do," she replied, sitting on the edge of the bed.

"Oh, I know what I'm doing with my life," he replied, setting the mug back down on the table.

Gabi felt his arms wrap around her waist just before she went airborne and came to rest on the bed with him on top of her.

"Karl!" she squealed as he playfully mauled her neck. "The neighbors will hear."

Sigurdsson raised his head up and stared into her eyes.

It felt as if a thousand butterflies had taken flight inside her, as she brushed an errant stand of blonde hair from his face.

"I don't recall you being concerned about the neighbors last night," he replied.

"That was different," she said sheepishly.

"Oh yeah, why is that?"

"Well, I needed to know just how *changed* you were."

"Oh, and does the new me meet your expectations, Countess?"

"Mmmmm hmmmm," she said as she bit her bottom lip. "Very much so, Karl."

"Good, then tonight I won't go so easy on you," he laughed.

Gabi grabbed the pillow from behind her neck and swung it around at him, but he caught it in mid-air.

"Show off," she huffed.

Sigurdsson laid the pillow down next to her and kissed her gently on the lips.

"I thought you liked it when I showed off?" he asked as he glided down her body, kissing her chest, and opening another button.

"I do," she moaned.

The moment was interrupted by Sigurdsson's cellphone vibrating on the night table.

"Seriously?" he groaned as he reached over and picked it up.

"Who is it?" Gabi asked.

"Work," he said as he took the call. "Sigurdsson."

"Good morning, sunshine," Avery White's voice chirped on the other end. "It's time to rise and shine."

"So I've been told," Sigurdsson said grumpily, as he sat on the edge of the bed. "What's going on?"

"Well, before you head over to your tea party with the feds, the L.T. wants you to take a ride over to the One-Eleven and take a look at a case they just got."

"Boss, I get that I'm Vega's *homicide whisperer* now, but that's not even in the same borough."

"Look, Karl, I know it's been awhile since the academy, so let me break this down for you. The chief calls Vega, he calls me, and I call you. You think the chief cares which borough she sends *her* detectives?"

"Obviously not," Sigurdsson replied.

"Now you're learning," White replied.

"So what has the chief rankled at...." he glanced over at the alarm clock. "0523?"

"One-Eleven got a call for a house fire and they found a body."

"Tragic, but that's hardly earth shattering."

"Apparently there are *extenuating circumstances* involved, the details of which they will supply to you upon your arrival. *Capiche*?"

"*Si, sergente*," Sigurdsson replied.

"Good, but don't milk this thing. You still have cases waiting for you back here."

"Understood," Sigurdsson said and ended the call.

"Is everything all right?" Gabi asked.

"They want me to look at suspicious death before I get to the office," he said as he stood up and headed to the shower.

"Yeah, but at least you know that the suspicion lies with the mortal world this time," she replied.

Sigurdsson paused in the doorway and looked back at her lying on the bed.

"Maybe I should interrogate you on what you were doing last night," he joked. "You know, just to be certain."

"Mmmmmm, I'll be here waiting for you when you get home."

"I like the sound of that, Gabi."

"What? Interrogating me?"

"No, goofy, just that you will be waiting here when I get home."

"Good, because you're stuck with me, Karl," she smiled. "I'm not going anywhere."

"I can live with that."

CHAPTER FORTY-FIVE

Sigurdsson pulled up to the sprawling home on Shore Drive just as the last fire truck was leaving the scene. He showed his shield to the cop guarding the door and was waved inside. The interior of the home was dark, the only light coming through windows that overlooked Little Neck Bay.

"Are you Detective Sigurdsson?" a middle-aged woman in a business suit asked.

"Yes, I am," he replied. "And you are?"

"Lieutenant Carbona," she replied. "I'm the C.O. of the One-Eleven Squad."

"Pleased to meet you, boss," he said, shaking her hand. "Did FD cut the power off?"

"No, the power was already out when they got here. The electrical breaker was tripped and we didn't want to reset it till Crime Scene shows up to take prints."

"So do you have any idea why I'm here?" he asked.

"It's probably easier if I just show you," she replied. "Follow me."

Carbona pulled out a flashlight and led him up the staircase to the second floor of the home. The air was thick with acrid smoke, and the carpets squished with each step they took, but as they drew closer, the smell grew much more familiar.

"Let me introduce you to Mr. Alexi Zharkov," she said, motioning to the charred remains on what was left of the king-sized bed. "At least that's who we think he is."

"Why is that?" Sigurdsson asked.

"Take a closer look," she said, handing him the flashlight.

He made his way over to the bed and glanced down, the light shining on the man's torso. "He seems to have lost something."

"Yeah, we noticed that too, which is why we only *think* he's Zharkov."

"Russian mob hit?" he asked. "They tend to have a flare for the dramatic, like beheading."

"That was our first thought as well," Carbona replied. "It's apparent that someone was sending a message, but then we did a search and realize it's a bit more twisted."

"There's more?" Sigurdsson asked.

"Oh yeah," she replied. "There's a lot more."

"I can't wait."

Carbona led him back down the staircase and to the rear of the house where the door leading to the basement was.

"And this is where it gets really interesting," she said, activating the flashlight.

The light flickered off the stone walls and the old wooden staircase groaned under their feet, adding to the already eerie feeling of the moment. As they neared the back of the house Sigurdsson caught a whiff of the distinct acrid tang that reminded him of pot being smoked.

"Drugs?" he asked.

"We haven't found any," she replied. "Patrol did a search of the house, to make sure there were no other people inside, and that's when they found this."

Sigurdsson stopped dead in his tracks as he stared down at the cement floor.

"Can I have that for a minute?" he asked, motioning to Carbona's flashlight.

"Sure," she said, handing it to him.

In the flashlight's beam he could see a large crimson circle with a pentagram painted on the concrete. In the spaces between each point was a symbol. Within each of the five points was an object: A shard of wood, a gold coin, a silver chalice with ash, a half-burned bundle of what appeared to be pale green leaves, and the remnants of a black wax candle and thread. Scrawled beneath the pentagram was:

But it was neither the disconcerting symbols nor the unrecognizable writing that bothered Sigurdsson, but what was in the middle; a small black cloth that covered a large oval mound.

"I assume you found the rest of Mr. Zharkov?"

"That's our guess," she replied as he carefully removed the cloth to reveal the grisly image.

The rest of Carbona's words slowly faded away until they were nothing more than a distant buzz. Sigurdsson exhaled sharply, an icy chill coursing through his body, as he stared into the blackened eyes of the being he once knew as Michael Orlov.

ABOUT THE AUTHOR

Andrew Nelson spent twenty-two years in law enforcement, including twenty years with the New York City Police Department. During his tenure with the NYPD he served as a detective in the elite Intelligence Division, conducting investigations and providing dignitary protection to numerous world leaders. He achieved the rank of sergeant before retiring in 2005.

He is the author of both the James Maguire and Alex Taylor mystery series' and has written several non-fiction works about the New York City Police Department's Emergency Service Unit and the aftermath of the September 11th, 2001, terror attack.

For more information please visit us at:

www.andrewgnelson.org

ANDREW G.
NELSON